RESTLESS SPIRIT

RESTLESS SPIRIT

An erotic novel

Sommer Marsden

Published by Xcite Books – 2012
ISBN 9781908262271

Printed and bound by CPI Group (UK) Ltd, Croydon, CR0 4YY

Cover design by Sarah Davies

Dedication

For the man. I love you. Forever and ever. Amen.

Acknowledgements

For the readers who love my tainted, damaged bad boys.
Shepherd's for you.

Prologue

HE PULLED ME TO him. Really pulled me. I slid across the crisp white sheets on my belly, randomly grabbing at folds of cloth as Stan pounded into me.

'Stay with me, Tuesday,' he said.

I knew he didn't mean keep up, or come with him, or fuck with the same enthusiasm. He meant don't go and *don't go* wasn't something I could consider.

'Shut up, Stan.'

I felt it curling like a flame in my belly, my pussy, my thighs. The flashing, pulsing heat that always means I'm going to come. When Stan got behind me and manhandled me, fucked me hard but said sweet words, it always worked me up. When his fingers dug into the meat of my hips and he moved like a man possessed, my entire being seemed to thrum with the pulse in my neck and my belly.

'Don't tell me to shut up,' Stan said, laying a hard blow on the flushed skin of my ass. But it only made it worse. It only made me worse.

I shoved my hand under my body, finding my clit with slippery fingers. I rubbed hard, way harder than I normally would if anyone were watching me. I thrust my body hard against my hand even as I tried to toss myself back against him. Impaling myself on Stan's big cock. Throwing myself back into his strong hands. The sexual version of the Nestea plunge, just giving up and hurling myself back into empty space. The unknown.

My pussy started to seize up around him and he grunted, 'Not yet, girl,' and pulled free of me.

I made a noise like something feral, but the world turned suddenly and he had me on my back. The bulk of him, six foot three-ish of huge man, hovering over me and prying my legs wide. Stan settled himself between my thighs, finding my slippery slit with his fingers and then his cock.

His mouth came down hard and sweet and needy. 'Don't leave, Tuesday,' he said again. 'Or take me with you.'

'Shut up, Stan,' I said again. And to help him shut up, I wrapped my legs around his thick waist, opened my body to him, tightened my cunt muscles and as an afterthought, I turned my head, sucked his big finger into my mouth and licked it like I always licked his cock.

Stan, good old Stan, hissed like a scalded cat and whispered, 'Christ.'

'Fuck me, Stan,' I said this time and he buried his handsome face in my neck and set about doing just that. His stubble scraped my flesh raw, his fingers bruised my skin, his bulk crushed the air out of me and it was perfect.

It was what I needed. To forget and to get lost. To open my body and close my mind and feel Stan's broad slippery cock ramming into me like he was punishing me, but in the most delicious way, for leaving him.

When he pinned my wrists down by my sides and damn near smashed me flat with his 200 plus pounds. When he sucked the whimpers and the moans off my lips and swallowed them down. When he ground his hips in that way he has and rocked from side to side. That's when I came.

'You're leaving me, Tuesday, aren't you?' he said.

'Honey, we were never really together,' I told him.

He sighed, his finger running over my dusky nipple making it stand up like some well trained thing.

'I know.'

'I know you do.' I brushed my fingers through his reddish brown hair and he flared his hand over my belly so the muscles twitched.

'Why, Tues?'

'I'm too fucking damaged, Stan.'

He didn't argue. Stan had been fucking me for months. And we'd been having this post coital back and forth for almost as long. He didn't argue because for the most part, Stan knew I was right.

When he left he threw his final say over his shoulder on his way out the door. 'You're not damaged, Tuesday. You're restless.'

Chapter One

WHERE I LIVE IT seems they frown upon a woman sticking up for herself. My ex, Phil, is the size of a tree. An angry tree. We tangled more than once and at first, the fucking and the danger and the thrill was enough to let me overlook the occasional drunken swing he'd take at me.

When he connected a bit too hard one Saturday night, I went to get checked. The white-haired, kind, emergent care doctor applied a butterfly bandage over my right eye where the skin was split and said softly – almost conversationally – 'You know, bad things don't usually get better.'

I'd swallowed hard and made up my mind. Fucking and danger and a tiny bit of thrill wasn't worth this. Because Phil was just going to get older and broader and angrier, probably. And the hits would get harder and the instances more often.

I went home to pack. He made a deal of it. I dealt with his temper tantrum with calm determination. Phil decided I needed a lesson. He actually said that, 'You need a lesson, Tuesday fucking Cane.'

I grabbed my baseball bat from grade school and gave him a good whack in the knee. When he didn't stop, I did the other – just to even things up. Then I left.

I'd moved into the local boarding house while I decided what to do. A lot of the locals in our sorta-big-but-not-big-enough-to-be-a-real-city-suburbs thought I was a rogue. Thought I'd taken the law into my own hands. Funny, but no one thought twice about Phil whaling on me if he saw fit. But what can you do? Most people are fucking crazy.

I hooked up with Stan for several reasons – he was pretty cute, he stuck up for me with the gossiping busy bodies, he was hopelessly gaga over me and he was a wall of man who'd provide good muscle should Phil come sniffing around.

I ended up deciding to drive to Allister Lake and take care of my grandmother who'd been in failing health. She'd been asking forever, I'd been putting it off. I made up my mind to just do it, and then she died. A sudden heart attack had taken that option from me. My nan was gone. Her house was mine. And I had a chance to start a brand new life.

I threw the last of my clothes in the suitcase on my final night at the boarding house and looked up to see Annie in the doorway.

'So, you're really going then?'

'I am.'

'Stan looked pretty upset.'

'Stan was pretty upset. But Stan wasn't my knight in shining armour.'

'He wanted to be.' She compressed her already thin mouth into a hot pink-lipsticked line to show her disapproval.

'They all do until they take a swing at you for being too loud or wearing a too-short dress.' I zipped my bag.

'They're not all like that,' Annie said.

'Enough of them are.'

I kissed her wrinkled cheek, smelling of powder and lavender toilet water, and off I went. Into the wild blue yonder. Just me, a beat to shit black and tan '76 Grenada, and my overstuffed duffle bags.

'What will you do out there?' she called after me from the front porch. The sky was whipping itself up into a sudden August storm.

'Whatever I can,' I yelled, pulling out. 'It's not like waitressing at Dom's Diners is anything to beat.'

'You gonna write?' Her dyed red hair whipped back from her too-thin face. Annie had been dropping weight. It worried me. She smoked like a chimney.

'I'm gonna try. Thanks for everything, Annie!' I yelled. 'You know I love ya.'

She waved me off but at the last minute she yelled, 'I love you too Tuesday Cane … you lunatic.'

I hit the road. I had a three hour drive before I hit Allister Lake. It rained cats and dogs the whole damn way.

Allister Lake is huge. The surrounding town not so much. The locals who own the original plots around the waterfront refuse to sell of any of their lots for new building. What survives is the original layout from the 50s. With the exception of a few in-law houses and guest homes that locals had added on over the years, looking at original photos of the town you see pretty much the same landscape. Very odd, very rare and very cool.

I pulled into Nan's gravel drive feeling that twinge of guilt that came when I thought of her. All the shoulds crushed down on me. How I should have visited more often, how I should have made up my mind sooner to come stay with her, how I should have come immediately. Nan had been my only family left barring some distant relations and now she was gone too.

'Orphan. Fucking orphan,' I said to myself.

I saw movement in my headlights but couldn't make it out and then it was gone. The white light painted abstracts on the A-frame home that I remembered fondly from my childhood and teenage visits.

'Home sweet home,' I said to my car and climbed out.

I dragged my duffle bag in and found the key on my ring. The lawyers had sent it along, but it didn't matter, I had my own from once upon a time.

The last time I'd been here I'd been eighteen and had managed to snag three locals before travelling back home. I remembered them vaguely. Big corn-fed men who did things like hunt, fish and swim in 'cricks' to cool off. I snorted and rolled my eyes.

'Let's try not to do that this time, Tuesday,' I said. 'But then again,' I sighed, dragging my bag behind me, 'What the hell.'

'What the hell what?'

I jumped, screamed and dropped my keys. I took a swing at the guy before he could dodge and ended up cuffing him good upside the head.

'Jesus, Tuesday, your nan would spank you if she saw you hitting your friends.'

'Wha–'

He held something up and I saw it was a small lantern. It had sorta kinda been behind his bulk when I clocked him.

'Hey, Tuesday.'

'Adrian!' I yelped and threw myself into his arms. Those three local boys I'd mentioned? Adrian had been one. Tall and leanly muscled like a street fighter, he stood about a head taller than my five foot ten. His shoulders weren't broad but strong as hell and the lantern lit up his brownish red hair and his dark brown eyes.

'Kiddo.'

'You're the same age as me,' I said.

'Three months older.'

'Wow. Ancient.' I unlocked the door and before I could do it, he stooped to grab my bag. 'What are you doing out here in the dark?'

I flipped the light inside the front door and nothing happened. Shit.

'I was in the barn and saw your car.'

'Why were you in the barn? And where are my goddamn lights?' I growled, getting frustrated. I flicked the switch again as if I could magically pump power into the house.

'Your nan's lawyer hired me to be the caretaker until the house was occupied. Out here at the lake, damn, the critters move in fast.'

He moved past me in the dark and I felt the brush of his hard body against mine. A surge of lust rose up in my belly as I remembered our few nights together. Naked, sweaty and rolling around in the oddest places. An unfinished house, the bed of his pick up, under Nan's apple tree out back. Heat flooded my cheeks and when I said, 'Where you going?' my voice sounded funny.

'I'm gonna go flip the breaker so you have juice. I had to shut the place down but for the sump pump. No use in paying for electricity that no one's using.'

He opened the cellar door and turned at the last minute. 'And Tuesday?'

'Yeah?'

'Sorry about Nan.'

'Yeah, me too,' I said around the lump in my throat.

'Be right back.' Then he was gone like a hero in a horror movie. His big fine self, his kind smile and his lantern. And me standing in the dark.

'Hurry,' I whispered.

I heard him moving around below the wide planked floors like the world's largest rodent. I shivered. Way to freak yourself out, Tues … My mind had conjured images of rats and mice, water bugs and spiders. All the creepy crawlies that came with shut up cabins and lakeshore living.

'OK!' I heard Adrian call but nothing had happened.

'OK what! There are no lights!'

'Flip the switch again,' he yelled and I heard a deep chuckle that slithered to the pit of my belly making me feel horny.

'Great,' I growled. I flipped the switch and my grandmother's sconce lights lit up her living room. Correction – *my* sconce lights.

'Work?' he said from the doorway.

'As you can see.'

'Good deal.' He walked into the kitchen and I followed, leaving my bag by the entertainment centre in the living room.

The thing about A-frames is they have very few vertical walls. The walls tilt and it can be unsettling at first. But the main room was big and wide and open, with ceilings that arched way over my head. I passed the small nook on the left that my grandmother had used for an office and then I was in the kitchen, a fairly open space split into an eating section and a cooking section by an island.

I sat in the wicker rocking chair while Adrian checked the pilot light and the stovetop. He made sure I had candles and matches and turned the water back on in the sink.

'If you need anything, you let me know. I'm still out in the barn. I guess I'll be moving out soon, though.' he said and smiled.

'Do you have somewhere to go?' I asked softly. The economy had been shit. I imagined it was the case even in a small place like Allister Lake.

'Not at the moment.'

'Then stay as long as you want,' I said. 'It's not like I need the barn.'

He took my hand and said softly – in a tone reserved for lovers, or at least former lovers –'Stand up, Tuesday. Let me see you in the light.'

I stood and he studied me. My cheeks grew hot, my pussy wet, my belly buzzed with nerves. Nothing quite compared to the feel of a man's intent gaze on you. Especially one as good looking as Adrian Weston.

'You look damn good, kid.' Then he kissed my forehead and turned to go. 'There's some wine in the pantry. Some hard stuff too. Tons of canned and packaged food. You know your Nan, always stocked for an–'

'Event,' I finished. 'Weather or social,' I laughed. My grandmother had believed in being prepared food-wise for any event, whether it be a blizzard or an impromptu dinner for eight.

'Right.'

At the door he turned and pinned me in the cage of his arms. My back was pressed to the green front door, his sinewy arms planted on either side of my head. 'Damn, you look good.'

'You too,' I said swallowing hard. My body insisted I hadn't just had sex with Stan. My body insisted that I hadn't had sex in months … nay, years!

'I'm right over there if you need me,' he said and kissed my lips.

It was a soft and proper kiss. Just enough to get my body revving like a muscle car engine. And at the very last second, he slipped his tongue between my lips to touch it to mine and I shivered.

'Night, kid.'

'We're the same age,' I whispered as he loped across the big lawn to the barn.

Great, how was I going to fucking sleep knowing that Adrian – hot, talented, willing Adrian – was asleep on my property? I had no idea.

Chapter Two

THE UPPER ROOM THAT had been my grandmother's was now mine. The walls tilted in and at first it threw me off. I felt a bit off balance, but then it all came back to me – my love for the A-frame. Looking out of her upper windows to see bright sunlight throwing diamond shards of light off the lake water. Hearing geese and ducks when the weather warmed.

I stared at Nan's bed and sighed. 'It's going to be weird.'

When nothing happened, I dropped my bag and kicked off my boots. I shimmied free of my dark grey jeans and unbuttoned my plaid shirt. In panties and a tank top, I wandered Nan's room, remembering sitting on the small bench at the foot of her bed while she did her make-up at the vanity.

Out in the dark night, on her big plot of land, was the potting shed she'd loved so much and the barn. I saw a light in the potting shed and froze. Then it winked and was gone. That couldn't be right. Adrian was in the barn. And if Adrian was in the barn then who was in the potting shed?

I craned my head, pushing my forehead to the cool window glass so I could see a bit of the barn. A light burned inside.

Weird.

'Maybe it was a reflection, you goof.' I was too tired to worry about it. I climbed into bed and stretched my arms and legs to work out the tension built up from the drive. My body made a lazy starfish shape in the bed. I reached as far as I could, groaning, releasing all my stress from being behind the wheel and from my life in general. Then I cut the bedside lamp off and waited to fall asleep.

And waited.

After an hour of listening to every creak and pop and groan

of the old house, I considered a night cap. But laziness won out and I lay there waiting for my nerves to calm and my body to relax and my fatigue to take over.

I shut my eyes remembering my times with Adrian. His warm lips on mine – thin but soft lips that made him look like he was angry sometimes when he wasn't. But when he smiled it touched my heart and my belly … and my cunt, to be honest. That grin of his showed the true nature of the man – good-hearted, funny, ornery and sexy.

Willing the image of his hands on me, I shimmied free of my panties and dropped them to the floor. My fingers slipping coolly over my clit made me shiver and I pressed a bit harder as I circled the swollen nub.

Adrian had done this thing where he clamped my nipple between his sharp white teeth and tugged, drawing the rosy tip out and away from my body. Biting down until it felt like too much, like the pain was too great. Then he'd release it and bury his face between my thighs, licking my pussy, sucking my clit, all the while his capable fingers stroked the tender nipple he'd just caused to throb.

I slid my fingers deep in my cunt, grinding my clit to the palm of my hand as I moved them. Slowly, fucking myself and rocking my hips up just enough to give myself deeper pleasure.

He'd had a talented tongue and he'd loved to drive the rigid tip into my wet slit until I bucked and danced for him and then he'd slide his hands under my ass and concentrate on my swollen clitoris. Licking with the flat of his tongue before tickling with only the tip. When he'd push his fingers deep inside of me – much like I was then – and suck hard and I would come. Fistfuls of hair clenched in my greedy fingers as my body shivered.

I came, a long slow slippery orgasm that unwound lazily in my pussy and curled up into my belly so the muscles trembled. But I wasn't done. I flipped on my stomach, remembering how Adrian would roll me. He'd fuck me, face to face, prying my thighs wide, then he'd flip me on my belly and take me from behind. His fingers – strong from working outside and fishing and hunting – would dig into my flesh and I swore I could feel my flesh bruising. And then, just when I was about to come, he'd roll onto his back and make me climb aboard.

I thrust my fingers deeper and rolled my hips, back and forth, to grind my tender clit to my palm. Pretending I was astride him. Calling up muscle memory and mental images of his tan hands on my pale breasts as I rode him. And just at that crucial moment, he'd pull me in, kiss me hard and suck my nipples until the resounding pull was felt from breast to cunt and I'd come.

And I came again, against my hand, my face pressed to the pillow.

I rolled to my back, tired and spent, but now considering running over to that barn and trying to find out if he was still as talented between the sheets as he was once upon a time.

Fatigue won. I was asleep before I could sit up and find my pants.

Allister Lake was a greenish blue mirror. The clouds reflected in its nearly still surface and sunlight twinkled like tiny fairy lights. I sat on Nan's deck with a cup of her coffee, so fucking strong that even I couldn't water it down by using less grounds. The first few sips made me grimace but then I started to enjoy the in-your-face bold flavour.

'So you're the infamous Tuesday?'

I jumped, coffee splashing my black sweater. Thank God it was black. I hadn't heard him sneak up on me – and by the size of him that was a fucking miracle.

'Jesus, who are you?' I gasped. 'I mean, I'm sorry–'

Clearly he was a neighbour of Nan's.

He smiled and it did something strange to me, I felt bristly and flirty and too hot in the face. He was about six foot six, the size of a small tree to be honest, and his dark brown hair was just long enough to technically require a cut. He sported a beard that hugged his lean face and it was shot with grey and silver.

Older man, yum …

I shook the thought off when he said 'Sorry. I'm Shepherd. I live next door. Well, as next door as that is,' he said, pointing to a white A-frame similar to mine but with huge mirrored windows that made me think of blind eyes.

Dark brown eyes regarded me and he grinned when I opened my mouth but managed to say nothing. My words had gone right of my head as I studied him. Broad shoulders, flannel shirt, jeans, big work boots that had actually been worked in. And that grin.

'Um … hi,' I said.

Brilliant!

He laughed softly and I clenched my hands into fists at the rush of attraction. It was rare for me to feel so drawn to a man. Especially a stranger, but here I was, attracted to Shepherd.

My brain kick started. 'Shepherd?'

'Moore.'

'That's an unusual name, Shepherd,' I said, smoothing my hair. I took great pride in my bottle blonde cap of hair with nearly black roots. I figured one day I'd outgrow the pseudo punk rock I-don't-give-a-shit look. But not yet.

He shrugged, putting one boot up on my floating deck. The term floating deck had always made me laugh but it was nothing more than a low wooden deck usually built off the back of the house. Still, it somehow sounded magical. When I motioned with my hand, he came all the way up and dropped into one of Nan's-now-my padded deck chairs. 'They wanted me to be a man of the cloth.'

'And you are?' I managed. I was having trouble breathing with him so near. There was maybe a foot between his jean-clad knee and mine and I swore I could feel the heat baking off of him even in the chilly morning air.

'I was an ultimate cage fighter. Now I'm a handy man.'

I cocked an eyebrow. 'A handy man?'

'I'm handy, I know how to do lots of stuff.' He winked and I had to shift in my chair.

'I see.'

'And you are …?'

'Tuesday Cane.'

He laughed again and I wanted to climb in his lap. I bit my lips to force the dirty image away.

'I know that, Tuesday Cane. You are a …'

'Oh, I am currently unemployed. Former waitress. I sling a mean breakfast special.'

'Ah,' Shepherd said. 'Well, I do know that Irving down at the restaurant is looking for a fill-in. Might not be full-time but if you know your way around a diner, he might go for it.'

'Thanks,' I said.

'I'm sorry about your nan.' He pinned me with that gaze of his. Dark eyes full of kindness. And something else underneath it all.

'Yeah, hey, thanks,' I said. I looked away, out at the lake for a moment. Letting it dazzle my eyes so I wouldn't cry.

'She loved you a lot, Virginia did,' he went on. He stood, went into my kitchen, came back out with a cup of coffee.

He was stirring up emotions – things I did not do very well – and I wanted to be angry and pissed and snarky, but instead I just watched him move. Slow, economical, self-assured movements that made me wistful for a time when I might be so comfortable in my own skin. His time using his body for a weapon and knowing how to control it was completely apparent in his demeanour.

Shepherd Moore, big bad handy man with busted up boots, dropped back into the chair and said, 'She thought you hung the moon. I heard you're going to become a huge bestselling author.'

I snorted so suddenly I started to choke. And then I was laughing, but I was crying too. 'Oh, yeah?' I managed shakily.

'Yeah,' he said, and winked at me.

There was that urge again – to curl into his lap and just be held. Very strange feeling for me, to be blunt. I tend to shun any contact not directly related to sex. Or any contact directly related to simple comfort.

'I guess to Nan a few stories published in semi-pro magazines is the big time.'

'I guess so.' He continued to watch me.

'That's funny. She did think I had talent,' I sighed, determined not to cry. 'But honestly, when she read my shit, it freaked me out. I'm not exactly kid- or elderly-friendly.'

He shrugged again and I watched those huge shoulders shift. 'She thought you were awesome. Always bragged about you. Always talked about seeing you and–'

I dropped my cup and rushed inside. The wave of guilt and pain and loss that swept over me left no room for rational thought. My only instinct was retreat – run – get away.

I turned to yell I was sorry or I'd be back or something along those lines, Christ anything, and turned right into a flannel-wrapped mountain of a man. His hands came down on my forearms and squeezed reassuringly. 'Hey, Tuesday, I'm sorry. We don't even know each other–'

'It's OK–'

'And I come over here and make you cry–'

'It's OK–'

'And upset you and it's not even nine in the morning.'

'It's OK!' I said again, almost angrily. But it wasn't and we both knew it because I was crying so hard I was shaking. But for his hands on my arms, I'd probably shake apart into a hundred girl pieces.

This was a great start to getting to know your neighbour.

He pulled me in and crushed my face to his chest. Under the flannel he wore a faded blue tee that looked like it had been washed about a million times. He smelled of cold air and clean cotton and leaves. I wanted to snuggle against him and the thought made me cringe inside. What a horrible needy thing I'd become.

'I'm sorry,' I whispered. 'This is so … fucking weird.'

He laughed and it rumbled through his chest against my ear. 'It is weird. But it's thanks to me. How about you let me make you dinner tonight?'

'You're an ultimate fighter, a handy man and you cook?'

'I told you I know how to do lots of stuff.'

When he said it there was an undercurrent of sensuality. I don't know how I knew other than all the fine hairs on the back of my neck stood up and I had to suppress a shiver.

I looked up at him and he wiped under my eyes with his thumbs. I realised then I hadn't let him go. I was hugging this stranger and letting him wipe my raccoon eyes and worst of all, he'd seen me cry. 'What time?' I managed though my tongue felt three sizes too big.

'What time is good for you?'

I shrugged, and yet, Jesus … I was still holding onto him. 'I have no job, I just moved in and you're holding me while I cry six minutes after we just met. Just give me a time.'

'Six?'

'Six is good.'

'Do you eat meat?'

I blushed and felt so fucking juvenile. He meant food not … cock.

He smirked at me and it was in that moment that I realised he could read my mind like a newspaper. 'I do. I eat meat,' I said and then turned my gaze away when my cheeks caught fire.

'Steak it is. I'll see you at six. Just …'He waved a hand. 'Walk across and come in if I don't answer. I tend to crank the music when I cook.'

'Right,' I said.

He shocked me by pressing a kiss to my forehead before he left. 'And I am sorry I upset you, but …' He pawed his hair.

'But?'

'But you needed to know. About Virginia. How much she loved you.'

Then he left and I put my face in my hands and cried. I'd never felt more grateful and more upset by a bit of information in my life.

So I started doing dishes and talking to my nan. Maybe it was crazy but it was my house now and who was here to eavesdrop anyway.

Chapter Three

'AND I SHOULD HAVE come here way long ago, Nan,' I sniffled and washed the final dish. 'I'm sorry I didn't. I'm sorry I didn't get to say goodbye.'

I flipped the light on because the sky was getting overcast; the bulb flared and then blew with a soft pop.

'Fabulous. So now I need … light bulbs.' I pulled open every drawer and every cabinet, even the pantry. Adrian was right; the entire pantry was stocked for Armageddon or a massive surprise dinner party. But no light bulbs.

I could waste a whole day rummaging the entire house or I could just ask Adrian. I looked at the bulletin board over the phone but saw no number for him listed or any indication that there was a phone in the barn.

'Because you would have known the number to your own damn barn phone if you even have one, right, Nan?' I shook my head and pulled on my lace up boots. Time to walk across the yard and find my temporary caretaker.

The wind was whipping hard and the sky had darkened further. It looked like rain and the oncoming storm had frapped the lake into lazy little peaks. I stood to watch the water for a moment, trying to fully absorb and appreciate that this was now my home. That my grandmother had given me this gift of lake life.

'What ya doing? Day dreaming?'

He leaned in the open barn door, tall and wiry and sexy as sin. He gave me that look that said he'd been thinking bad things. We hadn't dated long, Adrian and I, and it had surely been nothing more than a fling, but the look in his eyes was pretty much universal.

Aroused man.

I gave him a wave and walked toward him, into the wind. Feeling my hair lift up and sway in the suddenly strong gust.

'I came to see if you know where the light bulbs might be,' I said. 'Seems Nan didn't keep them in any of the places a lowly former boarding house dweller like me would think to keep them.'

'Ah, she kept 'em in the cellar,' he said, taking my hand and pulling me out of the wind into the looming darkness of the barn. 'But while you're here I'll give you a few just in case you get home and it turns out she was out of them or something. Come on.'

I followed him past what once had been operative animal stalls but now served as storage. One held a tractor, one a small plough attachment for a truck though my grandmother didn't own a truck.

'It's Shepherd's,' Adrian said. The growl in his voice said maybe he wasn't a fan of my new neighbour. 'He hooks it up and ploughs around the lake for most locals. Did your nan's driveway for free since she lets him store it here. He stores some of his tools here too.'

I nodded, chewing my lips and smoothing my long bangs. Whatever was up with Adrian and Shepherd I wanted no part of it. I'd had enough drama in the last year to last me a lifetime.

The last stall was stacked with supplies. Across from it was a stall that had been enclosed with a door.

Adrian handed me a box with two bulbs in it. 'Kitchen right?'

'Yeah.'

'Those should be the right wattage then.'

His fingers stroked over mine before breaking the contact. Exhaustion, fear and good old fashioned attraction all added to the sudden urge I had to kiss him. Apparently, trying to start a new life meant you wanted to jump every man who was nice to you.

'So!' I said brightly, moving away. 'What's this here?'

Before he could answer, I turned the knob and pushed the door open. I took three big steps into the now enclosed stall before my eyes truly registered the inside. A double bed, a dresser, a flat screen TV and a laptop. Basically it was a small dorm room complete with an easy chair and a TV tray with breakfast dishes on it. Through a small doorway was a toilet, sink and stand up shower. No kitchen.

'Oh, shit. Oh, God. I'm sorry! This is your room.' I said. But when I turned I was face to face with a smiling Adrian. His strong jaw stubbled with new growth, his eyes bright.

My pussy clenched remembering the night before and getting off to dirty, dirty thoughts of him.

'Your grandmother had it closed in to possibly be a small office or craft room. She was never sure which she wanted most. Just said renovating it gave her a project to set her mind too.'

I nodded. That was Nan. And knowing her it was probably a precaution should she need to hire on-site help. Which made my throat close up a little. I should have come sooner.

Adrian touched my chin gently. 'Want coffee?'

He pushed me back and I moved with him, my mind already talking me into what I was going to do. I mean, I was a free agent. We had a history. We were sexually compatible. I was a big girl. I was horny. It was cosy in here. I could go on …

'Sure.'

But he didn't get me coffee. He pushed the door shut and locked it. I watched his big hand pluck the box of light bulbs from my hand and then he grabbed my upper arms, held me still and kissed me.

I parted my lips for the kiss and when his tongue touched mine the jolt of want was so sudden, I groaned. My hand closed over the front of his chinos before I could even really form the thought to do it. It moved on its own and when I felt the hard curve of his erection I squeezed. This time, it was Adrian who groaned.

'I know this is forward.'

'It's fine.'

'But I really can't forget the memory of fucking you now that you're back,' he said against my neck. His fingers, big but agile, worked at the hem of my sweater. He pulled it up and growled to see my lacy white bra and the tops of my pale yellow panties peeking out of my jeans. 'Jesus, Tuesday. You've always gotten me hard. And mindless.'

'Good combination.' I grabbed his top button and yanked roughly, forcing the entire row of brass discs to surrender to my grip.

I shoved my hand down in his pants, past his cotton briefs and found him hot and hard. Gripping him, I walked back slowly and we fell onto his squishy blanket crowded bed.

'It gets cold out here at night,' he explained.

'Hush.'

'But you're warm.' He worked my jeans down over my hips and found me with his fingers. Adrian slipped them inside of me with insane ease, curling against my G-spot so I sucked in a breath. 'So fucking warm.'

'Yes,' I said. And then, 'Condom?'

Adrian reached past me, pawing in his nightstand and then he was kissing me again as he ripped the package. There was a moment when we wrestled each other for the condom, but I surrendered and shimmied out of my panties while he sheathed his cock.

Naked, shivering a bit, listening to the wind lick at the barn, I waited while he studied me. I almost spoke, feeling strange and more naked than naked because Adrian was looking at me. I mean really looking at me. But he pushed a finger to my lips and said 'I just wanted to see you for a minute, Tues. You've gotten more beautiful over the years. You used to be hot. Now you're stunning.'

My cheeks bloomed with heat but he didn't seem to notice. He moved his well-muscled bulk over me and rubbed the hard head of his cock to my slick opening. Adrian drove into me on one smooth stroke, inch by fluid inch. I was so wet and so ready that the friction stole my breath and fluttered my heart.

'Oh,' I sighed.

'Oh *good* or oh *bad?*' He kissed me then, sucking my tongue gently so I felt an echoing tug in my cunt.

'Oh *good*. Oh *very good*,' I said. I thrust up under him, to open for him, to get him deeper. I gripped my pussy tight and he made a sound that made me smile.

'Good?' I asked.

'Not good. Fucking amazing.'

Adrian pulled free of me and I reached for him, but he moved down my body too quickly for me to snatch him. His mouth – hot and wet and perfect – settled on my engorged clit and he started to suck. His stubble bit at my swollen sex and the bursts of near-pain only accentuated the humid pleasure of his mouth. He turned from sucking to long languid licks, thrusting thick fingers into my cunt where his cock had just been. He curled his fingers once, twice, three times and I came. Grasping his hair, thrusting my hips up.

Then he was turning me and his bedding brushed my cheek smelling of him – warm and musky and masculine.

'What was that?' I breathed, curling my fingers against his soft pillow as he hiked me up by the hips. Adrian entered me roughly and I gasped when I went from empty to full so fucking fast.

'I just wanted to taste you,' he said. 'It's been years.'

'And?' I barely managed it. I could feel the pressure building in my pelvis. That runaway-train feeling of impending release.

'And you still taste like watermelons and green grass,' he chuckled and swatted my ass hard enough that I tossed my head back and hissed. 'My god, your ass, Tuesday,' he said and swatted me again.

I gritted my teeth but he wasn't stupid. What he was, in fact, was a very in-tune lover. He curled himself over me, still thrusting deeply but with more restraint. 'Touch yourself, Tuesday. Come for me.'

'I just did.' But I wedged my shaking hand under my body to obey his warm silken command.

'I'm greedy. Do it again.'

I played slick circles over my clit with my fingertip as he reined himself in even more. Thrusting in smooth even strokes so that I felt stuffed full to bursting with goodness. His cock was long and when he rotated his hips just the right way he brushed my G-spot with enough force to make my face warm and my heart shiver. And he knew it.

'Come on. I can feel it. Give it to me.' One more sound smack was delivered and another deep thrust and then I pinched my clitoris and gave him what he asked for. My body delivering a fresh rush of juice to lubricate his way.

And he was free of me again, leaving me feeling empty and needy. But not for long. Adrian dropped to his back, laughing softly – at me no doubt – and pulled me onto him. I straddled him and watched his handsome face as he started to move up under me.

'I forgot sex with you was a full contact sport.'

His dark eyes studied me and he gave me that half grin that made my belly tremble with nerves and want. 'It's been a long time since we've been together, Tues. Hell, it's been a long time for me period.'

His warm hands cupped my breasts and he started to pinch my nipples. Hard and sharp and then a soothing barely there pinch. Back and forth, alternating, keeping me off balance so I anticipated the pain with a rush of pleasure.

I worked my hips and he met me halfway by moving up under me. We were rocking our way to a finale orgasm, I could tell by the look on his face.

'You? Why do I find that hard to believe?'

'Because I am just that studly?' He tried to smile but I clenched my internal muscles and his eyelids fluttered closed instead. I held his hands to my breasts with my own and pressed harder on my left side so he could feel my heart.

'Yes,' I said.

'Just haven't been interested in anyone. And you know me, I don't just run around …' He broke up, forcing me to let his hands go and gripping my hips hard. His fingers bit into my flesh delivering little bursts of discomfort that only made the fucking that much sweeter.

'Banging just anyone,' I finished his sentence and leaned over him, moving a bit faster.

He craned his neck and kissed me, then captured a nipple in his mouth and bit. I came again. Adrian watched my face, touched my lower lip with his fingertip that smelled like my juices. I met his gaze, sucked his fingers deep into my mouth and then he was the one coming. Arching up under me, gasping for breath.

I had forgotten how beautiful Adrian was when he came. I could get used to having a man like him around.

Chapter Four

ADRIAN DROPPED THE LIGHT bulb box into the recycling bin. 'So what's on the agenda for you, Tuesday Cane?'

'You like saying my name, dontcha?' I handed him a cold can of soda. Nan was so well stocked I might not have to shop for weeks.

'Yeah. It's a cool name. All the girls around here are named normal regular names like Lisa and Kelly and Stacey. It's not every day you meet a Tuesday. But it is–'

'Every week,' I chirped, citing his old joke. 'Ba-dum-dum-duh! Thank you, ladies and gentlemen, I'll be here all week.'

'Ha ha. But really. What are you going to do now? Become a lady of leisure? Write?'

There it was again. Write. My Nan must have made me out to be some super scribe. I shook my head and sighed. 'Nope. Waitressing, probably until I figure something else out. Shepherd said the restaurant might be hiring part-time.'

Adrian's face grew dark, his mouth clamped down to a tight seam and his jaw flexed. Uh-oh. What had I said?

'What?'

'Nothing.'

'Oh, yeah, nothing. You go from happy man to grizzly bear face in less than a second. Sure, nothing at all.'

He shrugged, finishing off his soda and tossing it in the recycling bin after the light bulb box. 'You've met him?'

'Yeah, this morning. He popped over to say hi.'

'You didn't mention that earlier.' He sounded petulant. Now I remembered why Adrian and I hadn't hung in there longer. He could be jealous and petty and juvenile. Sweet and sexy and stunning in bed, but sometimes that didn't override the childishness of his ways in relationships. Maybe he'd grown some.

'I didn't think about it. What's the big deal?'

He looked out into the overcast day at the now-choppy lake and the leaden clouds. 'No big deal.'

'So what's your beef with him, Adrian?' Now I was curious. I wanted to know.

'I just don't like him, is all. You'd do well to stay away from him.' He stood suddenly and almost tipped the yellow ladder-back chair over.

'Ooh, small town drama and rivalry.'

Now he looked pissed and I felt bad. 'I've just heard shit about him, Tuesday. He's a sexual deviant. Stay away from him. I have to go. I promised my dad I'd help him repair a fence.'

And he was gone. Stomping out the front and trying to act like he was just fine with our conversation when clearly he wasn't.

'Wow,' I said to Nan. Or my imagined presence of Nan. 'He really doesn't like Shepherd. And I'm just nosy enough to need to know why.'

I showered, threw on clean clothes and laced up my boots. I'd go and apply for a part-time job and ponder this whole sexual deviant thing.

'So, Virginia's Tuesday, you want a job at Irv's Eats?' Irving Lieberman asked.

'If you have one, I'd love to be considered.' There was something about Irving Lieberman that made me smile. He was small, pale and had eyes so dark they were the colour of espresso.

He puffed up his chest. 'I need a hostess. To greet and seat our patrons.'

I looked around the restaurant which basically was just a diner. Inside the front door four booths sat to your left, five to your right and dead ahead was a countertop with padded stools that seated a dozen. Painted a pale butter yellow with coral and red accents, Irv's Eats was sunny inside despite the day being cold and overcast outside. White Christmas lights were draped along the ceiling, down the thin venetian blinds and across bunches of hanging plants. The overall effect was Florida eatery meets dorm room meets your favourite aunt's cosy kitchen come holiday time.

I loved it.

'I thought you were destined to be a writer, Tuesday.'

'Dear Lord,' I laughed. 'Did my Nan tell everyone that?'

He nodded, indicating a stool which I grabbed. Mr Lieberman walked around behind and poured me a cup of coffee. Then he took the dome off a cake tray. 'Pastry?'

I had a vivid flash of being eight and sitting at this counter eating a blueberry Danish that basically tasted like heaven made from flour, eggs, sugar and preserves. 'Oh, gosh. Thanks.' I snagged the lone blueberry.

'And yes, to answer your question, Virginia told everyone that. She was very proud of you. She'd bend my ear until the orders piled up.'

'Oh I'm sorry.' I bit into the pastry and rolled my eyes with pleasure.

'No worries, dear.' He patted my hand. 'Virginia was a looker. She could've bent my ear as long as she liked.'

I laughed. 'She was beautiful.'

'My, my yes,' he said. 'So ...' Irving clapped his hands together and rubbed them briskly. 'Do you think you can hostess?'

I looked around. 'Of course. This isn't one of those pity jobs, is it?'

'Heavens no! My main waitress Delores is pregnant. Ready to pop and mean as a bull. She's been missing time and I need someone who will be on staff who can fill in for her and hostess and even do little things like deal with distributors or hand out coupons.'

'A Jill of all trades,' I said.

'Or a Tuesday of all trades.'

'Mr Lieberman,' I said, sticking my hand out. 'I'm your girl.'

'Ah, wonderful! Wonderful,' he said, pumping my hand

gleefully. Then he tugged me in and gave my cheek a resounding smack. 'Welcome aboard, Tuesday. Glad to have you.'

I grinned and finished my Danish. I was glad to have a job and a purpose. Because if I didn't have at least something part-time to look forward to, I'd be spending a lot of my time talking to Nan.

'When do I start?'

'How about in two hours? The dinner hour is swiftly approaching and Delores just called to say her ankles have swelled to the size of Christmas hams.'

'You totally just railroaded me, didn't you Mr Lieberman?'

He held his first finger and thumb very close together. 'Maybe just a bit.'

'So what's the pay?'

It wasn't enough to live on but it was enough to get by. Adrian had reminded me Nan had left me money. I was her only grandchild and she adored me, the fact that I was her only heir was no secret.

'I'll be back in a few hours. What should I wear?'

He rubbed his hands again, reminding me of a greedy little gnome, and went back through the swinging door. Apparently the restaurant was open from six to two for breakfast and lunch and then shut down until five when it reopened for dinner. Small town, private owner, his rules.

He emerged with a red tee that said IRV'S EATS in big yellow script. I grinned and took it.

'Just jeans and this. Or khakis. Or whatever floats your boat. As long as you wear my sporty tee you can be comfortable. And a tip, wear tennis shoes or shoes that you're really comfortable in. We're open from five to ten for dinner and the joint gets hopping. Especially in this weather, folks like to come in and chat and drink coffee or bring their wine and watch the rain.' He smiled, the proud papa of a very cosy eatery.

'They can bring wine?'

'Oh sure, sure. We have the BYOB thing. They bring some nice wine, get some pot roast, schmooze. End the night with some pie or some of my cook's coconut cake and everyone's happy.'

'I'll be back, Mr Lieberman.'

'Please, please, call me Irv.' He thrust the shirt at me and I took it.

'Irv,' I said.

On the drive home the Grenada's windshield wipers were thumping hard. The sky had opened up. 'Oh, shit. Shepherd.'

I turned off onto the lake road for Nan's and parked by his house. I ran up to the door, screaming – very embarrassing – like a girl due to the deluge. I was soaked by the time I rang the doorbell.

I rang it again and hugged myself, chills racked my body. 'Hello?' I banged on the screen door and glanced at my car. Maybe there was paper in my purse. Maybe I could leave a note. I started for the steps.

'I wouldn't do that if I were you,' he said from behind the screen door.

'Jesus! I didn't even hear you open the door! Are you making it a habit to scare the shit out of me?'

He grinned, pushing the screen wide. 'Sorry. I guess I'm quieter than one would expect. Come on in before you get pneumonia.'

I looked down at myself. Water dripped from my shirt and my jeans. It ran in rivulets from the end of my hair. My boots were so wet when I moved my toes they made squishy sounds. 'Um, I'm kind of … damp.'

'Goodness me, don't ruin the cashmere carpets,' he growled and grabbed my wrist and tugged me inside.

I squeaked with surprise but found myself standing inside his warm and cosy house on a very threadbare, very old but still very colourful rag rug. 'Stand here. I'll get you some towels. Take your boots off.'

I stayed on the rug and bent to unlace them. The main room in his home had the sweeping ceilings like my main room – it was very similar. But his sofa was coffee brown instead of cream like mine. There were tons of throw blankets on the back that made me want to curl up and hibernate among his cushions. The sofa was flanked by huge overstuffed chairs and matching ottomans. A rough raw wood coffee tale completed it. The windows that made me think of blind eyes were transparent once you were inside. I watched the lake dance under the driving rain and waited on the rug like a good girl.

'Here. Let's get you warm.'

'I really only came to say I was sorry.' I tried to go on but my teeth were chattering and I realised that I had broken out in goosebumps. A shiver worked through me and I said 'whoa' without thinking.

'Come on. You're going to seriously catch a chill and then you'll have to let poor Irv down.'

I blinked at him but dumbly stood and let him unbutton my plaid shirt. 'How did you know?'

He grinned and I fought an insane urge to touch his beard. I failed. So I did reach out and touch it.

We both stilled for a moment and I felt a rush of wetness that had nothing to do with rain. Maybe Allister Lake had turned me into a sex pervert – that was what Nan always called it. *That man's a sex pervert* ... And thinking that way made me smile.

Shepherd smiled back and popped the button on my jeans. Hadn't I just been doing something similar to this with good old Adrian?

He's a sexual deviant ... I heard Adrian's warning in my head, but instead of fear, I felt nothing but curiosity and lust.

'Irving called me to thank me for sending you his way. So ...' He pushed my jeans down but didn't touch my panties. Pale blue, soaking wet, clinging to me. Leaving little to the imagination, clearly accenting a very properly trimmed bit of pubic hair and I swore I could feel my clit – engorged and at attention – pressing to the damp fabric.

His intense brown eyes studied me and I saw the tension in his jaw, barely restrained but sexy as shit.

'So?' I barely managed.

'So, I know you won't be here for dinner like we'd planned.' He dropped my jeans on top of my shirt and started to towel me off. First my hair, then my neck. When he dried my shoulders and then over my bra, heat flooded my nipples and my collarbone. I knew that if I looked in the mirror my chest would be flushed a brazen red, the way it gets when I am turned on beyond belief.

'Oh,' I said.

Brilliant.

His towel – a well-worn green swathe of cotton – slithered down my belly and then caught my arms up to dry them. He dried over my panties and my hips and when he looked up at me my heart seized up.

There was something about seeing a man that big down on his knees.

'So I thought we could eat late,' he said.

The towel joined the pile of wet clothes and I rubbed my thighs together, feeling more naked in my wet bra and panties than I would have were I actually naked. 'OK. We can eat late. I don't know what time–'

'Let's say eleven.'

Shepherd touched my navel and my body galloped with need. The fine muscles in my belly fluttered and my pussy flexed with anticipation. I bit my lip hard to try and focus. I failed.

'OK.' I rubbed my legs together again and thought what a stupid thing to do. It only made the full and swollen feeling in my cunt worse.

'Am I scaring you?' He was still on his knees.

'No,' I lied.

'Does it help?' He touched my hip bones so gently I wouldn't have been sure he actually touched me had I not been watching.

'Does what help?'

'When you clench your thighs together does it help you not want to come?'

His hands were spanning the tops of my thighs and I felt my sex release another rush of fluid. A wet surrender flag waved for him so he would put me out of my misery. I felt a blush rise up my cheeks. 'No.'

'And now you're thinking dirty things aren't you,

Tuesday?'

How did we get here? How did we go from my back deck to a dinner invitation to me shaking and wet and might-as-well-be-naked on his faded rag rug?

'Yes,' I blurted.

'Do you want me to touch you?'

'I'll be late,' I said as if that would save me from myself.

'You won't be late. Now answer the question.' His eyes were so fucking dark. His body so goddamn big. He had a presence – it was the only way to describe it. You could not be near Shepherd Moore and not be 100 per cent aware of it. At least, I couldn't.

'Yes,' I said.

'Too bad. I don't want to touch you,' he said, looking up at me and grinning.

I thought my cheeks had been hot before, but now they blazed like small furnaces were hidden under my skin.

'Say please,' he said. 'Because there is something I want to do.'

I shook my head, anger and embarrassment and wariness warring in my chest. I gnawed my lip and realised that I could feel his hot breath on the front of my cold wet panties and instinctively, I clenched my thighs … damn it.

'Say it.'

'Please,' I said. I said it fast, like ripping off a band aid. Like swallowing a pill. Like jumping into cold water. I did it fast and tried not to pay attention to the fact that I was doing it at all.

Chapter Five

SHEPHERD PUT HIS HANDS on my hips and his grip was so strong I had no trouble believing he'd been an ultimate cage fighter. I expected smoke to rise off my skin where he touched me but promptly lost the image when the velvet humidity of his mouth clamped down over my sodden panties and I felt the heated nudge of his tongue to my clit.

So I was right. My clitoris was so engorged that it pressed to the pale cotton underpants. I had thought it was just my imagination but he went straight to it his tongue a heat-seeking missile that slammed me with a rush of pleasure so intense my knees sagged.

He covered my knees then with the span of his large hands and squeezed as if to tell me that if they did unhinge and threaten to dump me on my ass, he'd hold me up.

I made a sound I didn't recognise. It wasn't a word, it wasn't a cry. It was an utterance that could only come from surprise mixed with bliss.

He sucked the cotton and me into his scorching mouth, pressing that tongue of his to that hard nub of flesh until I squeezed my eyes shut so all of my awareness was focused solely on that point in my body. I moved to grip his shoulders and he said in a gentle but brusque voice, 'Hands down.'

I pushed my fingers restlessly to my own thighs and his hands came up to clamp my ass. He pulled me roughly forward, pressing his mouth to the maddening cotton that kept him from actually touching me.

'Shouldn't we–'

'Hush.' He squeezed my ass just hard enough for a jolt of pain that quickly bled into pleasure to startle me.

He licked and nudged and sucked in alternating rhythms with different pressures until I was sure the floor was tilting under me. I had to focus on holding my hands down and when he pulled back and looked at me, I was muzzy headed and confused. My pussy throbbed with my racing heart and I felt so swollen I wanted to weep.

'Does that feel good, Tuesday?'

I could only nod.

But Shepherd wasn't satisfied and as I was starting to piece together, he liked to be satisfied. 'Say it.'

'Yes.'

'Do you want to come?'

'Yes?'

'Are you uncomfortable?

'Some.' I put my eyes down, looking away from his probing gaze.

'Look at me.'

I forced my gaze back and swallowed hard. I was on the verge of begging him. Begging! Asking him to finish me off. Pull me down, climb on top, put it in me. Anything. Missionary, doggy style, suspended from the ceiling. Just do it – make me come.

'Why are you uncomfortable some?'

'I was just about to come. And now …' I shrugged.

'And now you've had a tiny break so it will be that much better,' he said and smiled. It was the smile of a predator. A beautiful, frightening monster who I wanted to kiss so badly I could taste the wet cotton on his tongue if I concentrated.

He pushed his mouth back to me, sucked, sucked, sucked and then pressed his tongue to that hard bit of flesh and when he bit me, I didn't sense it coming. A quick controlled nip to my clit that sent a buzz-flash of pain through me and I was coming. Gripping my fucking thighs with my crazy-restless fingers and trying not to cry out. What came out of me was a sigh and a whimper and a moan that made me feel so ashamed and yet so liberated.

When I opened my eyes he was standing. 'I'll get you some clothes to run home in. You still have time for a shower and to get back to Irv's.'

'But … you …'

Were we done? I didn't want to be done. I wanted to get my hands on him. Among other things.

'Will be here tonight when you get back.'

He handed me sweats and a hoodie and I laughed when I pulled them on. I looked like a toddler in her father's clothes. He stooped, rolled the sweats and I hugged myself with the soft hoodie keeping me warm.

'I've heard–' I broke off. What had I been thinking?

'You've heard what?' He tossed my wet clothes in a side room. I assumed it to be a mudroom because I could see boots and a washer and dryer and a coat rack.

'Nothing.'

'Come on. We've just been intimate, Tuesday. Can't you tell me?'

I studied him and could see the smile in his eyes though it barely touched his lips.

I shrugged and almost whispered. 'I've heard things about you and your … sexual preferences.'

'Goats?' he asked, straight faced.

'What? No!' I yelped. My entire face now blazed with mortification.

He laughed outright and I felt my body let loose more moisture. Shepherd Moore did weird fucking things to me – literally and figuratively.

'So people are telling tales already? Interesting.'

'I'm sorry. I never should have said. I don't listen to gossip anyway.' I turned to go. I had a job to get to. And a weird oral sex experience that still had me buzzing to ponder and analyse.

He put his hand on the door so I couldn't open it and a splinter of fear stabbed my chest. And I kind of liked it, I realised.

'You can listen all you want, but what you need to consider is it's up to you.'

'What's up to me?'

He kissed me under my ear and I shivered. He'd yet to kiss my mouth. Then he pulled his hand away and opened the door for me. 'Whether or not you let what you hear scare you off. Whether or not you're going to find out about me for yourself.'

I showered and tried not to overthink what had just happened. It had been oddly erotic having him make me come without seeing me naked or putting his mouth or hands or anything else directly on my nether regions.

'That's talent,' I snorted, and rushed out of the shower. No time to dry my hair. I wrapped it in a towel and left it while I pulled on jeans and my new work tee. I swiped my eyes with mascara and my lips with gloss and put some cheeky pink crème blush on my cheeks. Then I braided my crazed hair into two braids and set about finding my motorcycle boots in my mess of moving stuff.

I still had time, no need to panic. And I didn't feel panicked. At least not about Irv's or working or any of that. That atmosphere of his place made me feel at home and calm. It was what would come later that made me feel panicky. I'd be alone again with Shepherd. Would it be odd? Would I want to jump him? Did he only get girls off while they had clothes on? Did he shun traditional sex? Is that what Adrian had meant?'

'Jesus Christ, Tuesday, stop it!' I said, pulling on striped ankle socks and then my black leather boots. 'Shit kickers, just for you, Nan!' I yelled to my empty house. Hey, until I got a dog or a cat or a boyfriend, I'd talk to my grandmother all I wanted. Probably after that, too.

I didn't even let myself analyse it when I pulled on Shepherd's hoodie, zipped it up against the wind. The rain had stopped but the fall wind continued to rage. I pushed my face to the soft cotton and inhaled the scent of him. Wood shavings, cold air, leather, and whatever his signature Shepherd scent was. It was all there trapped in the fabric, a dizzying mélange that went to my head and my pussy. Calling up memories of that big man on his knees, his dark serious eyes studying me intently, his mouth knowing where to go instinctively.

I blew out a shaky breath and tried to calm my thumping heart. 'Good lord. Go to work,' I told myself.

The Grenada spat gravel as I headed out to Irv's. I would be on time for my first shift.

Irv hadn't been kidding. The place was mobbed even though I was just walking in. 'Am I late?' I gasped taking off Shepherd's hoodie and tucking it carefully in my oversized purse. I put it inside the office where Irv pointed.

'Nah. It was just raining buckets. I opened up a few minutes early so folks could stay dry.' He pointed to the board. 'Specials. Order window's there. Here's your pad. Waitresses pull their own drinks but everything else is kitchen. I'm the cashier so that's covered.'

'I thought I was hostessing,' I said, trying not to laugh.

He rolled his eyes at me and patted his bald head. 'Enh. What can I say, with the weather being what it is and Delores is out again. You are her tonight, got it?'

'No problem,' I giggled. 'I was joking. Breathe, Mr Lieberman.'

'Irv!' he corrected. 'And you're a good egg, just like my Virginia,' he said.

I cocked an eyebrow at him. 'Your Virginia?'

He blushed and I had to bite my tongue to keep from laughing. He looked ready to burst into flames. 'Hush, no pestering an old man.'

'So did you and my grandmother ever–'

'Oh, look! A customer!' He pointed me toward them and scurried away.

I was going to like it here.

Chapter Six

HE CAME IN AT about nine o'clock and stood out like nobody's business. Beautiful in a nearly fragile way. Soft brown hair shot with gold fell to his jaw line. Big blue-green eyes below full lashes that put most women to shame. Black jeans, blue button-down shirt, a loosely knotted red tie, a striped vest and well-worn brown Doc Martens on his feet. He did a double take when he saw me, gave me a half smile that made me curious.

I looked away, suddenly flustered. Was Allister Lake a magnet for oddly attractive men or was I just on some mission to start a whole new life, between my legs and otherwise.

'That's your table. You trying to wait on him with your psychic powers?' Irv was smiling at me.

I snorted, quickly covered my nose and shook my head. 'Sorry,' I said and hurried over.

'Hi, there. I'm Tuesday, what can I get you to drink?' My tongue felt too big and my brain too small. Plus I had the most bizarre sensation of déjà vu when I looked at him. Like I'd met him before.

'Tuesday. Like Wells?' His eyes were shiny and kind. His demeanour friendly but subtle. He seemed like the kind of man who thought about everything that was said to him. And then thought carefully about what he wanted to say in response.

'Like Cane.' I smiled.

'Ah, I was close. Was it your grandmother who just passed?'

Had everyone known Nan? Then I considered the size of Allister Lake proper and even the small surrounding town, and I realised they probably had.

'Yep. She did. That's me … her granddaughter' I walled off the wave of grief and smiled at him. The door opened and the bell jingled and Irv cleared his throat and I leaned in,' I'm sorry, but it's my first night, we're super busy and Irv thinks I'm lingering. Can I get you a drink?'

'I'm very sorry for your loss,' he whispered back and then, 'Dr Pepper.'

'Thank you.' I smiled.

He nodded. 'Alas, the gods finally drop an interesting woman in my lap here at AL and she has to rush off.'

'AL?'

'Allister Lake.'

'Duh,' I said.

He winked at me, and to my shock and dismay, I felt that wink in my belly and lower. 'Hey, you're new. Give it a few weeks and you'll be a local and you'll be abbreviating it too.'

'Ahem!' Irv said.

I pointed to pretty boy with my pen. 'I'll get your Dr Pepper … um … Mr …'

'Reed,' he said. 'My name is Reed Green.'

'Like Mr Green Jeans!' I said. Then I turned fast and prayed to drop dead. Because that always impresses a good looking man … a Captain Kangaroo reference.

I pulled his Dr Pepper and took his order, fish sandwich with lettuce, mayo and a toasted roll, an order of fries and lemon meringue pie for dessert. When I delivered the pie I blurted, 'Undercover Father!'

He grinned at me and I felt that curl of heat in my gut again. Which made me think of Shepherd and what he'd done to me. And that made me think of meeting him in an hour and that made me antsy.

'Good job.' He tucked into the pie, rolled his eyes, took another bite.

'And then–'

'And then some other nothing-special, average TV shows and two movies and I got bored.' He smiled as if to say end of story.

'Oh, sure. I'm sorry. And now you …'

Why had I started that sentence?

'Now, I write screenplays sometimes – if I feel like it – and have a berry picking farm.'

I laughed. 'A what?'

'A berry picking farm.' He gave me a teasing smile.

'Ah, see, I look at you and immediately think berry farmer.'

The traffic into Irv's Eats was slowing down and Irv did not clear his throat at me. 'As you should. Former TV star and now berry man.'

I smiled, realising when I glanced at the clock that in less than an hour I'd be at Shepherds. I had a vision of him on his knees, my fidgety fingers clutching my thighs as I came, water dripping from my hair, rain on the windows. I sighed without thinking about it.

'You OK?'

'I am. Sorry. My brain is racing, I just moved here, new job … just new everything.'

'Ah, let me take you for a drink tonight and calm you down.' His features were fine and almost delicate. High cheekbones, flawless skin, and Lord, those October sky blue eyes. I almost said yes and then, 'I can't. I have plans.'

'Of course.' There was that boyish smile, smooth silken voice that wasn't too deep and manly or too soft and feminine. It was a liquid silver voice that flowed and calmed and made you think happy thoughts. 'What was I thinking? A gorgeous young thing like you moves to town and I think I'd get first opportunity to woo you? Crazy old man.'

'Old? Like what? Thirty?'

'Thirty-three. See? What do you know?'

'That you're a whole four years older than me. Are you calling me old, Mr Green?'

'Would it earn me a drink?'

'No.'

'A smack?'

'Maybe.' I took the tab and the money he offered.

'How about you just let me take you for a drink on a night you don't have plans and I can tell you how you don't look a day over twenty-two.'

'Deal,' I said. 'I'll go get your change.'

'No need. The top bill is yours. The rest are for Irv. Tell him the pie was perfect.'

The top bill was a twenty and it had a phone number scrawled on it. I tucked it in my apron pocket and went to the cash register. When I turned to say goodnight, Reed Green was gone.

I pushed my hands to my belly when I parked outside Shepherd's house. Lights burned behind those opaque windows and now they made me think of haunted eyes. 'Haunted, Nan,' I sighed to my grandmother.

Another sudden fist of guilt punched me in the chest and I sobbed out loud before gritting my teeth.

'Jesus, don't cry,' I hissed. I undid my braids in fast angry motions to distract myself. I so did not want to cry.

But I did cry. So I sat there with my hand gripping the steering wheel, head down as if praying, and let myself cry for all I was worth. My make-up would be ruined, there would be no hiding this little fit of emotion, but what else could I do. I missed my grandmother and I couldn't shake the feeling that I'd let her down. Throw in all the fucking and attraction and new life and I was a basket case of feelings.

Bleh.

The door opened suddenly and I sat up startled. 'What?'

'You coming in or are you going to sit outside all night?'

'I'm sorry,' I sniffled and wiped my eyes with my trembling fingers. 'I was trying to save face.'

'No need.' He put his hand out and I took it, a warmth that came to me only with comfort slid across my skin warming me inside and out.

That struck me as funny and I giggled all the way to the front door as he led me. It had started raining again. The drops on my skin triggered a sensory memory of his hot mouth pressed to my damp panties. I curled my fingers against his skin and followed.

Inside he took a towel from a small chair in the foyer and

wiped my face. 'Virginia?'

There was no use denying it, so I simply nodded. 'I miss her. And I failed her.'

He laughed. 'Not to hear her talk. You were the light of her life and the talk of this town.'

'I haven't come for a proper visit in ages. She either came to town to see me or it was a drive through on the way to somewhere else.'

'You were living the life she wanted you to.' He touched my bottom lip but then turned suddenly and led me down the hall.

'Oh yeah? My grandmother wanted me with a douche bag who slowly but surely decided his favourite form of entertainment was taking a swing or two at me?' I said it under my breath but the venom in my voice was as clear as the lake air.

His eyes went dark and he leaned against the wall. 'Is that what you lived like?' Even I couldn't miss the fact that his big hands reflexively clenched into fists. Very large fists that were trained to do damage.

I had a burst of fear and it must have shown on my face.

'Are you afraid of me?'

'No. I'm afraid for whoever those fists are for. But I don't get the feeling that's me.'

That made him smile and my body relaxed.

'How did it end with that man? The one I should go find and beat within an inch of his life?'

'I took my old Louisville Slugger to him. He walked funny after that.'

Shepherd grinned. He reached out and stroked my hair. I held my breath for a heartbeat but then it went wild in my chest and I had to suck in some oxygen. I sucked in even more when his hand quickly twisted in my hair and he tugged me against him. His mouth crushed down on mine and I didn't think, didn't consider, I parted my lips for him and let his tongue thrust along mine so that I felt the kiss in my cunt.

'I can picture it,' he said softly. His lips grazed my jaw line and my entire body tingled with the sensation. He plucked my nipple roughly through my tee and I sighed, sagging a little in his arms. 'I can picture you all fired up and angry. Violent. Someone to be reckoned with.'

His arms crushed me against him and I felt the hard hump of his cock between my legs. I wanted him. I wanted him in me and over me and rocking against me so I said his name when I came.

'Shep–' was all I managed when he kissed me again. Big hands cupping my ass, trapping my front to his front. I could feel his heartbeat wild and unmanageable like mine and the heat of him seeping into my pores and helping me shake off the chill of the damp night.

'Food,' he said, pulling free. 'Steak like I promised.'

My nipple still throbbed in time with my pulse and my pussy was doing the same. I shook my head to clear it and tried to steady my racing mind. 'Right. I am starving, actually. Hard to believe that I spent all night working around food and didn't eat a single thing.'

On the eating side of the wide kitchen-dining room combo, warm sconce lights shone. The table was set with mismatched china and placemats. Wild flowers graced the centre of the table, rising up out of an antique milk glass pitcher. I smiled – my kind of décor. Laid back, easy and comfortable.

'You sit, I'll serve.'

I obeyed, touching the pale yellow plate that rested on a blue and white checked placemat. His was a red plate on a pale green and white striped mat. The napkins were white, the salt and pepper shakers shaped like a chicken and an egg. I ran my fingers over the rough wide plank wood table. I loved his house.

'You don't mind that they're mismatched, do you?'

I shook my head. 'No, I like it. It's how Nan was. If it was pretty and still serviceable, you used it. She called it shabby chic or sometimes country charm.'

He nodded decisively bringing in a platter bearing two beautiful T-bones and baked potatoes.

'Can I help?' I shifted in my seat wanting to please him – an odd and somewhat unwelcome urge in my current state of life.

42

'Nope. You sit. Let me grab the salad and the water pitcher.'

I studied the sconces to realise they were cut wine bottles set into bases over light bulbs. Shepherd put the water pitcher down – speckleware which again made me insanely happy for some reason – and then snapped his fingers.

'You can pour our water; I'll go get the wine.'

Then he was kissing me. A sweet and somehow familiar kiss that I imagined husbands and wives shared often. But we weren't married and we'd just met and that fact stole my breath because when he pulled back and left I realised … it had felt right. That kiss had felt perfect and wonderful.

And it scared the shit out of me.

I poured our water, determined not to think about it.

Chapter Seven

SOMEHOW I MADE IT through dinner, though sitting across from him had me on edge. Not uncomfortable on edge, lust-laden on edge.

'Are you OK?'

I was eating my apple pie, fresh bought I was told, from Caitlin's bakery which kicked the formal bakery's ass all over town. Apparently if you lived here, you ate Caitlin's pies. And when he'd said that, I fucking blushed like a virgin.

'I'm fine.'

'You seem uneasy.'

'I'm not uneasy.'

'O-K.' he dragged the word out. His eyes never stopped though. It was as if he were analysing every breath I took, every move, every nuance. 'Good.'

Shepherd started to trace his fingers in and out of the dips between my fingers. Slowly. Every inch his fingertip travelled was another spike of heat in my pelvis. I swallowed hard and smiled.

'Meet anyone interesting tonight?' he asked. He gave me a small half smile and I realised he was teasing me. He knew I was on edge and he was playing with me. He knew how badly I wanted him and he was fucking with me.

'I … um …' Each sweeping touch wiped my brain so I could barely focus or form a thought. I forced myself to see faces and blurted. 'I met the Andrews. You know they have twins and–'

'And triplets.' He nodded. 'Good, and?'

'And I met Mrs Gabriel. She has the worst–'

'Wig,' he said and lifted my hand to kiss my fingers. I

44

opened my mouth only to snap it shut. A thrumming pulse had started between my legs and everything else in me was just background noise. I was nothing more than my lust for Shepherd Moore at that moment in time. I embodied it.

Think, Tuesday. Think!

'I met the reverend and he did not like my h–'

'Hair at all,' Shepherd finished. He sucked my finger into his mouth and the pull of his tongue on me sounded in my cunt. I shifted in my seat and it only made the wet need worse.

'It's whore hair,' I whispered

He straightened up a bit. 'He said that to you?'

'No,' I laughed, able to take a deep breath since he was distracted. 'I heard him telling the woman he was with. Her name was …'

'Mildred. That's his sister. Seriously, sometimes I think they're doing each other.'

I let out a joyful shriek, but then his mouth was back on my hand and he said, 'Go on.'

His tongue was hot. And I knew what that fucking tongue could do. Through panties, no less. 'I … um …'

'Cat got your tongue?'

'No, your tongue's got my brain. All locked up,' I admitted in a breathy whisper. Hearing the state of my voice I felt even more flustered.

'Just one more.'

He held my hands now. Over the table. Very proper. His thumbs sweeping back and forth over the surprisingly tender flesh above my own thumbs. My nipples spiked against my bra, reminding me that all I really wanted was to have him in me. Holding me down and fucking me. It had been in my mind a lot, when I wasn't fucking Adrian, or flirting with Reed, for God's sake.

Greedy.

But it made me smile, all the attraction and want and joyous flirting and more. I had lived a bottled up life for a while. I'd broken free and had moved on. My only regrets were breaking Stan's heart and not getting to Nan in time. But I knew what Nan would tell me if she were here: guilt is a wasted emotion.

If you must entertain it, make it quick and get on with it. I wanted to go forward in my life with ballsy bravery. Right now I owed nothing to anyone but myself.

'Reed Green,' I said.

His face shut down on me. He released my hands. His eyes went from open and warm to shuttered.

What had I said?

'Oh yeah?'

'Yeah. Why? What's wrong with you two? What did I say?'

He stood, clearing the table. 'Nothing. You said nothing. I just don't like him is all. He's a womaniser.'

'Oh yeah?' I laughed. 'Uses his fame to woo them, does he?'

He cocked his head at me and then shook it in disgust. 'You could say that. And he's so goddamned pretty, so you know they all swoon.'

I chewed the inside of my cheek to keep from laughing. I had a feeling that would upset Shepherd even more. First Adrian had an issue with Shepherd and now Shepherd had an issue with Reed. Either there were women in their history or this was small town life.

'And for fuck's sake,' he said, taking a pile of dishes to the sink. 'Who stops acting to run a berry picking fucking farm?'

'Is that the official term?' I asked, pressing my lips into a tight seam. I would not laugh.

I was right on his heels and he whirled too fast and knocked me off balance. I clutched the wine glasses and pitcher but started to lose them. Shepherd righted the pitcher and me. I let out a startled whoop and then laughed.

'It is,' he growled. 'It is the official term.'

He plucked the dainty wine glasses from me and put them in the sink.

'Well who stops ultimate cage fighting – not just fighting but cage fighting – to be a handyman?' I put my hands on my hips and waited.

'I do.'

'So he can't pick berries?'

He shook his head. 'Never mind. You'd have to live here to

get it.'

His eyes were riveted to my red tee and I was starting to feel naked. 'I do live here,' I whispered.

I touched his beard. I couldn't resist. Normally I despised facial hair but with him it fit so well. It was so aggressive and yet seemed like something he hid behind. I petted it with the tops of my fingers feeling its wiry yet soft texture against my skin.

'Just for a while,' he said. He caught my hand, stilling it.

I stood on tiptoe and kissed him. 'I'd like to live here a long time.'

'Maybe you should go,' he said.

'Why's that? You don't like me any more?'

'I do. I like you too much. And I'm not a good pick for someone like you.'

'What kind of someone am I?'

I tried to pull my hands free but he wouldn't release them so I played the sneaky card and pressed my body tight to his. I rocked my hips and felt the press of his erection to the split of my sex.

'A nice person.'

'You're nice too. What you did earlier was nice. And I want to be nice with you again.'

His eyes were so fucking dark. Impossibly dark. And full of lust so staggering I felt it run along my skin like an electrical current.

'Take your clothes off.'

I stood up straight and did my best to meet him eye to eye. 'You take them off,' I said.

He bully-walked me back, trapping my hands between his much bigger ones at my chest. He nudged me along until the backs of my thighs met the lip of his table. In front of one of those big blind-eye windows. I wondered if people could see our silhouettes outside. I wondered if they could see what we were doing.

The possibility that they could sent a thrill through me and my pussy clenched up tight, wanting him, wanting this so damn bad I could taste it.

Shepherd pushed me back – rough enough to make me break out in goosebumps. He tugged my red tee over my head and dropped it in my dinner chair. He worked my button and zipper with ease, shocking for such big fingers, and tugged my pants down.

'Black,' he said.

'What?' My head was buzzing. From him, not wine. I stared up at him, relishing the feel of his palm sliding along my belly just above my panties.

'Your panties are black.' He stroked them. From waistband to gusset making sure to scrape along my clit. I arched up mindlessly, holding my breath and feeling my heart in my temples. 'And silk.'

'Satin,' I laughed.

'Same thing basically.'

He tugged them free and I was aware of every inch that scrap of soft fabric slid. Shepherd dropped those on top of my jeans and slid his hands under my ass. I felt shy and bold and so fucking light headed I feared I'd lose consciousness.

'Open your legs for me, Tuesday.' His eyes were already penetrating me. A wave of pleasure flooded through me at just his eyes on me. It felt like he was touching me when he stared that way.

I let my thighs fall open and his eyes were there. Between my legs. On a place I rarely ever looked – but he was studying me the way I'd seen people study rare flowers or beautiful butterflies. I wriggled under his gaze.

'Stay still,' he said. His hands pinned my thighs wide and stilled my restless movement. 'I want to look at you. Before I suck you.'

I moaned then. Just as if he'd touched me. I made that noise and waited to feel ashamed, instead I felt honest.

A man had never said that to me before. It was always lick or kiss or God help me one time suckle. But suckle made me think of distinctly non-sexy things. And all of that ran through my head as I tried so hard to stay so still but continued to undulate and sway like sea grass in a stormy lake.

His hands were huge, spanning my hipbones, anchoring me

to the rough wood table. He dropped to his knees, so tall he still almost looked like he was standing from my angle. His head dipped, beard scratching my inner thighs and he took my clit in his mouth and sucked.

My fingers tangled in the placemats. My hair swished under my hand as I moved it back and forth to try and find some kind of equilibrium. 'Jesus,' was the only brilliant thing I could think to say.

'Hush, Tuesday.'

He sucked softly and then harder when his fingers, unimpeded by panties this time, slipped into me and began fucking me. Deep thrusts that he curled up perfectly on the upward motion. My hips tried to rise up and he used his forearm to shut me down.

I whimpered, frustrated but so, so turned on.

His tongue speared my wet hole and then his fingers slid back home, filling me and nudging me into a slow sweet orgasm that took all the noise from my throat and all the air from my lungs.

Shepherd stood, eyes glazed and darker than I'd ever seen them. The low ethereal light from his sconces backlit the bits of silver in his beard and his hair. He licked his lips and I reached for him.

He took a step back. 'Don't move.'

He unbuttoned his jeans and shucked his dark boxer briefs. His cock was big. I don't know why that surprised me. He was big. All over. Easily six foot six, two hundred and thirty pounds, give or take.

Surely he could palm a basketball or someone's skull if he was in the cage. And yet, I was still surprised at the size of him. The length and the girth. When he took himself in hand and stroked, my whole body rippled with desire. I became kinetic.

He toed off his socks and opened a door in the sideboard and pulled out his wallet. I watched him rip the foil packet and roll the condom on and all the time, his fingers on his own flesh was a mesmerising sight to me.

I spread my legs, baring my sex for him as he advanced –

shameless, needy, restless, like I might die if he didn't touch me.

'Stop moving,' he said.

I froze. It took all of my energy to keep myself still as he traced my labia with his warm fingers. He tested me then, thrusting deep, my pussy so wet we both heard the accepting noise it made when he fingered me.

My cheeks flared hot but I kept my gaze steady.

Shepherd pushed the head of his cock to my slit and gripped my hips. 'Do you want this?'

'Of course.'

'Say it.'

'I want this.'

'It's not too soon?' he asked, looking both aggressive and sincerely concerned.

'I'm learning there's no such thing as too soon.' I let my legs fall open just a bit more and he made a noise that came from deep in his chest.

Shepherd didn't drive into me. He inched into me. Slowly. The rough pad of his thumb pressed my clit as he slid home and I watched him. How his stomach muscles flexed and his biceps moved and his jaw clenched tight. He gripped my breast with his right hand and lightly plucked the nipple until it stood up straight. Then he bent his bulk over me and took the nub in between his sweetly sharp teeth and nipped me.

When I gasped and moved he slid all the way in, forcing his cock deep into my body. Making my cunt adjust and grip up around him. We froze that way, sprawled over the wooden table – face to face. His breath hot on my face, his hands rough on my skin.

'Move,' I whispered. 'Oh God, Shepherd, please move.'

He started to rock into me. Languid even thrusts that inched me across the table top until he gripped me tight and held me still. I couldn't remember being that boldly honest before. Not naked, not face to face, not fucking.

I had needed him to move, to quench the need inside of me, and I had asked for it in a raw and honest voice. It startled even me.

His thumb pressed and rolled, spreading my own fluids over the hard knot of my clit. Shepherd drove deep, watching me as I watched him. His hips pistoning so the small cut muscles along his flanks stood out and danced.

He grabbed my ankles, bringing them up to rest on his shoulders before returning his thumb to rub me some more. I arched up some, using his broad shoulders for leverage and he never batted an eye. His cock slammed my G-spot repeatedly, brushing all the sweet spots along the way and he gave me one final press and rub and I was coming, trying so hard not to drum my ankles against his skin.

He didn't care. 'You ripple when you come. Like tight warm water on my cock.' He laughed softly when he said it and then pulled free. Offering me a hand he said, 'Up.'

I stood, holding his hand – and glad I was, because my knees felt weak and watery.

He turned me, bending me over the table, spread between our still present placemats: my body lying down the centre between the two colourful swatches of fabric. Shepherd kneed my legs apart a bit more and then leaned over me again. Placing my left wrist as far as it would go and then my right. 'Grip the table,' he said and I did. I curled my fingers around the rough wood and realised I was panting.

I was terrified, mortified and entirely turned on. I was being studied like some girl-specimen and normally that would make me run. For whatever reason, with Shepherd, it made me stay just as he'd placed me. I could feel his eyes on me and my heartbeat sped up to the point of dizziness.

Fingers pushed into me and thrust in and out so that I could hear the soaking wet evidence of my want between my thighs. He drove a finger gently but effortlessly into my ass and I bucked then. Not from pain, from surprise.

I pressed my face to the wood and waited to see what he would do to me. What I would let him do to me. The thought of that cock of his trying to fit into me there was enough to make my stomach buzz with anxiety. The realisation that I would let him try was enough to send an army of goosebumps marching up my spine.

Shepherd grunted, gripped my hips and hiked them high so just my tippy-toes were on the floor. He drove back into me, my cunt gripping him tight, greedy from its brief respite. His fingers continued a steady tempo in my ass and when he pressed so that I could feel finger and cock warring against that thin membrane that separated my two holes, I came.

This time Shepherd came too. A few heartbeats after my final spasm, he clenched my skin so tight I gasped and he emptied into me with a growl.

He pressed himself over me, his warm chest laid along my back. I felt his heartbeat banging my shoulder blade and the bite-tickle of that beard of his. He kissed the back of my neck.

'You can stay if you like. But you don't have to.'

It surprised me when I said, 'I think I'll go home.'

What the fuck was wrong with me?

Chapter Eight

I LOVED WHAT WE'D done. I loved how raw it was. I loved how I felt when I was around Shepherd. Even in a day he called to all the hidden parts of me that were fascinated by men like him: strong and sort of silent and kind of gruff. But good.

However, I did not like how fast I was feeling this way. Phil had only been dispatched a short while ago. And Stan was a broken heart in my very recent past. Like the 48 hour range.

True to his word he walked me to the door. It was past one and I was tired. My first shift followed by a rousing fuck with this man, had put me in the "so tired I felt like a zombie" zone.

Shepherd zipped his hoodie up to my neck and yanked the drawstring. The hood closed in on me so when he tugged gently I had to step forward into his arms. He kissed me hard and I let him.

I almost changed my mind.

But this was my new life and my new life could not begin tethered to someone else.

'You can have your hoodie back,' I whispered mentally crossing my fingers that he'd say no.

'It's cold out there. And you need it. Plus, you look sexy as shit swimming in my clothes.'

'I was hoping you'd say no. I like the smell of it,' I confessed. Standing on tiptoe, I kissed him.

I turned to the door but he caught me up in his grip. 'What's it smell like?'

'You,' I said.

He gave me that half grin that now had the effect of turning me inside out. Didn't matter that I'd shared myself with two different men today. Didn't matter that I'd only been in town a mere 24 hours. I saw that smile and my insides turned to hot liquid.

Which was why I had to go.

'And what do I smell like?' he prompted.

'Good,' I said. 'Really fucking good.'

Then I kissed him once more and bolted out the door before I changed my mind. I started the Grenada feeling like I'd wake the whole lake up and they'd witness me leaving Shepherd's house so late. And so flustered. And so clearly fucked.

My second day at Allister Lake started with bright sunlight through a skylight. Nan's bed was a big queen size deal in a brass frame. I'd never even had a frame on my bed before. Not even at the boarding house. It had simply been a mattress and box spring combo that sat directly on the floor. There had been nights that I'd been glad for it, too, because the likes of Phil had left me worried about monsters under the bed, and in the closet, and sometimes wearing boyfriend suits.

I rolled onto my belly and refused to give those bad thoughts room to grow.

'Good morning, A-frame. Good morning, sun. Good morning, Nan!' I shouted the last one.

I still had a lot to say to my grandmother it seemed, and since I was the only one here (though sometimes I felt she still was) I figured I was free to say it.

I padded to the bathroom and took care of business. Then I pulled on leggings and a football jersey that had been Stan's. I would run today. It was chilly in the house so it was perfect running weather.

The coffee pot gurgled and hissed at me as I braided my hair in a fat, messy French braid. I rummaged in a duffle bag and found my tennis socks and my beat-to-shit running shoes.

A cup of coffee, a piece of cheese and I was ready. I brushed my teeth and pulled a cap on and took off down the gravel road. I would rediscover the wonders of Allister Lake on foot.

It's tricky to run on gravel for someone like me. By "like me" I mean clumsy. I started out slow so I wouldn't fall. Once

I found my stride I looked around. That was right around the time I came level with Shepherd's house.

I was almost past and I heard 'Tuesday Cane!'

I stopped, shielding my eyes despite the cap. The sun off the lake was dazzling and almost painfully bright.

His breath puffed out of him and he was wiping those big hands – hands that had been manhandling me just hours before – on a rag. 'Good morning. Don't want to hold you up.'

I shivered. 'Morning, Mr Moore,' I said coyly. I was blushing and it felt good. The heat in my cheeks warred with the biting air.

He waved. 'Hi.'

He seemed almost shy and sort of irritated by it, which made it that much more enjoyable for me. 'I have to move,' I said bouncing.

His eyes flashed predatory as he took me in. 'You should have worn the hoodie.'

'I couldn't,' I admitted, blushing even more.

'Why not?'

'Because I'd sweat on it, and then I'd have to wash it,' I confessed.

'So?'

'So then it wouldn't smell like you any more, would it?' I launched myself at him, kissed him boldly and took off before he could grab hold. 'Off I go.'

'I'm working at the school auditorium today. It's not in use while we renovate. Stop in if you're bored.'

'Will do,' I said and waved.

It had felt good to kiss him but it also felt good to run from him. I was not ready for anything more than fucking. The three Fs – fun, flirting, fucking.

I ran, harder than usual but it felt good to get my heart racing and my body sweaty and flushed. It felt good to run like I was trying to beat the devil. Because maybe I was.

I ran along the gravel road until gravel turned to dirt with little bits of blacktop. Like they were going to pave the road but couldn't quite commit. The lake was still visible though much farther off.

The wind lifted my long bangs and then dropped them in my eyes. I ran through the stitch in my side, the cramp in my calf and a sudden staggering wall of exhaustion that rose up out of nowhere. But I kept running.

Then I hit a divot in the dirt, lost my footing on the funky half-done road, and I twisted my ankle.

'Motherhumper!' I sank down and rubbed my ankle, praying no one would come along and run over me. Even in a bright purple jersey with my bottle blonde hair I could be missed. At least I feared I could be.

I flexed and relaxed my ankle several times and finally stood and put a tiny bit of pressure on it to test my strength.

Pain. Not excruciating pain, but pain.

'And you, genius, have a cell but not a single God damn number of anyone you can call in Allister Lake!' I put my head back and gritted my teeth.

I shut my eyes, trying to breathe, still standing in the middle of the road like a doofus. The bright sunlight penetrated my eyelids and turned the sight in my shut eyes blood red.

'Dumb, dumb, dumb,' I sighed.

'Not dumb. Really cute and possibly injured. Good thing you decided to hurt yourself outside my place. I did give you my number on your tip. Remember?'

I opened my eyes and smiled. 'Mr Green.'

'Ms ... well, Tuesday is all I know.'

He stepped into the road and put his hand out. It only took a second for me to assess him. Expensive navy blue sweater, black jeans, worn brown work boots that probably cost what I used to make in a month. He'd tucked his hair behind his ears and his lean face was clean shaven. I grabbed the offered hand and he hauled me up. Where I promptly stated to lose my balance again.

'Whoa. Hold up.' Reed laughed and slung my arm easily around his neck.

I tried to pull away, flustered.

'Do I smell?' he asked, putting his arm around my waist. We took one tentative step together. There was a flare of pain in my ankle but nothing extreme.

'No,' I snickered. 'But I'm afraid I do.'

He grinned and I noticed how plump his lips were. I wondered about kissing them which made me bristle. I was turning into a horn dog. Must be the lake air.

'You do not smell, Tuesday.'

'Cane,' I said.

'Pardon?'

We were slowly making our way to his home. It was gorgeous. A wood shingled two-storey home that had three decks I could count from here – top floor, main floor and a floating deck that swept off from the side of the house toward the lake shore.

'My name is Tuesday Cane,' I said. 'My grandmother was Virginia Cane.'

'Ah, sadly, I'm new. I don't know the locals very well – new or otherwise. I knew of her passing, and vaguely of you, but not the details.'

We'd made our way to the porch and he turned to me, sliding his hands along my waist. 'Ready?'

'For what?'

'To go up the steps. I want to ice that ankle. It's swelling a little. See?'

I glanced down and damn if it wasn't slightly puffy. Sighing mightily, I turned back into a walking stance, held on to former TV star Reed Green and followed his lead. 'Of course it is,' I growled.

His house was simple but expensive. I'm not money hungry but I do recognise real paintings and fancy googahs (as my Nan called them) when I saw them. The side table in his foyer held a bowl big enough to hold me. An antique mirror presented me with my own dishevelled reflection and I cringed.

Reed caught me, his eyes fixing on mine in the mirror. 'You look gorgeous, 'he said.

I laughed out loud then. A loud, bawdy laugh that shook me in his arms. 'Yeah. I am fierce.'

He winked, nodded and propelled me toward the kitchen which I could see at the end of the narrow hallway. 'You look like some wild thing. A huntress maybe.'

'Are all TV actors full of shit?'

'Yes,' he said. In the kitchen he helped me sit before getting ice from the stainless steel freezer fridge combo. 'But you do look great. I'm not bullshitting you.'

He waved a homemade ice pack at me. 'May I?'

'Go for it.'

Reed plucked a cloth napkin off the table and set it over my bare ankle. Then he nestled the bundle of ice on top. 'Never on bare skin. You can burn yourself.'

'With ice?'

'Yes, with ice.'

I watched his long fingers slide along the ribbon of exposed skin between my anklet sock and my legging. 'You're cold. Would you like tea?'

'Sure.' It came out breathy. He really was a stunning man up close. No doubt why the camera loved him. Delicate cheekbones and fine features threatened to make him pretty, but the startling eyes and intense brow served to remind you he was a man.

'Lemon herb or chamomile?'

'Lemon herb. The other might put me to sleep.'

'Sleep indicates comfort,' he said. 'I'd have to take it as a compliment.' The copper kettle went on and he pulled two mugs from the shelves. They were black with red insides and made me think of vampires.

Reed Green's house was comfortably neat. A place for everything and everything in its place.

'How did your night go last night?' he asked.

'Fine. I had a nice time.'

'Anyone I know?'

'I don't know. You said you're new. Do you know everyone?'

'I'm getting there. I've only been here a little over a year.'

'And you're new?' I laughed.

'At Allister Lake if you've been here under a decade, you're new.'

'Well hell, I'm not new then. I'm freshly minted.'

He inclined his head and smiled. 'Now you get it.'

The ice shifted and I moved to grab it, wincing with the effort.

'How about some pain reliever to go with your tea. Get the swelling handled before it even sets in.'

'Sound like a plan.' I sighed.

Then he was placing two white pills in my hand. 'You're good at changing the subject. So, was it anyone I know?'

'Do you know Shepherd Moore?'

His face went sombre and those pretty feline eyes narrowed.

I snorted, and shook the pills like dice. 'That face says yes. And that you don't like him.'

'Why would I like anyone I consider competition?'

A tremor ran through me and I did my best not to let him see the effect his words had on me. I mentally calculated: Adrian, Shepherd and now Reed. That was an equation that clearly equalled juggling too many men. I knew I didn't want to get bogged down or any of that stuff, but wasn't that a bit extreme.

And yet when he bent to reposition the migrating ice pack and his fingers brushed my bare skin again, I wanted to know more about him. And more about what his hands felt like on me. Possibly something higher than my ankle.

'Competition?'

He leaned in so we were face to face. His long fingers that reminded me of a pianist travelled my cheekbones so that my lips tingled as if he'd kissed me. I wished he would kiss me.

'Every sighted, able bodied man in Allister Lake is competition to me right now.'

'Oh yeah?' I shifted in his oversized kitchen chair and it had nothing to do with my ankle or pain.

My cunt was thumping as hard as my heart and the heart rate was due to Reed not the run. He was handsome and funny and kind. He was so fucking close and he smelled so freaking good. Sandalwood, roaring fire, snow. That's what he smelled like. I wanted to suck as much of that scent into my body as I could.

'Yeah.' His lips were soft and his mouth tasted of peppermint.

I let him kiss me gently for a moment and then when he leaned in further and tugged my braid, I parted my lips and let him slip his tongue inside. When he thrust it over my own, I gently sucked the length of his tongue the way I would a cock.

'My, my. I was right about you.' He whispered it against the slope of my throat and goosebumps spiked along my skin. My nipples went almost painfully taut in my sports bra.

'You were?'

The tea kettle started to scream and he straightened up to turn it off. 'Yes. I want you just as much as I thought I did.'

'You're Max Torrent, TV's favourite undercover son. You could have any girl in Allister Lake.'

There was a petulance in my voice I didn't like. Why was I doubting he'd want me? Just what the fuck was wrong with me? Nothing. My flaws existed only in my head and were spurred on by the phantom voice of boyfriends past. Phil.

I shook it off and watched him prepare the tea. 'I don't want any girl at Allister Lake. I want Tuesday Cane, newest citizen in our fair little fucked up town.'

'So why don't you like Shepherd?' I asked, changing the subject.

He set my tea in front of me and sat in the opposite chair. 'More like Shepherd doesn't like me.'

'Why not?'

He shrugged. 'You'd have to ask him.'

I sighed. Men. So fucking tight lipped.

We chatted about TV life versus lake life. What it had been like to play the son of a super spy and how it was to be a child star and beyond. He wrapped my ankle in a bandage and joked about boy scout training. He plied me with two pounds of fresh berries and then he drove me home in his antique Chevy truck.

'Sure I can't walk you up?' he asked, putting the truck in park.

'I'm sure. I need a shower then I need to call Irv and see if he needs me to work today.'

'And if he doesn't?'

I shrugged. 'I'll write.'

'That's right. You're the writer.'

I shook my head. 'Only in my imagination and apparently my Nan's.' I got out, clutching the bag of berries. 'Thanks for rescuing me.'

'I'd rescue you any day of the week,' he said. 'Come pick berries tomorrow?'

I imagined us picking berries. And somehow it ended with us rolling around covered in squished berry juice, fucking. I tilted my head down to hide my red face.

'Sure. If I don't have to work.'

'Give me your phone.'

I handed it over and watched him push a bunch of buttons. Then he handed it back. 'I'm in there now. Come here.'

I never thought about denying him. I leaned over the seat and let him take my face in his hands. He kissed me softly and then ended with a nip of my bottom lip that made me jump a bit and gasp.

'Call me.'

'I will.'

He drove off and I stood in my driveway. To one side the barn. To the other, across an expanse of lawn was Shepherd. Was he watching? Did he see? Was he angry?

I needed a shower and to think. I hobbled inside and put the berries in the fridge. I shucked my clothes and climbed into the shower.

When I got out, I threw on leggings and Shepherd's jacket. I'd made up my mind.

Chapter Nine

HE WAS IN THE barn working on the lawnmower.

'I need a favour.'

Adrian looked up and grinned. 'Good morning to you, runner girl. I saw you take off. Good run?'

'If you call an almost twisted ankle a good run.'

'What do you need?'

'The door to the storage room is stuck. Can you get it open?'

'You should have just called me if your ankle's hurt.'

'Didn't punch it into my phone,' I said, shrugging. I started limping to the house so he'd have to follow. And yes, I exaggerated it a bit. It would make the whole outcome better, I thought.

Damsel in distress. Adrian ate that kind of shit up.

Halfway to the house, he laughed suddenly, danced in front of me, bent low and scooped me up.

'Adrian,' I hissed. My first thought being a watching Shepherd.

But he kept laughing and jogged to the house, jostling me in the fireman carry he was using. 'You were taking too damn long, slow poke.'

He took the steps fast and I shut my eyes to avoid vertigo. In Nan's room, he set me on my feet and steadied me until the world stopped moving. His eyes were dark and kind and I could tell he wanted to kiss me. Instead, he tucked my still damp hair behind my ears and said, 'I'll fix that door.'

'About the door–' I leaned against the bed and watched him.

He turned the knob and opened the door. 'The door appears

fine,' he said, cocking an eyebrow at me.

That look of his made my stomach hot and my pussy hotter. 'I … um … yeah.'

Adrian was in my face then. Smiling, his eyes sparkling and as I watched, his nimble hand reaching toward me. A gentle line of fire raced along my skin when he touched me, tracing my clavicle with just a fingertip. The touch of his skin to mine so subtle it was as if I were imagining it.

Back and forth, back and forth. I was the cobra in the basket. But then he went from clavicle to belly button and the startled muscles in my belly flickered and danced. 'Do you need something from me, Tuesday?'

Heat and moistures pooled in my panties and I shifted a little. Cleared my throat. 'I do.'

That finger ran up and down, up and down, drawing an unseen zipper on my stimulated skin.

He leaned in and kissed me softly. His tongue tracing my lower lip, mimicking his finger. 'What do you need?'

'I'm worked up,' I confessed.

'Are you, now?'

'I am.'

I let him push his hand into my leggings and my slippers whispered on the hardwood floor when I spread my stance. He found me instantly, zooming right in to those tender, agitated nerve endings that needed his touch.

'Do you need me to fuck you?'

I shook my head. That wasn't what I wanted. There'd been tons of fucking, and the consideration of even more with Reed this morning. I wanted to mess around. I wanted fast and easy. A release. 'No. I just want to get off.'

I could say that to Adrian. There was an honest ease with him. I could ask him to take care of business and he got it.

'Ah, you want to get off. What if I want to get off with you?' he asked, pushing me back.

I ripped at the buttons of his jeans with shaking hands. 'I think we both can get off.'

'I think you need to lie down, Tues. Your poor ankle.' He grinned at me and the Big Bad Wolf sprang to mind.

'I think so.'

Adrian shed his jeans with serpentine ease. The boxer shorts went next and I chewed my lip to see his hard cock standing at attention. For me. The power of arousing a man never failed to startle me. There was such raw joy in seeing another person's naked need. Their desire.

I reached for him and he stepped into my touch. His cock smooth and warm in my hand.

'Lose the tights,' he said.

'They're leggings.' I grinned.

'Whatever. I don't care if they're just really tall socks. Take them off.'

I released him just long enough to shimmy free of the black fabric and the tiny red panties underneath.

'I like it better when you go bare under there.'

'I'll remember that.' I sighed because he was already covering me with his strong body. His head dipping between my legs to taste me, his own legs straddling me so I barely had to crane my neck to take his cock into my mouth.

His mouth was soft at first and he licked gently because Adrian knew it made me crazy. I could tell he liked torturing me. I thrust up under him but he clamped his hands to my hipbones and held me. Forced me down flat and at his mercy. I couldn't move and I had to just let him – let him have his way with my pussy.

'Behave, Tues or I might have to get back to that pressing matter of a lawnmower.'

I sighed and concentrated on sucking him into my mouth. I licked up the back of his cock and nudged his balls with my nose. Adrian stilled and I heard him inhale a great shuddering breath. I laughed. 'Hey you pinned me down. I can play that game.'

I ran my lips, slightly parted, along the side of his shaft before dropping a proper kiss on the tip of his cock. Then I ran my lips, wet and pliable for him, back up the other side. When I thumbed the small slit in the head of his cock and sucked his balls gently into my mouth, one at a time, just to give him some torture in return, Adrian drove his face back between my

64

thighs to eat me in earnest.

'Jesus, woman,' he sighed and sucked my clit hard enough that tiny little sparkles of white light firecrackered behind my closed eyelids.

'Jesus right back at you, stud,' I sighed.

I licked the letter W into his balls and then reversed it for the letter M. For whatever reason the sensation of that drove most men to near madness.

Adrian was no different. He thrust his fingers into me, pushing against my G-spot with drenched ease, thanks to my arousal and his mouth. When he returned his tongue to me, licking roughly, I started to come. That first flickering spasm that made me go tense under him as I sucked harder.

I was trying to time this in tandem. I needed to give as much as I got here. Reed had left me flustered and confused. Shepherd had left me soothed and horny and needy. Adrian just flipped my switch.

I worked him with my hand and my tongue and he swirled wet circles around my clit before kissing it gently. It was the gentle kiss, the shy suction on that tiny organ that did me in.

I came, squeezing him with my spit-slick fist and he came. I did my best to drink some of him in but he was too much and the salty white fluid baptized my face and my hair and I was laughing and coming all at once.

Adrian collapsed on me and rolled and then we were laying head to foot on my grandmother's pretty quilt.

I sat up pushing my sticky hair away and grinned.

'Does your ankle feel better?'

'It does.'

'Are you trying to kill me?' He pushed his reddish brown hair back and blew out a big breath. His cheeks were rosy and his eyes were shiny and I touched the tip of his cock to watch him jump.

'Not at all. You'd be no fun dead. You wouldn't be able to do that dead.'

'Fuck, Tuesday, I'd come back from the dead to do that.'

'I have to call in now,' I said. I got on my knees to kiss him. 'Thanks.'

'No problem, pretty girl.' He grinned. Behind the grin seemed to be a tiny hint of something more, though.

As long as Adrian didn't get attached we'd be fine.

He left and I washed my face and brushed my teeth and pulled my hair back into a messy knot and arranged my bangs. They were just a bit crunchy in the front and I smiled at myself in the mirror. I liked having little secrets.

In the storage room that Nan had converted into an attic of sorts, I found a trunk with some of Nan's old clothes in it. Sweaters and a few dresses and balls carved from cedar to keep moths out. I even found a pair of brown suede boots that came almost to my knees.

'Score,' I said, pulling them on. Perfect fit.

I walked to the front window and looked down into the yard. By the barn, Adrian was giving the lawnmower a test run. He glanced up toward my room I think. He didn't know I could see him or that I was at a different angle.

Shepherd walked out and climbed in his truck. When he backed up to get on the road, he spared a glance toward my house. He was going to the school he'd said. Maybe I'd drive out and see him. I could take him lunch.

I rotated my ankle and the small bit of fringe on the boots swayed joyously. No pain. Seemed all I needed was an orgasm and some endorphins. I grabbed a sweater and a vintage top of Nan's and shut the door behind me.

I had a lunch to pack, I decided. And a big strapping man to visit. A surprise would be nice for my soul, I thought. It would be good for both of us to have a little spur of the moment chat and nibble. No sex to complicate it. I could ask him why he hated Reed and he could tell me it was none of my business.

I hurried downstairs.

Chapter Ten

THANKS TO NAN'S MAGICAL pantry I was able to make nice submarine sandwiches with crusty rolls I found in the freezer. While they warmed in the toaster oven I found roasted red peppers and artichoke hearts, olives and pepperoncini. Some hard pepperoni was on the second shelf and I chopped off some nice slices to add to the veggies. Parmesan cheese from the fridge (it lasts forever) and some Italian seasoning.

'Tada,' I whispered to myself. Then I found a bag of chips and a six-pack of soda. Some cookie dough sat beckoning me in the freezer. Long homemade rolls of raw dough wrapped in wax paper and clear wrap. Each was neatly labelled with Nan's handwriting. *Butterscotch Oatmeal Raisin, bake at 350 for 10-12 minutes.*

So I did. I cut nice clean discs of cookie and put them on the toaster oven tray.

I realised the heady smell of sex was coming off of me so while they baked, I hopped in the downstairs shower. The first floor bathroom had a toilet, a sink and a shower stall, no tub. I didn't owe Shepherd anything, or even Adrian for that matter, but I didn't want to show up to meet him smelling of another man. It was just … rude.

Unless he was into that sort of thing. The thought made me snort and I said aloud, 'But you don't know yet, do you? So show up clean and smelling of …' I glanced at the shower gel. Lilacs and cotton.

Who thought up these scents anyway?

I'd washed my body but left my hair dry. I towelled off and the toaster oven dinged just as I walked in. 'I should have a theme song. I'm that good.'

I packed all the other crap in a picnic basket – yes, God bless my Nan, she actually owned one – and when the cookies were cool enough to put in a shallow dish I packed those too. But I left them uncovered so they could cool. Plus the bonus of spreading fresh baked cookie smell wherever I went.

The sky was getting just a bit overcast as I climbed into the Grenada. Welcome to fall at the lake. I backed out and got way down the road toward town when I realised I had no idea where the school was.

I pulled over by an idling mail truck and gave him a short honk of the horn. The mailman tossed me a wave and leaned across to his open Jeep door. 'Can I help ya?'

'I'm new here, well, I'm new as a full-time resident, and I was wondering if you could tell me where the elementary school is.'

He grinned. 'Virginia Cane's granddaughter. Wednesday is it?'

'Close.' I laughed. 'Tuesday.'

'Right, right. I'm Ben Mitchell your mailman extraordinaire. But anyhow, you know where the bank is?'

'Sure. Right across from Irv's Eats. My new employer, FYI.'

'Ah, congrats! Best corn chipped beef in the world. My Sunday breakfast every week.' He rubbed his hands together as if anticipating his next dose of that good stuff. 'Anyway, if you go past Irv's, take your first right on to Poplar Land and you'll see the school from the road. You'll be able to tell just where to go from there. Follow the American flag.'

'Thanks for the help.'

Ben sniffed the air and I snickered softly. 'You smell like cookies, little miss.' He had greying hair, sharp green eyes and high cheekbones. His skin was ruddy from being in the sun so much. I wondered if Nan had a thing for him too. I saw no wedding band.

'No, I smell like Lilacs and cotton. These cookies smell like cookies.' I popped the lid and snatched two still-warm cookies. I held them out to Ben and he stretched even further to get them.

He smelled one. 'Are these Virginia's Butterscotch Oatmeal Raisins?' he sighed with audible lust.

'They are.'

He bit into one and said, 'She used to make these for me all the time.' Then he blushed.

'Thanks again.' I waved and rolled up my window before I laughed out loud. 'Oh, Nan,' I said, following the road to town. 'You dirty, dirty girl. Good for you.'

I pulled into the school just as final buses were pulling out for the day – they must have had a short day because it was only 1.30. Days went fast when you were settling into a new town, a new house, a new life. And new men.

I parked by Shepherd's truck and took the basket to the front door. I rang the buzzer, asked for the auditorium Shepherd Moore and the disembodied female voice told me to go straight and make two lefts. The auditorium was marked.

The echoes of my boot heels chased me down the hallway. When I walked into the gaping space of the auditorium I froze. I felt tiny and exposed. I felt naked.

'Hello?' I practically whispered.

'Hey, there Tuesday,' came his warm gruff voice and my body responded by rippling with energy.

I followed his voice. 'I brought you food.'

'Come on up. Hurry. I'm starved.'

I stopped, squinting against the stage lights in my face. But behind the light all was dark. I couldn't see him but I could hear him. Varnish fumes were in the air but not overpowering. I started up the steps clutching my basket like Dorothy going down the yellow brick road. Or Little Red Riding Hood walking into the wolf's lair on the way to Grandma's house.

'Keep coming, Tuesday,' he said and then chuckled. Shepherd was being dirty on purpose, I knew it and yet I still reacted. A ribbon of arousal uncurling deep in my belly and filling my womb. My pussy was swollen and ready and that was just from his damn voice.

I climbed and out of the darkness a hand grabbed my thigh and I started but then laughed. 'There you are.'

'Here I am.'

That strong hand pulled me down and I found myself sitting in his lap. With the lights out of my eyes, I could see his shadowed face. We were now in darkness looking down on the lit rows of chairs below.

It was like being hidden in plain sight.

'Hi,' he said and kissed me. Forcing his fingers into my hair, holding my head, kissing me hard. A pleasurable sound rumbled in his chest. The kiss was possessive and rough and aggressive and … perfect.

'Hi,' I gasped, pulling back. I sucked a deep breath into my lungs and managed, 'I brought you food.'

'So you said.' His fingers zeroed in to find my nipples – hard and sensitive – through the soft, worn navy blue pullover I wore. No bra underneath so when he stroked my breast, he rubbed the cotton over my sensitive nipples and I hummed.

God, what a needy sound. But I didn't care.

'I did. Sandwiches, chips, soda and–'

'Cookies.' Fingers rushed up under my shirt and goosebumps blazed along my skin where he touched. His palm skated the flat of my belly and up between my breasts. His fingers fanned out to cover the part of my breast above my crazily beating heart.

'Yes, cookies.'

'Is it wrong to want you more than food right now?' he asked, looking like some beloved villain from a comic book in the crazy light. 'Is it wrong that all day all I've had in my head is the memory of fucking you?'

'That's not wrong,' I managed. My tongue didn't want to work properly when I tried to talk but when he kissed me it felt just right.

'Good. What do we have here?' Shepherd tugged the waistband of my leggings and they gave.

'Stretchy pant kind of deals.'

He shoved both hands down the back and groaned when he found me bare under there too. The navy pullover was long enough to cover my hips so I'd gone without panties. 'Take them off. One leg at least.'

'Here? My God, we can't,' I said. But I was already

70

straddling him, facing him, letting him cup my ass in his big working-man hands.

'No one's here. Kids are gone for an early dismissal. Plus staff and students are banned from this area during renovation anyway. Safety first.' He squeezed my ass hard enough to make me wriggle and squirm. 'Too many fumes and a scary handyman.' He chuckled.

'But still anyone could ...'

He tsked. 'You are a city girl. Denise and Monica are in the front office with Principal Barns and that's that. And they follow the rules to a T. If they want me they page me on the overhead or call my cell.'

He pushed a hand in the front of my leggings and slid a finger into me. I held my breath. When he flexed that finger and found my clit with his thumb, I blew it out and shivered. 'Yeah?'

'Yes, ma'am. One leg out. Do it.'

Who was I to argue? I moved around to get one leg free, thanking the gods of Lycra for letting me get the legging out of my boot and then over my boot. I listened to the rustle and snap of a condom being opened and donned and when he grabbed me by my hips – one bare, one clothed – I went so fucking willingly it was ridiculous.

'Come here, sweet Tuesday,' he muttered.

I straddled him again, not letting him enter, just pressing us together so we both sighed. 'I came here to feed you,' I said. I wanted my intentions clear, which was comical.

'You will feed me.'

I rolled my hips and took the kiss he pressed to my lips. 'I made a really nice lunch,' I moaned as he thrust his tongue into my mouth.

'I bet. And you're feeding me right now, too,' Shepherd informed me.

'How so?'

He slid a hand between us and moved his cock so I could align with him. I sank down slowly, inch by inch. We were eye to eye though it was so dark his eyes looked like black pools of nothing under a strong brow. 'You're feeding my soul,' he

71

said.

I waited for him to laugh and when he didn't, something in my chest shifted and I had to look away. Just fucking. I had to remind myself. That's all it was – fucking.

I lowered myself quickly to break the spell and it worked, his eyes slammed shut, his fingers digging into my skin. When I was speared on him, I moved slow and easy, torturing us both and making it all that much sweeter.

'I'm glad you came.'

'I'm glad I came.'

Sharp pain flared and I felt his teeth dig into the thin skin along my shoulder. Before the throb could start he soothed it with his tongue and I rocked forward and then back. Finding my rhythm and that perfect pressure on my clit. When he nipped me again, I came. A long slow, wet spasm that shut my mind down. Blindly I found him with my mouth, kissed him hard. His beard rough against my cheek, his tongue hot as it warred with mine.

I moved faster, finding his tempo and keeping up. I wanted him to come. I wanted to feel the bulk of him go taut and still with his orgasm. I wanted him to want me more than food, more than talk, more than air.

I was discovering that when it came to Shepherd, I just wanted him.

He pinched my ass cheek hard enough for me to hiss and I surprised us both by growling. 'Fuck. Do it again.'

I ground my body against him, gripped his shoulders in my hands before moving them to tug his hair. 'Jesus,' he rasped and pinched me again.

This time when I came, his hands clamped down on my hips, anchoring me so I couldn't move away. He thrust up hard under me and came with a stifled roar. My knees were pinched painfully in the back of the theatre seats. Thank God they were roomy because we were wedged in there good and the way we were moving together, I wondered if we'd ever pry free.

Which made me laugh. So there we stayed, forehead to forehead, breathing heavy as the rush of it all passed a little. 'Hi, Tuesday.' He grinned.

72

'Hi, Shepherd. Hungry?'

'Starved,' he said. I found my pant leg and he helped me get my leg back through before getting himself put back together.

'Now, let's eat,' I said, and dropped into the seat next to his. Below us the empty theatre was big and bright and somehow golden.

Chapter Eleven

WE HAD OUR FEET up on the backs of the chairs in front of us. All you could hear at first was us munching – we'd worked up quite the appetite.

'So why were you up here anyway?'

'Taking a break.' He popped a chip in his mouth, chewed. Shepherd shut his eyes like he felt bliss and that made me happy. 'I hate that they're painting these seats. I hate that they're then coating that paint, sealing in the damage as it were. But it's a job and they'd hire someone else to do it if I didn't.'

'So you prefer the old school seats up here,' I said, patting the curved iron arm of my seat.

'Yes, I do. Much more character, don't you think?'

I nodded. 'I prefer worn in and a bit used – it means character,' I agreed.

'Ah, now I get it.'

'Get what?' I swigged my soda and let it fizz in my mouth for a moment.

'Why you like me.'

I punched his arm. 'You're not old or worn in.'

'Older than you.'

'How old?' I countered, finishing off my sandwich and licking the olive oil off the tips of my fingers.

'Thirty-nine.'

'Oooh,' I sighed. 'Ancient.'

'What? Seven years on you.'

'About. So?'

He shrugged. 'So nothing.'

'Since we're sharing.' I patted his leg and he took my hand

for a moment. A hot flash sizzled through me and I ignored it. 'Why do you hate Reed?'

He ran a hand through his hair. 'Why do you care?'

'Because I know him and I know you and I'm nosy.'

'A girl thing. We were together, but not for much longer if I'm honest. But then Reed Green showed up and she got stars in her eyes and I guess it ticked me off is all. But we were on the outs as it was, anyway. That relationship would have died a natural death had he stayed out of the picture.'

I nodded. 'Reasonable. Did he end up with her?'

He roared laughter. It echoed loudly, ricocheting around the auditorium like an invisible ball of sound. 'For like … a week,' he said.

'Ah, short lived.'

'Yep. Long enough to fuck her and then give her the boot.'

'She lives here?' OK so I was prying and I was sort of jealous. Whatever.

'Nah. She lived here because of me, left because of him.'

'Now, why does Adrian not like you?' I asked boldly.

He stared at me and I could see, even in the dim light, him considering whether or not to tell me the truth. Finally, he said 'Similar scenario. They were on the outs, she ended up in my bed. He didn't like it. It's a small town.' He shrugged. 'It can be a bit incestuous, if you will.'

I handed him a cookie. 'Thanks.'

'For what?'

'For telling me the truth. You could have told me it's none of my business.'

'True.' He ate the cookie in a single bite so I handed him another one. 'But then you probably would have withheld cookies, right?'

'Right.' I laughed.

'Not worth it,' he said and then dove over me to grab another.

Then it was my laughter bouncing around the big old auditorium.

I spent that night at home. I made myself some of Nan's tuna casserole that I found in the freezer. I figured when I ran out of her food, I'd mourn her all over again. Somehow eating her cookies and casseroles and treats from the freezer and talking to her all the time kept her alive.

When they were gone, so would she be. For real …

I dialled the boarding house. Annie was about Nan's age. Maybe a bit younger. She had been the closest thing to family I had back home. I needed to hear a familiar voice and feel loved.

'Annie here. We have two rooms available,' she said on pick up.

'Do you, now? That's odd. You're usually booked solid.'

'Tuesday!' she crowed. I heard the rustle-bang of her shutting herself and the phone in the pantry. She refused to get a wireless phone so she prowled the downstairs of the house with a regular wall phone on an insanely long cord. Which everyone who lived there was constantly on alert for so as not to trip.

'Hi, Annie. How's tricks?'

'Fine, fine. All the men folk still walk around all sad that our resident hottie is gone.'

'They'll thank me when they find hotties of their own.'

Annie snorted and I could almost hear her roll her eyes. 'And what are you up to?' Her voice grew softer. 'How are you holding up?'

'I'm fine. I still have moments of staggering guilt and regret … but I must say. The scenery around here is distracting.'

'Oh … men. Do tell.'

So I did tell. I told her about Adrian and meeting Shepherd. I told her about my bad behaviour between the two. About Reed and how he intrigued me and yes, attracted me. And I confessed to my klutzy fall. I even dished about my impromptu encounter in the auditorium.

'Whew. Girl, sounds like you are a busy bee. And it makes me wish I was 20 years younger.'

'Oh come on,' I said putting my feet up on the arm of the sofa. I wriggled my freshly painted toes and wondered what else I could eat. It had started raining again and I could hear it tapping on the slanted windows which I'd shuttered for the night. 'You could totally manage to get up to no good.'

'Yeah, yeah.'

There was a pause. 'You know Phil came sniffing around here for you.'

'You didn't tell him where I was, did you?'

Didn't matter, though. I would do that same thing all over again if he showed up looking for me. In fact, Nan owned a gun; I'd use one of those damn things if I had to.

'No. We didn't. No one said a word beyond you were gone. But you know he started pondering that. Saying the only place you had to go was your grandmother's and she'd been sick, and gee he wondered if you were up there at that fancy lake house.'

I took a deep breath and reminded myself to not get upset.

'Well, just let him try anything,' I growled.

'I know it. Don't worry. If I heard anything about him headed that way, I'd call your cell. And by the way, young miss, do you have a house number and an address you'd like to share with me?'

'Sorry,' I said and recited them.

'Got it. I miss you, kid,' she said a bit wistfully.

'I miss you too, Annie,' I said and realised it was true.

I didn't miss the city or the bullshit or the ghost of Phil, but I did miss her. She was my family. 'You should come visit me soon,' I said. 'Take a little vacation.'

'Are you kidding!' she cried. 'These fools would rob me blind.'

I laughed, but sadly, she was probably right.

'Maybe Joey could come babysit the house for you,' I suggested.

Her brother was five years her junior and had watched the house when she'd had to go in for ankle surgery. Between me and him, we kept the house under control.

'Maybe. I'll think about it.'

'No, you won't,' I laughed.

'I will!'

We both knew she was lying.

Chapter Twelve

WHO THE FRIG WAS that?

I turned onto my belly and pulled a pillow over my head. I'd had too much food, too much wine and not enough sleep. And someone was banging on my door.

Hard.

I sat up.

'What?' I shouted, shaking my feet with frustration.

The banging stopped. 'Thank you,' I sighed and flopped back down. Noise rose straight up from the great room and slipped over the loft railing into the hall. From there it insinuated itself into my room and my brain. Normally, it was no big deal. It was just a truck going by or a lawn mower or some boat out on the lake. But now it was ... I started to doze.

Banging. Again.

I sat up and pulled my crazed hair into a messy knot. Whoever it was at my door was going to pay. I mean, what the fuck time was it anyway?

I glanced at the clock and blinked to clear my vision. 10:01 in bright green numbers. 'Well, shit.'

It was late in the morning. Late enough to reasonably knock on someone door. But they weren't knocking. They were banging. And as if provoked by the thought, the banging started again.

I pulled on an eggplant coloured sweater robe and tied it off. I rushed down to the main floor and wished for socks or slippers or something. Winter was coming and the damn floor was cold.

I hit the bottom step, my ankle giving a twinge, and almost fell on my ass. I stagger-limp-hopped to the door and pulled it open. 'Jesus on a cracker! What?' I yelled before the door was even open.

On my stoop stood one very irate looking Reed Green with a bundle of mangled flowers and one pissed off, red faced, bullish looking Adrian.

'What the hell!' I yelped.

'Tell him to let me go. Or I swear I'm not responsible for what I might do.' Reed said this with a straight face and gritted teeth.

I flapped my hands around and gaped. 'What are you doing?' I growled at Adrian who had the good sense to look suddenly worried. 'Why are you … manhandling him?'

'He was prowling around.' Adrian shook Reed by the scruff.

For some reason I found myself inappropriately amused and I bit down on the inside of my cheek to keep from laughing.

'Prowling around?' Reed said, his voice somehow dangerous. My nape prickled from the sound and I crossed my arms in front of my breasts to hide the fact that my nipples had just spiked. 'I looked in one window when no one answered the bell or the knock. And I was carrying these!' he said, shaking the flowers violently.

And there was the laughter again, bubbling up in my throat so I had to swallow hard. I stepped back. 'Let him go, Adrian.'

Adrian pressed his lips together and his face got even redder. I felt bad for him, I mean the day before I'd been sucking his cock. But he didn't own me and he couldn't run around assaulting my visitors. Jealous or not.

'Come on in, Reed. I'm sorry.'

Adrian released his prisoner, tossed his hands in the air in agitation and promptly turned on his heels and stomped off. He was grumbling angrily under his breath as he went.

'Sorry,' I said again leading him into the kitchen. 'We used to … well, when I was younger we dated. And he's a bit of a worrier and he um … is the caretaker.' I was carefully avoiding the whole casual-sex-like-rabbits-since-I-arrived scenario. 'I'm making coffee,' I said. 'Want some?'

I nervously patted my hair and realised I had to pee and I

hadn't brushed my teeth. I bent to plug in the machine and my robe gaped, showing a fast but full flash of naked breast. I hurriedly stood and clutched the robe shut. 'Actually, I just got out of bed. I need to … um, use the facilities and then I'll come make coffee. I haven't even …' I rushed out. 'Be right back!' I yelled hurrying before I wet myself.

Upstairs I ran to the bathroom. Then I brushed my teeth, smeared on a little blush, and made sure to tie my robe a bit tighter. I never rushed to get dressed in the morning – in fact, I put it off as long as possible. But part of me wondered if this was a seduction thing, too. If it was, so be it.

In the kitchen, he was putting my bent flowers in a giant cookie jar he'd rescued from the top of the fridge. I hid a smile behind my hand.

He turned, chocolate hair swinging gently against his firm jaw. My God, he was so … pretty. And I rarely went for pretty men. But he wasn't pretty as in precious. He was pretty as in something you'd find in a painting by one of the Masters. Someone angelic and fierce but stunning to look at.

'Finding everything OK?' I asked. I opened the fridge to assess my food situation. I'd really have to actually go to a grocery store soon. I didn't trust the eggs but I found a hunk of cheese and some cured bacon and a can of mandarin oranges getting cold in the back. I remembered that about Nan, had to have her mandarin oranges cold.

'I did. I have put your lovely but assaulted, "hope you're feeling better" flowers in a cookie jar, as you can see.' He smiled big when he turned to me and my heart did a floppy little fish dance in my chest. 'And I put your coffee on. Kona. Nice. Nan had good taste.'

I cleared my throat, moving past him but brushing him with my arm just the same. 'And how do you know that's Nan's?'

'Well, there is zero fresh food on the counter or in the fridge. No fresh milk, no juice, no fruit, no bread. But there is a pantry fit for an alien invasion should we all have to hunker down here to stay.'

I put my head down covering a laugh. 'She was well prepared, my Nan.'

'I'll say.' Reed caught my hand up in his, tugging me gently. My entire body went on red alert and I turned to him, cool air rushing over my skin as my robe gaped.

I made no move to cover my breast. He made no move to hide his stare. 'Are you?'

'Am I what?' My mouth was dry with nerves but my pussy was swollen and thumping in time with my heart.

His eyes on me made me want to fidget. Squirm. Move like some restless creature.

'Better today? The ankle?'

'Oh, the ankle!' I blurted. 'Yes. A bit tender if I come downstairs too fast. Like when you were being …'I chewed my lip.

He grinned at me. 'Go on, give it to me.'

The dirty double entendre only served to make my belly and cunt that much warmer. That much more eager.

'Held hostage. For trespassing.' The repressed laugh turned to a giggle. 'I'm sorry about that. I think he–'

'Thinks he owns you for God's sake,' Reed finished.

I shook my head and moved to get two mugs. The motion only served to gape my robe a bit wider and Reed very slowly, very gently – giving me plenty of time to stop him – slid his hand inside and touched my naked skin.

'He doesn't.' I managed.

Something about him touching me made me think about Shepherd touching me. I had a brief exotic fantasy of them both touching me and blinked it away. 'Why does Shepherd hate you?' I asked to see if he would tell me the truth.

Reed froze, but his fingers didn't. They swept back and forth over the tender skin of my breast, teasing my nipple to attention and making my cunt tug empathetically at the stimulation.

'I stole his girl.' He smiled. 'I don't think she was really his girl, though. I think he was done with her.' He took his time leaning in to kiss me and right before he did he breathed in my ear. 'I'm not taking his girl again, am I?'

'I'm nobody's girl.'

His kiss was entirely different than Shepherd's. Softer and

more courteous but no less aggressive under the shiny veneer of manners. I turned into his touch and he slid his other hand inside my robe to cup my unattended breast. Plucking my nipples, he kissed me harder and I gasped into his mouth. Reed swallowed my sound and backed me to the counter.

'Nobody's girl. I like it. You only belong to you, right Tuesday?' His voice soft and teasing and I could hear his smile.

Without thinking, I parted my legs and he felt it, pushing his thigh into the gap I'd provided. His hip banged my pelvis. His cock, hard from the feel of things, brushed my thigh. My robe now swam around my upper arms, my chest completely bare but for his hands.

'I'm just mine. I don't like to belong to anyone.'

Phil used to mutter, "Nobody. You're nobody," when he'd been too in the bag to control himself and decided it would be fun to take a swing. Before I stopped all that bullshit. When I moved into Annie's and considered dating again, I'd changed that mental soundtrack to nobody's. I was nobody's but my own.

'Good girl. You shouldn't. Maybe that's why she chose me over Shepherd. Me, I don't care, do what you want. Him … possessive. Needy if you ask me.'

I kissed him to shut him up because I realised when he spoke that way about Shepherd a red knot of hot anger woke up in my chest. I didn't like belonging to anyone, I didn't like feeling I had to defend anyone. That was too close for comfort for me. I shut Reed up by rubbing the knuckle of my thumb along the ridge of his erection.

He stopped, biting my tongue gently and humming deep in his throat. I shivered at the sound. That was the sound of a man losing a tiny shred of control. Because of me. I loved it.

'Under it all he's a good man, so I'm glad I'm not taking his girl,' Reed said. There was a flash of that TV smile and then his hands on my robe belt. The tie whispered when he worked it and the robe slid down and free of me as I stood in the sunny kitchen.

'Dear Lord, woman.' His gaze felt palpable. The way he

looked at me made me tremble. Reed stroked up my arms and then down my sides. My skin flushed hot and then I shivered again from the wacky change in internal temperature.

'Kiss me,' I begged.

He did. Another soft kiss that somehow turned hard and claiming toward the end. One hand tangling in my hair and yanking me to him with a surprising strength. He didn't look so strong as to pin me to him, almost powerless to move. But he was.

He stroked between my legs with his free hand, almost petting me with that soft touch, until I whimpered. Then his fingers delved in deep, curled and withdrew. 'You're really fucking wet, Tuesday Cane.'

'It's because of you Mr Green Jeans.' I tried to laugh but he plunged his fingers deep again and I lost the joking lilt. It was nothing but an exhalation and a silent request for more.

He didn't give me more. Of that. Reed kissed my shoulder and surprised me by pinching my nipples so that I cried out. Then he dropped to his knees, tucking that beautiful soft hair behind his ear as he went.

'Let me see you.'

I blushed. I always blush when men say things like that. But it's not just blushing I do, I also grow wetter and more plump when they talk to me with dirty courtly words of praise.

I spread my legs and let him see. His breath hot and moist on my erect clit. His fingers commanding on my inner thighs as he held me wide. He dipped his head and touched me with this tongue. A phantom touch – so light I was sure I'd imagined it – until he licked me hard with the fullness of his pink tongue.

'God, I might come immediately.' It was a confession, short and brutal and self deprecating.

'That's OK. If you do, we can start all over again,' Reed said.

The coffee pot gave one more jovial burble, belched and then beeped to tell me it was done.

'Did you want to stop for coffee?' he asked, then shoved his tongue, rigid and slick into the wet slit of my cunt. He brushed my clit with his fingertips and my knees gave a little dip.

'No!' I chirped.

'Good. I was hoping you'd say no.'

Reed Green, TV star extraordinaire, berry picking farm owner, set his mouth to me and started eating me for real. My body splayed against the counter. One hand bracing myself, the other threaded through his silken hair. Watching his face as he went down on me, the elegant sweep of his dark lashes on the very tops of his cheeks, the arch of his cheekbones – it all became overwhelming.

So when he thrust three long fingers into my pussy and fucked me with them, I came. And I wasn't quiet about it.

Light warmed my belly and the tops of my thighs. Outside wind howled. At a glance, it was a sunny summer day. If you paid attention there was a crisp chill in the air and light wisps of cool air as the wind buffeted the A-frame.

'Very nice,' he said, praising me for an orgasm no less. 'Now–' He yanked my arm and I buckled. Folding easily down onto the pretty area run beneath my counter. 'Do you have any condoms, Tuesday?'

I was on the pill. I was clean. But I was also getting a lot of action and though thrilled, I wanted to be careful. I glanced around. 'Purse?'

He spotted it first, going to the kitchen chair and handing me the oversized plum coloured leather satchel. I fought my wallet and a rush of other nonsense to find my make-up case. Inside were several condoms and I handed him one.

Reed promptly grabbed my purse, tossed it and pushed me back so that I lay sprawled on the cool kitchen floor. He put his mouth back to work between my legs, muttering things I could not hear but the cadence of his voice turned me on. He got his cock free of his jeans and stroked himself long enough to make me feel irrational and urgent. And then he sheathed himself before crawling up over me, reminding me again of a giant gorgeous feline.

'Are you ready? Because I'm ready. I've been fucking ready to drive into you since you brought me my dinner at Irv's. If I could have, I would have driven into you while you served me my dinner at Irv's.' He grinned and I touched his lip.

Reed sucked my finger into the hot velvet of his mouth and I felt my pussy clench up tight. 'Fuck yes, I'm ready,' I said.

'Part those legs for me, then,' he ordered.

My legs fell open and I took him in hand, guiding him to me. Letting him in, I arched up and gripped him tight with my cunt. The jolt of pleasure from flexing those muscles stilled us both for a minute. And then Reed started to move, hard and fast at first but eventually slowing to an almost lazy rocking motion. Our own personal boat of fucking in the middle of a chilly floor.

I would have laughed at the mental image but he kissed me – my lips, my eyes, my nose. He tugged a bit of my hair between his shiny famous-person teeth and the unexpected spark of pain rushed through me and I came with a rush of noise and fluid.

He laughed. 'I wondered if that would work with you. You like a chaser of ouch to your ahhh, I see. I could be wrong.'

I shook my head. 'I don't think you're wrong.'

It was something I'd never really realised until recently. And now that I did, it was like a secret power or a hidden weapon. You could only hurt me if I let you … or in some cases, if I begged.

'Put your hands over your head.'

He waited and I considered. I studied his face and thought of his kisses and nodded, putting my hands high. He held them there and drove into me with more force. Hiking my leg high to my waist, pausing to draw back and watch his cock spearing in and out of me.

'I'm about done for. Watching you take me. Watching myself disappear into you …' He shook his head and then blue-eyed boy that he was, stared me down and said so sincerely I felt panicky. 'I imagine it would be easy to disappear into you, Tuesday. You get into a man's head and you take root.'

I shook my head. None of that. No niceness on that level. No serious words.

He caught my emotion, smiled at me and said 'But enough of that poetry and fancy talk. I think I'm going to come. Do you think you can come with me? I'd like that.'

His kiss was sweetly scented. A ghost of toothpaste and something sugary and Reed himself.

'Do it again,' I begged. 'Hurt me. Softly.'

So he wrapped his slender hand in my hair and we rocked together. When he was so close he was damn near growling, he thrust hard – harder than any other time – banging against every greedy nerve ending in my pussy. And at the same time he tugged. Tugged my hair just hard enough that a line of fire erupted on my scalp but started to fade as fast as it had emerged. The pain bled to pleasure, the pleasure to joy and I was coming with him. His hand still caught up in my unruly hair, his sweet mouth crushing down on mine.

Chapter Thirteen

'COFFEE?' I CHUCKLED AS we sat up. He looked stunned and my emotions mirrored his appearance. Outside, something scraped on the deck. When I started to stand, Reed grabbed my hand, squeezing.

'Just wind. It's tossing everything around out there today. And yes. I would fucking love some coffee.'

The phone rang and I snagged it on the third ring. Dancing away from him when he reached for me.

'Oh, hi, Irv!'

Reed frowned but then the frown bled into a smile and I winked at him.

'Sure, sure,' I placated my new boss. Apparently, Delores was dilating and the doctor had said work was done for. 'I can do dinner shift. No problem. I'll be there with bells on.'

'How about just your work tee?' Irv said.

'That too,' I laughed and hung up.

I took the cup of coffee a put-back-together Reed offered and sipped it. 'Perfect. How did you know?'

He shrugged those lanky shoulders and touched my hair. It was a sweet gesture that unsettled me a touch. 'You just look like a two sugars and dollop of cream kind of girl. Though this stuff is not cream. But I found it unopened in the fridge.'

'We can pretend.' I sat at the counter and he joined me. His foot knocked over a neatly stacked line of Nan's cookbooks. Who stored cookbooks on a bottom shelf, a counter meant to seat folks, I didn't know.

Someone who lived alone and set stuff up damn well how they pleased …

'Touché,' I muttered.

87

'Pardon?'

'Nothing,' I said. 'I talk to myself a lot. I guess that includes when others are here too.'

I leaned over to straighten the pile and he helped me. Reed studied one red and white chequered book. 'She had a lot of nice cookbooks,' he said.

'She loved to cook. And bake. And craft. All the stuff I suck at,' I said.

'Oh come on, I'm sure you can make ...' He randomly opened the book and smiled broadly. 'Ah, see, Kismet. Blueberry cobbler.'

I rolled my eyes and we righted ourselves, laying the book flat on the counter. 'Cobbler? How about we start with boil water?'

Of course, I was exaggerating. I had made a rather nice thrown together meal for Shepherd and I the day before. But Reed Green did not need to know that. And he didn't need to know I could sort of kind of be creative in the kitchen beyond fucking on the rag rug on the floor. I was more guarded with him than Shepherd, I noticed. I wonder if that was a TV persona thing or a, Tuesday is paranoid about men, kind of thing.

'Sure you could. What time do you need to work?'

'Four, I think.'

'Come home with me.'

'Wow you're randy,' I teased. 'We just–'

'I mean to pick berries. We'll take your grandmother's book, we'll pick some couldn't be fresher blueberries and I'll school you in the ways of cobbler.'

I raised an eyebrow at him. 'School me? That implies a vast knowledge of cobbler.'

He grabbed the ends of my hair and tugged me to him. Barely an inch remained between his lips and mine. I felt my mouth tingle with the nearness of his energy. I still smelled like him, and him like me.

'My aunt Ruth made the most kick ass cobber in the world. Blueberry, strawberry, peach and apple. Even cherry.' His hand slipped inside my robe and he pinched my nipple so I inadvertently gasped.

My body responded to his touch instantly. I wanted to fuck him again. I swallowed hard. 'Sounds yummy,' I managed.

'Her blueberry was the most kick ass, though. And I bet we could do your grandmother's cookbook justice. What do you say?'

He hefted my entire breast, not much bigger than a standard teacup, but pretty nice if I do say so myself. His touch was possessive and it thrilled me just enough to make me uncomfortable. 'I say let me get dressed and we can go pick some of your nice juicy berries.'

'You make it sound dirty,' he said, grinning. Those teeth flashed at me and I remembered the feel of them pressed to my skin. Wanted to feel them again.

And then Shepherd reared up in my mind, pinning me to his rugged wood table. Taking me.

I cleared my throat and shut my robe. 'Let me hop in the shower for five and I'll get some clothes.'

'Bring your uniform for Irv's in case we make a day of it.'

The look on his face made me think he had plans to make a day of it. A day of baking and a meal of me. I could live with that.

I hurried upstairs and from the bathroom window caught sight of Shepherd climbing into his truck. I turned the water on and waited by the glass for a minute, hoping he'd turn and I could wave.

The truck sped backwards in reverse and I realised that he could see whatever vehicle Reed had shown up in parked out front.

'You don't owe anybody anything,' I reminded myself. 'I belong to nobody. Nobody but me.'

Still, when he backed out fast, spewing gravel, I put my hand to the chilly glass and watched him go.

'Perfect time,' Reed said, holding the door to his car for me.

'What?'

'The berries, they'll be dying off soon enough. Now that the fall is really here. Once it hits Allister Lake and the first frost comes, that's it for me. I spend the winter just living on royalties.'

My brain kicked in and I stopped the car door with my boot. 'Maybe I should drive myself,' I said. 'I just realised I'd need to rely on you for a ride and then I have to get home somehow. It's too far to wa–'

'I'll bring you back here to get your car before your shift, OK?'

I hesitated and he good naturedly took the toe of his work boot and nudged my foot back inside the car. It was a vintage Corvette. Year, make and model escaped me but it was the kind my friend Mary's ex-husband drove. I used to call it his penis on wheels. I bit the inside of my lip to keep from grinning.

'OK,' I said and sat back.

When Reed got in the driver's side he buckled up. 'Plus, I eat at Irv's almost every night anyway. It's a social thing. Beats sitting out here on the outskirts of town by myself. Unless I'm feeling particularly monastic or hermit-like.'

'That would be me,' I confessed. 'I actually love being alone.'

'Really? I'd never guess it. You seem so … open and friendly.'

'Is that a sex joke?'

He snorted, eyes on the road, hands casual on the wheel. 'Not at all but I could make it one if you like.'

I punched his leg lightly to show I was kidding. I didn't feel the same ease joking with him that I did with Shepherd. And I wondered again if it was the TV thing or me. Either way, I wanted Reed to know I was kidding. 'I am all of those things. But given my druthers, as Nan would have said, I like to curl up alone or maybe, sometimes with one single person I feel totally cool with.'

'That's nice.' He tucked a stray piece of warm chocolate hair behind his ear and glanced at me before putting his gaze back to the road. 'I hope I'm on that short list.'

'You're getting there,' I said. Then I worried but he smiled and I knew he'd taken it the right way.

'So we're going to pick and bake and …'

'Eat,' he said. 'And a bit before four I'll take you back to your car and let you go spread your warmth and magic at the dinner shift.'

I snorted. 'I think I'll like Irv's. I love that he calls it a restaurant …'

'When it's clearly a diner,' he said.

'Exactly!'

We laughed all the way down the winding road to his pretty TV star house. I managed to only wonder about Shepherd and how his demeanour, even from a distance, had somehow been angry or upset.

And then I refused to question why the fuck I was worried about a man I'd just met and hadn't even seen today.

Reed parked by the front deck and opened the front door for me to drop my purse. He handed me a wicker basket that had a plastic liner and grabbed an identical one. 'Ready?'

'Berries, ho!' I called.

I let him pull my hood up – my own red one, not Shepherd's oversized grey one – and tuck my crazy white-blonde hair inside and tug the strings. 'It's windy and if you can feel …'

He put his hand out and I tilted my face to the greying sky. 'It's drizzling,' I said. 'That's OK. I love drizzle. I love rain and I love snow. I think I'm a freak.'

He took my hand and led me toward the copious bushes along the perimeter of neat rows of strawberry plants. Or an attempt at neat rows, it appeared that some time over the summer the plants had decided how they wanted to grow and had taken over. It was a nice wild sexy plot of land with lush berries peeking through green leaves and stems.

'Nah, I like it too. Something about bad weather instils a cosy feeling. And it gives you an excuse to lie around and drink warm things and read or watch movies.'

I nodded. 'Exactly.'

We started to fill our basket with berries. Reed said they were sparse, I couldn't believe that. Some of the bushes were so full, all I had to do was put my basket underneath and shake it. When our baskets were heavy he set them under a bush and tugged me along.

'Come look at the lake from here. This section of shore isn't sandy. It's overgrown and thick and goes right up to the edge.'

I followed and liked the feel of his warm hand over mine and the little flecks of mist that had settled in his hair. He caught me looking and when I blushed he touched my cheek. 'Hot,' he said.

I looked away and felt my cheeks grow even hotter.

Reed stopped at the edge in a gnarled thicket of bushes and overgrown vegetation. Strong hands turned me until we were face to face. 'Kiss me, Tuesday.'

I tilted my head back and kissed him. A sweet shy kiss that somehow turned intense and demanding in a heartbeat. My chest thumped with my incorrigible pulse and I went wet between my legs when he squeezed my shoulders hard enough to sting.

'Fuck me, Tuesday,' he said. Laying down another order to see if I'd obey.

I didn't think about it. I reached for his belt and tugged the worn leather. The buckle clanked and I pulled hard to get the metal prong from the hole. I managed to get a hand down inside his jeans. To feel the soft and impossibly hard terrain of his cock with my fingertips. Sweeping my finger over the divot at the tip of him, I felt a drop of wetness. I bit his tongue when I did it so the kiss faltered before raging again.

He grabbed me and moved me back and the sensation came. The falling-vertigo-tilting feel of him lowering me to the damp grass that smelled so dark and so green at the same time.

My jeans soaked with drizzle and dampness through the back, my body moving blissfully agitated beneath him. Reed filleted my jeans and pressed a heated kiss to my belly right above my mound. I didn't want his mouth on me this time. There wasn't enough patience in me for that. I just wanted him in me, filling me, splitting me.

He rolled me and tugged my jeans. My jacket caught up around my hips and he shoved. We were a wrestling match for sure: one woman, one man and a lot of clothes and finally, damp and tousled, we somehow managed to get ourselves bare

92

and pressed together.

'Condom,' I sighed.

Reed rustled through is pants and found one. 'I admit it. I stole one and pocketed it just in case …'

'Just in case your strawberry field, blueberry bush seduction worked?' I giggled.

He grinned at me with white even teeth, nodding and smiling in a way that turned something in my chest to a hot coal. God he was pretty.

'And it did. So now I win and you win and I'm going to–' He broke off, thrusting a finger deep into me to test me.

My eyes slammed shut, my head fell back and Reed's tongue lapped the skin above my pulse.

'Fuck me,' I finished.

'Exactly,' he said and I heard the roll and snap of latex and he was in me. Sliding deep on one slick thrust and filling me so completely all I could do was spread my legs, wrap them around his trim waist and move up under him.

He took my mouth in a kiss and I took his.

Chapter Fourteen

MY HOOD HAD FALLEN back and the wind tore at my hair. It tossed the bush that I faced and I was reminded of a film I'd seen on whirling dervishes. Had the bush not been rooted I expected it would spin.

'Big one coming,' he grunted, moving his mouth along my jaw and my neck. Hot kisses dropped on every available space he could find.

The big vehicle he'd predicted rumbled up the lake road and we froze. We weren't easy to spot but here we were sprawled on his land in broad daylight. And yet …

'Turn over,' he rasped, the heat of his words snaking across my earlobe.

I nodded, turning when he released me and got myself on hands and knees. Reed looped an arm around my waist and forced into me. His bulk – so underestimated since he was so damn lean – crushed me and I was sliding. My belly and my chest hit the dirt, my fingers combing through the low branches of the bush as he thrust into me, pinning me, pushing me. His mouth on the back of my neck, my shoulder and his free hand trapped between me and the ground. Fingers working my clit with a perfect rhythm that I couldn't ignore.

'I'm going to come,' I said bluntly.

The wind swallowed up my words and spat them in the opposite direction.

He scraped his teeth along the back of my neck and I shivered violently from the sensation. My nipples pointed rock hard and a chill worked through all of my skin despite being warmed by him.

'Say it again,' he said.

I didn't have to lie. I was already starting that long wet slide toward the first pretty spasm of release. 'I'm going to come' I said louder. 'Now!'

The orgasm hit me and I slammed my ass up with the pressure. Reed's grip increased and I felt like I couldn't get enough air and that only made my orgasm that much more sweetly devastating.

I trembled in his arms with the force of it and he kept his teeth on me, thrusting deep – so forcefully I could hear the wet marriage of our bodies even above the wind. And when I went limp in his arms, his voice snaked into my ear. 'Good?'

'Good,' I agreed. 'Good, good, good …' I chanted, mindless from the violence of my climax.

He chuckled and released me only to grip my hips tight and lean back. He thrust slow and easy until I sank my knees down and out a bit more. Changing his angle, changing his trajectory and apparently sinking him deep into something even more blissful. I know because he puffed out the word, 'Cheater,' and then groaned out his own release, sounding like a wild thing from the woods around his house.

I rolled to my back and let him kiss me softly. There was a tenderness with him that came after. I found it both intoxicating and terrifying.

Reed smoothed my angled bangs from my forehead. 'Um … before your shift?'

'Yeah?' I wriggled to feel the heat of his hand on my bare belly. More wind howled and we both saw my skin blanketed in goosebumps. He tugged a twig free of my hair and waved it at me.

'You might need another shower.'

I snorted, rolled to my side to find my stuff. 'I think you might be right. But first I need my clothes. All of them. Before I get pneumonia.'

My teeth had started chattering and the passion was gone so my skin was reacting to the deep bone-chill.

'Let's get those berries and get inside.'

I was wearing his sweats and a tee and watching him preheat

an oven. My clothing was now tumbling merrily in his dryer and I was trying not to be enchanted by his warm kitchen and cool blue eyes.

'So your mom must have baked a lot, then,' I said.

Reed's mouth went tight and he buttered a long glass baking dish. 'Put those three ingredients in that bowl,' he instructed. 'That way the berries can start to get happy in the sugar and lemon juice.'

I did as instructed, stirring the berries with a wooden spoon to give them a pretty coating of raw sugar that resembled champagne coloured ice clinging to their indigo skin. I thought he wasn't going to answer but as he bent to get the flour canister he said, 'My mother didn't worry about much beyond marketing me. She wanted me to be "on the TV" as she said it. So, I was her mission. Not baking, not PTA, not Little League.'

There was a bitterness in his voice that made me feel like a spy. I cleared my throat and wiped the counter with a rag. The Formica was perfectly clean but it gave me something to do.

'I'm sorry.'

'Not your fault.' He shook his head and his hair, silky to the touch – I knew that now – swayed around his jaw. His eyes held a world of hurt but his mouth showed his determination not to capitulate to it.

I knew that look. I had lived that look. I sympathised so much I chose not to coddle. It would only upset him more.

I pulled my hair into a ponytail but had no band, so I let it go. It tickled at my cheeks, completely out of control thanks to two showers, lots of fucking and rain. I grinned. 'And here I just thought you were a god for walking away from the famous life.'

He grunted. 'Never wanted the famous life. Don't get me wrong. Getting known for Undercover Dad was a jolt for a kid like me. And then moving on to being an adult star was cool … in some respects. In others it was maddening. It took several months to keep the men with cameras out of my fucking blueberry bushes when I moved here.'

'What finally worked?' I sipped the tea he'd made me and waited.

'I didn't do anything worthy for a photo. I think when they realised that I was actually … done. Barring going back to the city for charity events or occasional cameos, they left. I didn't have any picture-worthy scandals going on. No big parties, no gang bangs, no drunk driving. Just a man and his berries.'

'I hear your berries have wooed more than one woman.' I was sorry the moment I said it. I hadn't meant to do that, it was a problem I had. Open mouth insert foot syndrome.

He barked out a laugh that sounded anything but amused. 'Shepherd. Jesus. That woman had one foot out the door. And–' He dumped the berries in the glass dish and spread them out. He handed me flour and then butter cut in pieces and motioned for me to mix it. 'And he was kicking her ass out the rest of the way. Make it so it looks like chunky corn meal,' he said, keeping me on edge with his back and forth conversation.

I mixed it with the spoon and when he said 'might be easier with your fingers,' I gave up the spoon and dug in.

Reed leaned in smelling of some manly scent and sugar of all things. 'He didn't want her. He just got his alpha jockeys in a twist because she ended up banging me on the way out.'

I knew he was right. Shepherd had pretty much admitted the same.

'Men,' I said, rolling my eyes. I was trying to be cute and funny to defuse the situation.

He grinned that famous crooked grin at me and I had the urge to kiss his pale pink lips. Such a lush mouth for a boy, I thought.

'Yes, we are pretty stupid most of the time.'

'Just territorial,' I said. 'He should have just peed on her to mark her.'

'Oh, he did more than pee on her to mark her,' he muttered under his breath. 'But then he changed his mind.'

I wanted to ask what he meant. *He's a sexual deviant* echoed in my head from Adrian. But I refused to get sucked in. I refused to care. I had walked away from Phil and his bullshit and Stan and his cloying too-much-love. I did not want to care what Shepherd did or how Reed felt or that under it all I felt like I was shafting Adrian. I didn't want all that sticky messy feeling shit.

I just wanted sex. Was that so bad?

I put my hands up and laughed – letting the serious conversation fall away – and wriggled my messy fingers. 'So, verdict Mr Green. Did I do a good job or what?'

Chapter Fifteen

WE ALMOST DIDN'T MAKE it and I thought he'd have to take me straight to work. But he dropped me at my car as dusk was purpling the sky and I all but dove into the Grenada. I put my plastic wrapped blueberry cobbler – that had been to die for – on the seat and fired up the car.

Reed knocked on the window just as I was about to put her in gear. I rolled the window down and he leaned in to kiss me. I took the kiss, worrying and secretly hoping that the other two men in my life were watching.

Now what did that say about me?

'It seems silly,' he said, still leaning in my open window.

'What does?'

'Bringing you here. I could have just taken you to work. I'll be eating there later anyway.'

'I like it this way …' I dropped my words and shrugged.

'I know. No strings. No attachments. Tuesdays gone with the wind …' He sang a snippet of the old Lynyrd Skynyrd song to me.

'Something like that. I just … I'm not that girl. I'm not a settle down girl.'

'Until you find the right guy,' he said. 'I'd lay money on it.'

He kissed the tip of my nose, a surprisingly sweet gesture, and was gone. I rolled up the window and took off fast. The Grenada spat gravel and revved like she liked the fast life. The car was black and tan and very much like the one my mother owned when I was a kid. I'd called it the pimpmobile back in the day.

I made it to the diner with two minutes to spare. Racing in the front door I called my hellos. I dropped my jacket and my purse in the office and tied on an apron. Irv patted my arm, thanked me and thrust an order pad into my hand. Then he said, 'Work!'

It was only then that I turned to see Shepherd at my table. Big and hulking, looking hungry and pissed and like he had a few things to say.

My body tingled all over but especially my girl parts. I squeezed my thighs together but that only served to fan the flame of arousal that always scorched me when I saw him. Something about Shepherd Moore soothed me, and something else about him put me on edge. Tossed together, those two instinctual reactions made for a heady and confusing cocktail of hormones and emotion.

I steeled myself and walked up to him. 'Hi, Shepherd. What can I get you?'

He made me wait. Those dark brown eyes running up and down my body. I felt naked and panicky, trapped in that gaze, and it made me angry. Very fucking angry. Responses like this were why I didn't want to get involved beyond the bedroom.

'I can come back if you're not sure,' I snapped. There must have been real bite in my tone because even Irv looked up from behind the cash register. For his sake, I quickly plastered on a smile.

'No, no. That's OK. I guess I was just having trouble making up my mind,' he said. For the first time ever I heard a very soft, very faint drawl in his voice. It made me wonder if he was from here originally, because the tone almost suggested the deep south. Georgia maybe. 'I guess I wish I could take a bite of all of it.'

He was fucking with me. He meant men. He knew about Adrian, I was fairly certain. But now something – some intuition that was maddening under my skin like an itch – told me he knew about Reed and that ... that was what was really getting to him.

'Well, variety is the spice of life,' I said a bit too peppy. A bit too bubbly. A bit too in-your-face fuck-off.

He frowned but then he smiled. The sudden shift in his demeanour threw me off. 'Fair enough.' He shrugged. 'All's fair … Just like in love right?'

I blinked. 'I wouldn't know. I don't think I've ever been in love. Not really.' I shifted, feeling less bold and more unnerved by the minute. 'I'm not a love kind of girl. I think.'

'Me neither,' he said. 'Guy, I mean. There was the one time I thought …' He caught himself, shook that big head again, reminding me of a bear.

When Shepherd gave me a genuine smile, something in my lower tummy shifted and turned hot and liquid. Irv cleared his throat and I blushed and Shepherd chuckled. That laugh ran up my spine raising every tiny fine hair in its wake. 'Sorry. I'll take the meatloaf, mashed potatoes, green beans and sweet tea. See, once you see clearly what it is you want … it's not so hard to decide.'

I nodded, wanting to run but forcing myself to move at normal speed. I took his menu and his big blunt fingers brushed over mine for a second. The feel of his skin went right to my knees making me forget about cobbler and fucking and even sweet unexpected life confessions in a warm kitchen. It made me forget everything but that first moment his mouth had pressed down over my sodden panties and I felt the heat of his breath on me.

'OK,' I said in a shaky voice and then I hustled away. Afraid to look back. Needing to catch my breath.

I hustled around at Irv's urging to finish the rest of the dinner rush but felt Shepherd's eyes stay on me. Somehow not angry any more. Now it felt like an affectionate and amused gaze and that weirded me out even more.

I did not want to worry about what he thought. And I certainly did not want to feel happy that he was no longer angry with me. I didn't want to care one way or the other what he thought. We could fuck. We could eat dinner. We could joke. We could not … care.

'Here you go. Meatloaf and potatoes and beans and sweet tea,' I said. My voice high and watery, my body humming like I had swallowed a live wire.

'Thank you, Tuesday.'

I nodded, not looking right at him. I was so afraid that if I

101

did look right at him, I'd want to kiss him. To touch him. To feel with my hands that we were OK and there was no animosity.

'You're welcome.'

He grabbed my wrist as I went to pull back and like some well trained creature I felt my body hum to life and tingle. A warm wet release slipped from my pussy and graced the centre of my cotton panties. He didn't know ... he couldn't know. And yet, somehow I felt like he did.

'Yes?' I whispered.

The door swung open and the bell jingled and I looked up to see my world had just gotten a bit more claustrophobic. A bit more sticky. Reed stood there, mouth rigid, face dark but expressionless. He turned his head and made his way to a booth by the window.

'I want pie when I'm done.' Shepherd squeezed my wrist just hard enough to grind those bones. Just hard enough to remind me of his power and what that power did to me. Inside.

'Oh, OK. What kind?'

He spared Reed a glance but kept his face stolid and unreadable. 'Cherry of course. Cherry's my favourite. Sticky, sweet ... perfect.'

I knew he meant me. I knew he meant sex. I knew it as surely as I knew I was breathing oxygen and the world was round. But I managed to just say, 'OK,' before I turned away.

He squeezed my wrist one more time before I left and I gasped before I could stop myself. He heard it and smiled. I heard it and cringed inside. I glanced at Reed who looked up, frowning. It was clear he had heard it too.

'Well that was fun, Nan!' I boomed in my empty house. I dropped my purse onto the sofa – more like threw it – and tilted my head back and screamed into the soaring ceiling.

'I need a dog!' I raged. 'Or a cat!'

I kicked off my boots and slid in stockinged feet to the sideboard and poured a big fat glass of wine.

'So that I do not sound like a mental person talking to myself. Or my dead grandmother. No offence, Nan,' I finished.

I took a big swig and laughed. It was all very ridiculous. I was letting them affect me and that was my damn fault.

Someone knocked on the door and I groaned. No. No, no! I did not want to deal with this. And yet, I had to.

I tried the peephole but only saw an arm. Could have been any arm. I cracked the door to see Adrian standing there.

'You OK?'

He was angry. I could tell.

'I'm fine,' I said. 'Just tired.'

He grunted. That meant no sex. Adrian wasn't stupid. 'Just checking in.'

'Thanks. Everything OK out there in the barn?'

'Getting colder by the day,' he said.

If that was bait to invite him to stay in the house I wasn't taking it. I didn't need a caretaker. Me letting him stay was to be nice and because we had a history. 'Yeah, fall is in the air,' I said. 'Look Adrian, I hope you don't think–'

He held up a palm to stop me. 'Don't. I don't need the talk,' he said. 'I was just checking in. I'm a big boy.'

I smiled and let myself give a little sigh of relief. Then a huge awkward moment slammed down between us and I said, 'Well, if that's all, I need to take a shower. It's been a really bad day.'

'Sure thing. I'm out in the barn if you need anything.'

'Hey,' I said, remembering the potting shed my first night at the house. 'Have you seen anything in that potting shed?'

He shook his head. 'Nah. Haven't even been in there forever. Virginia never needed me in there so I stayed out of her stuff.'

'Just thought I'd ask.'

'I can check it if you want me to,' he said, eager to help.

'Nope. If there was anything in there, you'd know it. You're here all day and you're more in the know than any of us.'

He looked pleased at my assessment and that made me feel better. He finally said good night and turned to leave. I shut the door and locked it but not before a blast of frozen air licked my face.

I drank my wine as I made my way slowly up the steps. I

wanted a long hot shower, another wine, a bad movie and maybe a good orgasm. On my own, thank you very much.

I got three out of four.

Chapter Sixteen

I REFUSED TO ANALYSE why I pulled Shepherd's hoodie on with my orange and hot pink flowered pyjama pants. Or why tugging the hood ties tight so the whole thing warmed me made me feel less spooked. Shit, I had no idea why I was spooked to begin with.

Probably too much fucking, too many men in my life, too much stress and then there was the whole brand new life deal. The real question should be, why wouldn't I be stressed?

I put on one of my favourite horror movies. Probably not the best idea, but beloved movies tended to soothe me regardless of content.

I rummaged through Nan's pantry and came up with a hot air popper and popcorn. 'Sweet,' I said to myself – of course – as I fired it up and poured kernels in to the fill line.

The machine hummed and whirred and I put a big red bowl beneath to catch the end result. Melted butter pooled in the red saucepan and I nearly poured it on myself when I turned to see a face pressed to the kitchen door.

I screamed and the face laughed but then a small knock sounded. 'Sorry,' Shepherd called through the glass.

'Sorry!' I shouted, ripping the door open. 'What the fuck do you mean sorry? I almost had a heart attack.'

We stared at each other, me shaking from the sudden shock. Him in the doorway where the wind tossed behind his back like he was an archangel fallen to earth to exact God's vengeance.

It struck me that's what Shepherd reminded me off. A warrior. Someone with a quest.

'Sorry,' he said again, his eyes tracking over his own damn hoodie.

Shit. Why had I put it on? Why not one of my own fucking sweatshirts or a robe.

'Hi,' he said.

'Hi,' I breathed. I took a step back instinctively and he moved into the doorway, filling it, before stepping past the threshold and into my kitchen. He kicked the door shut and my nipples spiked to two hard points beneath his well worn clothing.

'I …' I shook my head.

'I came to say I'm sorry.'

'Why?' I asked, turning to pour butter on popcorn I didn't want any more.

'Because I am sorry. I'm an ass.'

'You're all asses aren't you?' I said, trying to make a joke.

'Are we?'

'I think so. Maybe it comes with the penis.'

He gave me a half grin. 'Or maybe it shows up with a woman like you. Women like you tend to make men like us stupid and caveman in demeanour.'

'Women like me?'

'Good women.'

I shook my head. 'I'm not.'

'You are.'

Somehow he'd walked into my kitchen, filled my field of vision and had me pinned, butt against the counter. 'Wrong.'

I slipped free of him and made my way into the great room. On the screen Neve Campbell screamed and a man in a smiling mask ran after her. 'I'm sorry,' he said from the doorway.

I nodded. 'I heard.'

'I had no right–'

'It's not you–' I started, but he cut me off with a big guffaw.

'It's you?' he finished.

I nodded. 'It is. I'm tainted. I'm damaged. I was with a man like Phil and it … demolished me for the whole love scenario.'

'Who said I could even love you?' he countered.

I blinked. 'You're right. I'm sorry.' I took a step back and he took a step forward.

'I'm not built for love either, Tuesday. I was once. But it

was ruined for me.'

'She broke your heart?' I asked, shocked to think of him as vulnerable and realising that was stupid. We're all vulnerable somehow.

'That depends on what you mean by broke my heart.' His hands found the ties I'd already tugged tight and he used them as leads to pull me to him.

I could have fought. I didn't.

His mouth was so close to mine I could smell mint on his breath. I could count the hairs bursting through his sun-darkened skin if I had the time and patience. I didn't. 'She left you for another man?'

'No.'

'She cheated with your best friend?' I gasped.

'No.' His lips grazed my jaw and then his teeth did too.

'She said she'd marry you and then ran off?'

He paused and then said, 'No.' Taking my ass in his big hands, he squeezed gently. Palming my cheeks with a strength that was exhilarating and scary to boot.

'What then?'

He pulled his head back to look at me. I could see – despite time that must have passed for him – pain in those dark, dark eyes. 'She fell out of love with me.'

'What did you do?' I asked, confused.

Falling out of love with a man like Shepherd? A man who exuded strength and kindness and all the stuff in between. The man who'd made me dinner because he made me cry. The man who smiled at me though I'd hurt him – intentionally or not. The man who was here confessing to me though it must be killing him.

'That's the whole damn reason, cupcake,' he said. He crushed me to the back of my sofa as someone on the TV screamed. His cock was hard, riding the cleft of my sex. His hands squeezed my bottom again and he nudged into me so my body burst with a hint of the pleasure I could have should I just take my damn pants off.

'She just fell out of love?'

He nodded. His lips crushed against mine and I parted my

107

lips for him. His tongue thrust sensually, bullying me with his kiss. Fingers curled to my hips and he rocked into me again giving me another short burst of arousal. My toes tingled and I shivered.

'Are you cold, Tuesday?'

'No. I'm just …' I shook my head. 'She just fell out of love? She just … left?'

He pressed his lips together hard but then he smiled. 'That's it.'

'That's crazy.'

'But true,' he said. 'Now tell me, if you're not cold … what are you?'

'I'm horny,' I said bluntly.

He grinned and ducked down. I was confused for a moment until he caught me on the up-thrust. Shepherd tossed me over his shoulder like a toy and carried me up my steps.

'Where are we going?'

'To your bed.'

'Oh,' I said, relaxing against him. My body confused by the hot and cold feeling of being in his grip, but hot was winning.

'Unless you don't want me,' he said. He had frozen, me over his shoulder, all of him tense under me.

'Take me upstairs, Shepherd. I haven't not wanted you since we met.'

He made a sound that indicated he was pleased. But it also sounded a tiny bit sceptical.

She just fell out of love …

How bad must that hurt? It hurts when someone leaves you for a reason, but for there to be no reason. I shook my head. I simply couldn't imagine.

He tossed me – yes tossed – but somehow gently so that I landed on my soft bed with a flustered sigh. My hair swam around me and I watched the mammoth, gruff and bearded figure that was Shepherd Moore. The light from the balcony backlit him and he looked angelic again. A rogue angel with a mission.

I parted my legs without thinking. Wriggled.

He unbuttoned his black and grey flannel, watching me.

Straight faced and stern but I realised that with this man I always felt something I rarely felt. Almost never even pondered.

Safe.

I felt safe with Shepherd. As scary as he seemed, as warned off as I'd been. I pushed the thought away as he grabbed each of my ankles in his big hands and tugged me ever so slightly toward him.

'I heard you were a sexual deviant,' I told him.

He froze. And then he surprised me by chuckling so long and so loud he straightened up and tossed his head back.

'Oh yeah?'

'Yeah. From more than one person,' I said, toeing his flat taut belly with my foot. He grabbed it and yanked me toward him harder.

I squawked, my best impression of a jungle bird, and that made us both laugh.

I shimmied to my belly, crawled to him, faced him on my knees. 'What do they mean?

'I think they mean they are as vanilla as nursing home pudding.'

I put my head down and swallowed a giggle. Shepherd grabbed hunks of my hair in his hand and moved my head so I had to look at him. 'Why do you ask, Tuesday?'

I shrugged, wanting so badly to seem nonchalant. But inside of me my emotions warred and twisted, my pussy grew wetter and I felt such a craving I could crawl out of my skin. 'I was just wondering,' I said on a breath. Then I chewed my lips to keep myself calm.

His eyes zeroed in on where my teeth met my flesh and he put my hand on his cock. He still wore his jeans and his belt. His boots he'd kicked off by the door. His shirt hung open and the smell of him – whatever the secret scent of Shepherd was, I could never put my finger on it – filled my head. I smoothed my fingers against his erection and he looked just a touch more stoic if that was even possible.

'Why do you ask?'

'I wanted to know.'

'Do you want something, Tuesday?'

'No,' I lied.

'Are you sure?'

I looked into the black depths of his eyes, surreally dark and shaded in the low light of my room. 'I ...'

He popped his button fly by pulling the fabric and opening them all in one long yank. 'Tell me,' he said. When his cock was free, he put just the right amount of pressure on the back of my head. No pushing. Not bullying. Guiding. It was more like he was giving me permission more than anything.

Permission I gladly took.

I leaned in and pressed my face to him. Smelling the salty, warm cotton smell of his body and relishing it. I pressed my cheek to his cock and finally moved my head to drop a kiss on the tip. Just the tip.

I felt the wetness there and darted out my tongue to collect the tiny prize of his precome.

'Jesus. You make me crazy,' he said.

A thrill worked through me and I smiled. There was that rush of power that came with making a strong man bend, a stern man shake.

I didn't respond, just let my hair swim and sway around my face as I took as much of his hard length into my mouth as I could. I sucked gently and then even more gently scraped my teeth along his fragile flesh

He yanked my hair and I whimpered but kept sucking.

'I'm going to flip you over and fuck you until your knees buckle if you keep doing that.' His voice was a predatory growl in the dark.

God, I hoped he was telling the truth.

I went down as far as I could. Letting him fill my throat, walking the fine line of my gag reflex. But if I sucked air through my nose I could get him deeper and his visceral response was to thrust just a touch into my waiting mouth.

I swirled my tongue and danced it over him but he pulled me back, still using my hair as a leash. 'Why did you ask me?' he demanded.

'I wanted to know.'

'Do you want something?'

I flashed back to sex with Phil before he'd turned into a douche. We'd experimented with some pain play. I had submitted. But when his need to hurt moved outside of the bedroom –outside of his control – I had dropped it. I hadn't trusted anyone since then beyond a little hair tug or gentle to moderate slaps on the ass. Normal sex shit.

I trusted Shepherd. I trusted him so much it frightened me and stole my words. I shook my head, oddly on the verge of tears.

He caught the look and dropped to his knees, bringing us eye to eye.

'Tell me.' It wasn't a request.

'I want you to hurt me.'

He blinked. 'Do you, now?'

'Yes.'

'How?'

I shook my head. Looked away. That wasn't for me to decide. Not if I really wanted to feel that rush of submitting to someone's will. He had to decide.

'I can't tell you that,' I said, eyes averted.

I caught his smile in my peripheral vision. 'Christ. You fuck with my head. How about we punish you? How about you pay for what you did to me earlier?'

He yanked my pyjama pants down and ripped them free. The zipper of his hoodie screamed when he yanked it down fast and hard. He turned me suddenly, his grips sure but a bit rough.

'What did I do to you earlier?' I gasped, aroused, in need and so fucking confused.

His hands positioned me up on to hand and knee and there it was. That proprietary touch on my ass. He smoothed his callused hand along the swell of one ass cheek and then the other. As the first blow fell I heard him grunt, 'I saw him fucking you. In your kitchen. I saw you with that twat, Reed.'

111

Chapter Seventeen

OH SHIT. OH SHIT. There was no time to say a word. I was lost in the feel of his hands on me.

I had asked for his punishment, to experience his "deviance". I had asked and he had agreed. I had no idea there had been any kind of impetus under it all. Other than I frustrated him, maybe. I frustrated a lot of people.

The blows landed one after another, firm and stinging but controlled. He was not going to hurt me for clearly hurting him.

The realisation that seeing me fucking Reed had hurt Shepherd registered only fleetingly before another blow chased it away.

Like any good man he didn't let his anger control his hand. He let his hand control his anger. Delivering hard but well-tempered blows so that my back bowed up and my head fell back.

I sighed low in my throat feeling that blissful place where pain bled quickly into pleasure and amplified the need between my legs.

'Shepherd,' I gasped.

'That fucking made me crazy, you know.' He said it conversationally. Like we were having coffee and he was sharing a secret.

His hands smoothed mesmerising circles over my skin – the skin he had just tortured – and when he dipped a finger into my pussy to test me, all of my body responded. I moaned – a mournful desperate sound that had him growling in the darkness – and then the blows began again.

On the meat of my ass cheek, then down to my thighs. When he delivered one smart blow upward between my legs, smacking my clit so it tingled and throbbed, I sobbed out loud. 'I'm sorry I hurt you.'

'You didn't hurt me,' he said.

He pushed me to my back, his eyes darting around the room.

'Nightstand,' I said. 'And yes I did.'

He gritted his teeth and spread out over me to reach the drawer. When he wrestled the condom on, he faced me. Anger rippling beneath the surface of his skin, trying so hard to imprint his face with a whole slew of emotions. He stilled his expression into a mask and said, 'You. Did not. Hurt. Me.'

His fingers dug into my hips and I opened my legs for him. Opened wide so the heated rod of his cock could press to my wet centre, so he could feel how fucking wet I was. How much I wanted him. Just what he did to me.

The muscles in his jaw danced and bunched again as he controlled his emotions. 'I did hurt you and I'm sorry.'

He put his hand over my mouth, almost – but not quite – blocking my air, and shoved into me. It was a brutal welcomed thrust that had my entire cunt flexing up around him.

'Shut up, Tuesday,' he said gruffly but not unkindly.

I had no choice. He was cutting off my air and yet I did not struggle as he drove into me. The heady buzz, the tiny spots, all of it heightened the feeling in my pussy as he nudged my G-spot with every long thrust.

I gasped gently when he moved his hand up for a heartbeat. He shoved a meaty hand under my ass and angled me and when I curled my thighs around his waist to get him deeper he growled. The growl made the hair on the back of my neck stand up and my nipples prickle.

He dipped his head to snag one hard spike of flesh in his sharp, sharp teeth. He tugged it to the point of perfectly controlled pain and I came. I struggled accidentally for a moment when the air did not flood my lungs as usual.

Shepherd moved his hands to rest against my throat, his thumbs pressing my pounding pulse as his movements became more frantic. More animal than man.

'I'm sorr–' I started again. Maybe partially to provoke what he did next.

He squeezed my neck just enough to stop the words. To make me choose air or speech and I chose air.

His hips rocked as his bulk covered me. Instead of feeling smothered, I felt secure and I parted my lips and he took my mouth in a kiss. 'Shut up, Tuesday,' he said in my ear as he came.

I let myself hold him for a moment. I let myself enjoy the heated weight of him pressed over me. But when it became too nice, too lovely, I moved out from under him.

'I know it's late,' I said, feeling suddenly claustrophobic. Anxiety sizzled through me and I didn't really know why. 'And I'm sorry, but I want to go to …' I waved my hands indicating my bed.

My throat was too small and my eyes burned with what I feared was the beginning of tears. What was wrong with me? I was hurting him again, I could see it in his eyes. He'd nodded once and stood to pull on his jeans. The light from the balcony hit him square in the face and I could see the pain there as plain as day. Buried way down deep but recognisable if you looked.

'I'm sorry, Shep–'

'It's cool,' he said. He even smiled at me. When he touched my face my heart broke. 'I get it.'

When he moved his hand away and I felt the absence of his touch, my heart broke again.

'I'm confused, is all. I am so …'

'You just lost your grandmother. New life. Ex behind you. I get it.'

I wanted to change my mind and ask him to stay. I wanted to tell him I was stupid and confused and would he please hold me. Instead I watched him go.

I slipped my pyjama pants up over my hips and tied them. Pulling his hoodie back on I felt a stab of some brutal emotion in my chest. Jesus. When I heard the front door shut, I raced down to lock it. Now that he was gone I felt on edge. On edge and nervous and yes, stupid. I felt stupid and horrible for hurting him. It dawned on me as I turned the lock with shaking hands.

'You just had a bit of a reaction to the pain, you ass.' My voice sounded hollow and wounded even to me. 'You got freaked out after the fact. Because of Phil. Because of how it turned last time.'

I shook my head and did allow myself a whole minute to cry. I had just hurt Shepherd because I had wigged out post pain, post orgasm, post … trust.

There was trust and there was trust. There was I trust you to be in my body and fuck me but using my boundaries and rules. And then there was what I had just offered him. I trust you to be in my body and for you to fuck me and I trust you to know where to take me … how to take me … how far to go to get me where I need to be.

I dialled his number and no surprise, it rang and rang and rang. I left a message when his outgoing snippet simply said, 'Go for it.'

'It's me. I'm sorry. I'm sorry, Shepherd. I freaked out. It was … other stuff. Not you. It's a long boring story involving a girl who waited too long to leave a guy who lost his way and got heavy handed and stupid with the hitting. And I'm sorry. Even if I didn't hurt you, you said I didn't …' I stammered. 'I'm still sorry. I think I had a little post traumatic freak out there. And I am sorry.'

I hung up quickly before I could make a bigger fool out of myself by saying I was sorry for the millionth time. Which was ironic because Nan used to tease me I was damn near the perfect person if only I could learn to say that I was sorry.

'I learned, Nan!' I yelled.

I ran a hand through my hair and something banged again on the deck. Maybe Shepherd had come back. Maybe he was out there now. I raced to the door and threw it open before thinking.

Nothing but wind. Nothing but wind and darkness and empty night. I shivered and went to shut the door. I pulled the blinds down to shut out the blackness that pressed to my window.

'Nothing,' I said. But I had seen that all the deck furniture was pressed to the wall. None of it had moved along the wooden slats. So what had I heard?

'You heard your own damn guilt stomping around in your head, crazy ass talking to yourself motherfucker,' I said in my best Samuel L Jackson voice. Then I laughed and dragged myself up to bed.

I shut the lights off along the way and when I got into my room I happened to glance out. Hoping Adrian was warm and hoping soon he'd find a good woman. He deserved one.

There was that flash of light again in the potting shed. A warm glow that I somehow lost when I moved the wrong way.

Maybe it was a reflection of light from somewhere else, I thought for the second time. I'd have to check. But for now, the weight of the day was heavy on me and I curled into the bed, holding a chunk of sheet that smelled particularly like Shepherd to my nose to calm my nerves.

'It is completely normal to sniff the scent of a man you just shunned. That is totally normal, to feel better having the smell of him in your nose. You idiot …' I mumbled.

Usually I drop off into sleep like a rock falling from a bridge. This time I felt myself drifting. Felt myself falling. The floaty surreal feeling rushed up to grab me with pliant hands and in that instant I felt his hands around my neck again. And the odd but overwhelming trust and safety I had felt at that moment.

My grandmother was a beautiful woman. Snow-white hair she liked to dye penny red. But when she let it go it was the colour of fresh untouched snow.

I stared at her. I knew it was a dream. Even in the dream I was no fool, but I hadn't gotten to say goodbye so I let it play out, cherishing the feel of her here with me.

She kissed me. Her lips and skin so very cool and dry, the way they'd always been in life. When she kissed me it always made me think of leather or silk smoothed by time. There was such comfort in a kiss from my grandmother.

Even one that wasn't real.

'A man can be aggressive without being violent.'

I blinked at her. Nodded.

'And you can be scared but honest.'

Another nod. My eyes were going haywire, tears I fought doubled and then trebled my vision. I swallowed, my throat painfully tight.

'But most of all Tuesday Child, be honest with yourself.'

I woke long enough to brush the tears from my face and zip Shepherd's hoodie all the way to my neck. Fall wind – violent even according to the locals – nipped and whispered along the eaves of my house. I clutched the man-scented sheet back to my face and slid back into slumber.

This time I dreamed of trolls in small houses, phantom lights, ghosts with bad intentions and pain that had nothing to do with orgasms.

When morning came I was grateful to wake up. I felt less rested than I had in days. And it had nothing to do with Shepherd or hurt feelings or fucking too many guys or confusion. Something was wrong and I simply didn't know what.

Beyond all the obvious stuff, I mean.

Chapter Eighteen

IT AMAZED ME TO a degree how easily I'd slid into lake life. I shuffled down to the kitchen after pulling on some big wool socks. Fall did not come to the country the way it did to the city. In the city you got little licks of cool temperatures and then slammed with Indian Summer. The blacktop and the building and the chaos tended to trap the heat and keep it there longer.

At Allister Lake the cooler temperatures swooped between buildings, rushed off the water, rubbed itself against redwood siding and A-Frame abodes. It ripped through the lakeshore neighbourhood squealing like a banshee. And I loved it.

I poured my coffee slowly after sitting in a stupor and watching it percolate. When I saw the rug out of place by the kitchen door I pictured Shepherd standing there. Grinning. Imposing and full of intense energy that always made me feel alive and a little bit kinetic.

'Jesus, Nan,' I whispered, recalling my dream. 'I need to go say I'm sorry to his face. Like a big girl.'

My mind supplied a vivid image of my grandmother's smile and that made me smile. She always wrapped her arms around me from behind, peeking her face over my shoulder. She was shorter than me so the hugs had always made me laugh. I nearly felt that phantom hug and was grateful for it. My grandmother was the only real family I had, even dead. So feeling her presence, true or imagined, made me calmer.

Some frozen pancakes heated in the toaster oven with warm syrup served as breakfast and I promised myself I'd go to the grocery store today. Irv had called bright and early to say that his niece would be filling in for Delores today but could I do tomorrow. I'd called back to confirm.

A quick shower and then I hunted for clean clothes. Jeans and boots and a big grey sweater seemed good for a day the colour of pewter. But I loved this weather and I wouldn't complain. Stomping across the gravel to Shepherd's house, I remembered the light in the potting shed and made a mental note to ask Adrian for the key. But the thought floated from my head as I got up on Shepherd's front porch.

Jesus. My heart was pounding.

I knocked. For a split second I wondered if Adrian was watching. Or my ghost in the potting shed. Or Nan?

I turned, feeling the hair on my nape sway with nerves, but saw no one. No one to see because no one was there. I was just being a freak.

I knocked again, pounding harder.

Nothing.

The truck was parked by the front as usual. Maybe Shepherd was out back. I walked back down the wide wooden steps and made my way to the side. When I rounded the back I saw a door in the ground open and heard music.

A door in the ground? Was he a hobbit?

For some reason my own confusion struck me as so amusing I started to giggle. Until I approached the hole and the music came into focus. Jeff Buckley's haunting voice. *Remember when I moved in you* ...When he sang Leonard Cohen's Hallelujah my entire body went rashy with goosebumps. Always had, and when I studied my arm I saw it still did.

'Hello?' For some reason I whispered. Possibly I was afraid, possibly intimidated. Possibly I did not want him to know I was coming.

'Shepherd?' I whispered, trying to force my voice louder and failing.

I moved down three steps and realised it was a storm cellar. Dug into the earth not far from the house, it was set to the left of the house, just a few running strides from his back door.

'Shep?' I managed to be a bit louder but nothing compared to the music.

Hallelujah ... Hallelujah ...

I shut my eyes for a moment, drinking in the song. Trying to get my damn heart to stop pounding so that when I got the chance to say I was sorry I didn't sound like a moron.

My body swayed lightly due to anxiety and rotten sleep. I steadied myself and walked to the bottom step. The overhang was so low I had to duck my head.

His back was to me. Broad and muscular in a navy blue pullover with a touch of leather on the collar. I had no idea why that was so fucking sexy but it was. His hands, big and dusty, glided over a medium sized bookshelf as he sanded layers of old paint off. I watched him move, how at ease he was. How his hands could make the sander behave and how after he sanded, he stroked the wood almost gently with the other hand. I watched him and remembered those hands on me. The blows of each spank rocking my body but then the gentle throbbing that he soothed with a callused hand.

'Shepherd?' And still my voice refused to behave and I went unnoticed. He stood and stretched, dropping the sander as the track changed and a whole new song filled the small stone space.

'Shepherd?' I managed in the brief moment of silence. He didn't startle or tense, he just turned with a smile.

The smile went right to the centre of me. A white-hot lightning bolt of lust wracked me and I hugged myself against its impact.

He didn't say anything.

'Hi,' I said.

He nodded. 'Hi. Did you sleep well?'

He wiped his hands with a shop rag and tossed it on a stool. My eyes ticked off everything I could find just to distract myself from my nerves. A shelf overhead full of small boxes, jars of screws, a bag of shop rags. A handmade wooden counter ran the right wall and the shelves beneath held everything from heavy duty glue to knots of rope to rolls and rolls of tape.

'No,' I whispered.

I looked up to find him watching me. I felt slightly drunk

120

and entirely off kilter. 'That sucks,' he said, giving me a half smile.

I wanted to stand on tiptoe and kiss his mouth. Fist my fingers in the short brown and grey of his beard and tug. I wanted to beg him to take me again and promise that I'd do it right this time. The trusting part. Not fuck it up and panic and push him away.

But I also did not want to give my heart to anyone. I refused. Even if I felt those small stirrings, the urge to give him that part of myself, I pushed it away. I could not get to that place again and be mangled. I could not handle any more damage.

And there was always damage, wasn't there?

'It does suck. Did you get my message?'

He nodded, tugging a new rag from his back pocket and wiping his already clean hands again. He was feeling what I was feeling. A tense but heady energy that rushed around us, an invisible presence making it nearly impossible not to move toward him and then against him. Just to feel him.

I took two steps forward just as he did and we stood there in the middle of his work space as if in a standoff. I imagined if I shut my eyes I would see crackles and pops of purplish white energy arcing between us.

He touched my lip with his fingertip while my eyes were shut and my whole body jerked. My cunt gave up a small sluice of fluid and I prayed for him to say it was all OK.

'I got your message.'

'And?'

'And it's fine.'

He was lying to me but I let him.

'Why won't you look at me?' he asked.

'Somehow it's easier to say stuff right now like this.' I smiled but damn if I didn't keep my eyes closed.

'So you pushed me away because ...' Then his lips crushed down on mine and I felt like I was swaying in a stiff wind.

'Because of a very bad man who I took way too long to get away from. We ... experimented. And at first it was fine. But when he got ... troubled–'

'He took the pain out of the bedroom.'

I nodded. Eyes still closed. When he touched my nipple through my sweater I tensed and hissed and immediately felt such astonishing want in my pussy it scared me. 'Yes. And when you ... when I ... trusted you to do that to me I was happy. And it was good. Really good. And when it was over ...' I shook my head. Tears threatened because I was frustrated and frustration always made me cry.

'When it was over all those sensations and fears and bullshit rushed over you.'

I nodded and cut him off before he could go on. 'And I felt like I was drowning and I needed–'

'To take back control.'

I opened my eyes and he was watching me. His eyes so intense on me I felt utterly bare despite my warm clothes. Was he seeing my soul? God, I hoped not. I was sure it was some dark and twisted thing.

'Yes, to take back control.'

'Well then I guess you have to decide whether or not to trust me,' he said, leaning in. 'You seem to trust that actor pretty boy putz.'

I narrowed my eyes at him. I felt it. My ornery snake look, Nan had called it. 'Fucking is not trust.'

He nodded decisively. 'True enough. But it's time you decided.'

He was pushing me and I didn't know why. 'Oh is it? All several days into our ...' I almost said relationship and caught myself at the last moment. 'Knowing each other.'

'Yes.' He took that final step in and we were nearly belly to belly.

'Who the fuck are you to tell me what to do?' I growled. I pushed him. Didn't even think about it, I just pushed him.

I became very aware in the tight space that I was provoking a very strong man. Men can be aggressive without being violent ...

I needed to stop. But I didn't. I pushed him again. 'I am not yours to order around.'

'I'd like it if you were,' he said with that sexy and irritating

122

half smile. 'Because I'd tell you to get down on your goddamn knees and suck my–'

I swung. I swung and in that still-awareness moment that preceded movement I thought, oh shit. I realised I didn't want to do this. I didn't want to be this person. I had people like that in my family and this was not the woman I wanted to be.

Shepherd caught my hand before it connected and he stared down into my eyes. Burning a hole through me – a hole full of shame and regret and worry and at the bottom of it all, sagging but not dying … hope.

'Will you trust me?'

'What?'

'Will you trust me? Yes or no.' He squeezed my wrist and the sparkle-bite-burst of pain made me shift on my feet. My pussy flexing greedily against nothing but itself. I would have given a million dollars to have him bury himself in me to the root at that particular moment.

'I don't know,' I stammered.

He still held my arm. He still squeezed. 'One more chance. Will you trust me?'

I didn't hesitate.

'Yes.'

Chapter Nineteen

MY HAND SLAMMED THE rock wall and there was a moment where confusion made my head ache. Shepherd used a bungee cord to loop me to the brace for the overhead shelf.

'Shepherd,' I whispered.

'Hush.'

My other arm was moved overhead and he took another bungee cord from the counter. When I was secure, despite some struggling, he stepped back.

Dropping onto the stool, he sized me up. 'See, I think you took control with that baseball bat with that loser ex of yours. Even now you're actually in control.'

I laughed. It was an angry laugh tainted by a vein of fear. 'Oh yeah?'

'Yeah. Say kitchen and I let you go. That's your word.'

Kitchen. Kitchen where he'd seen me with Reed. And still he'd come to talk, apologise at the restaurant and then later in bed he gave me what I needed when I asked.

And I'd freaked and tossed him out. I hadn't allowed myself any solace in him or him in me.

'Say it,' he said.

I shook my head. Instead I said, 'I told every one of you that I wasn't interested in–'

He held up a hand. 'Yep, I know – a commitment. I get it. And I had no interest in one, either. Trust me. And I still wish I didn't …' He looked up and away. Finally those eyes settled back on me and he said 'I wish I didn't have these flashes of … wishing.'

I got that. I knew what he meant.

'What do you want from me?' I hissed. I truly did not want

to have this conversation. I truly did not want to have to … face him.

'Your trust.'

'You have it,' I said, shaking the cords and thusly the shelf over my head.

'I don't think so.' He scratched his beard and walked to me. We were so close again I could feel the heat radiating off him. It was in direct opposition to the cold that seemed to seep from the stone wall to my back.

'I'm tied here aren't I? I haven't said … that word.'

It did not escape my notice – or his, judging by his face – that I did not say "kitchen".

'But last night instead of letting me see your fear – instead of explaining to me what you felt – you ran me off.'

'Shepherd, I didn't even know what I was feeling,' I growled.

'No excuse,' he said and kissed me.

His tongue and teeth and lips bullied mine and he cut off any of the protests I might have tossed at him. I didn't see the knife in his hand until he pulled back.

'What's that?' My tongue was clumsy in my mouth and my heart raced with sickening speed. I tried to take a deep breath and failed.

'A fork,' he joked and winked at me. 'Don't worry. There's no bloodletting in my home. But I owe you some new digs,' he said.

'New–' But then I got it because he sliced my sweater from neck to waistband and I stood very, very still to let him do it. I was no fool. Then he cut the little piece of lace that held my bra cups together in the front.

'And a bra,' he said, looking up from where he knelt.

I had enough time to pray he didn't plan to do that to my jeans too when he undid my button with his big fingers. Then the zipper hissed and he shoved the denim down to my ankles. The knife was back to ruin my pale green panties.

'And panties,' he breathed, pressing a hot kiss to the swatch of skin right above my mound. My belly fluttered, my pussy got more slippery still and I willed him with the power of my staggered mind to put his mouth two inches lower and make me come. Give me that rush and buzz of release.

Instead he stood and wiped his hands on his jeans. 'I'll be back,' he said.

'You ... what?' I struggled enough to make him smile. 'That is so not funny.'

'It's not meant to be.'

'I ... where are you going?' I asked, forcing myself calm. Making myself take a deep breath and hold it for a count of four before I passed out.

'I was just about to make some lunch when you showed up. You want any?'

I looked at myself pointedly and then glared at him. 'Sure. Naked and bound in your hobbit hole is totally a place to eat lunch.'

'I could feed you,' he said and to accent his words he placed one lone fingertip between my legs and pressed my clit like a button.

I gasped. Furious. Aroused. And damn it, now I realised, hungry.

'No,' I whispered.

'Fine by me. But I am starved. Be back in a few. And while you're up there, ponder this. What's with you and Adrian? He's a boy. What's with you and pretty boy? You're smarter than that. It smacks of fear and running and denial.'

'Oh and you are the perfect man for me?' I snapped, again staring at my bonds.

He shrugged. 'I don't believe in perfect. I don't even think I buy that soul mate shit. But I do believe in connections. I do believe in energy recognising compatible energy. I don't have a word for it,' he said, shaking his head. 'But I believe you can look at someone – maybe one someone in your whole life – and feel this instant ...'

Zap, I thought. Lightning.

He shrugged those massive shoulders. 'I'm doing a really bad job of explaining this, but I bet you dollars to donuts, you know what I mean.' He pressed his lips to mine once more, pushed his finger back between my legs for one heart stopping

126

second and then he walked up the stone steps and out into the unseen day.

'Well, shit,' I said to no one but me and the four walls.

Just when I was about to start screaming at the top of my lungs he returned. 'Want some?'

I eyed the sandwiches on the plate and a cold soda. Refusing to answer, I shook my head no.

'Closest thing to heaven food-wise,' he said, settling on his stool and studying me. 'Ripe end of summer tomatoes. The kind that go red and juicy on the vine as a fuck you to the cold snaps that come with the beginning of fall.' He took a bite, his eyes never leaving me and mine never leaving him.

Shepherd chewed and his eyes slid over me. I wanted to dismiss the fact that with the hunger in his gaze I felt a certain flair of pride. He did not strike me as the kind of man who often got that look. In fact, he struck me as the kind of man who let a lot of sexual opportunities pass him by because he knew that he could have them ... and he only cherry picked the ones he wanted the most. That got me right in the gut if I was honest.

'Then you smash them between two pieces of squishy white bread.' He took a swig of soda and swallowed. 'Some folks like toast, but I think toast just ruins the whole thing. But whatever, squishy bread, toast ... whatever floats your boat. Tons of mayo and some Old Bay. Best sandwich on planet earth.'

In three big but neat bites he finished off the first sandwich washed it down and wiped his hands. When he was in my face I could smell the tomatoes on him. They smelled like earth and greenness and outside. It fit Shepherd perfectly.

'You sure you don't want some?'

'No,' I said. My stomach chose that moment to grumble and he smiled at me.

I rolled my eyes when his back was turned but straightened my face when he returned. He tapped my bottom lip and without thinking I popped my lips open for him. Then Shepherd tucked a bite of sandwich into my mouth and said

'Chew.'

It was heaven. My stomach grumbled greedily and he put another bite in my mouth which I chewed without prompting. A rivulet of juice ran down my chin and I was powerless to wipe it away. He gave me a swig of soda and then kissed me. His mouth hot and sultry where the soda had been cold and crisp. His tongue lapped at mine and then traced my lips. When he licked the ripe juices from my chin before bending his head to my nipple and giving it one gentle kiss a rush of heat seared my body, rolling through my pelvis.

He straightened, towering over me and said, 'Say kitchen.'

'No,' I said.

When had this war between us flipped? Now he wanted me to say it and I refused. He was just as worried as I was about this connection we felt. He had just as much fear.

That gave me power so when he pinched my nipple and said, 'Say kitchen,' it was very, very easy for me to stand my ground and say, 'No.'

Chapter Twenty

'BUT YOU DON'T WANT to trust me, we both know that,' he said. His mouth crushed down on my other nipple and he made me sweat. Where I wanted pain – and I was convinced he knew it – he gave me tender gentle kisses on that rosy prickled flesh. I wanted him to pinch and scratch and bite and he was lapping at me with a lazy kind of reverence.

'You don't want me to trust you,' I said, staring him down.

That threw him and I felt a bit gleeful to see it. He froze, looking into my eyes and then he smiled almost like he was embarrassed.

His hand danced along my collar bone, whispering over the skin like he was washing me with an invisible washcloth. All of me wanted to press up into that touch but I made myself stay still. But for the small slick of moisture that slid from me. There was nothing at all I could do to still that.

'Say it,' he said, following his hand with his mouth. Small, hot kisses along every inch of my skin until my nipples were pinpoints of flesh so hard they hurt. I wished for him to put me out of my misery – suck them, bite them, lick them. Something.

'No,' I countered.

Shepherd bent his knees and kissed down between my breasts. His hands firm and proprietary on my hips. My jeans were still shoved down around my ankles so when I wiggled just a bit they whispered to give me away.

'Say it. You know you want to be free of me.' A row of kisses was laid around each breast until I was positively vibrating. Pushing myself back to the cold stone wall to anchor my body. I would not beg.

'I don't want to be free of you. I'm just … skittish.'

He skated past a nipple but did not touch it. Not at all. I had to swallow a sob of frustration.

He rose to his full height and I caught a glimmer of frustration in his gaze. 'Why are you teasing me?'

'I'm teasing you?' I laughed. 'I'm the one strapped to a wall under a shelf, that honestly – I'm afraid is going to crash down on me and kill me at any moment. Not you.'

I straightened up despite my disadvantage and his lips twitched like he wanted to laugh but wouldn't give in.

'Say kitchen,' he said, pinning my upper body with one big forearm as he leaned in to bite my neck. Not a little love bite. Not a nip. This was a bite that made me gasp and made my pussy give one hard flex. This was a bite that would leave a mark and I felt such a surge of joy it startled me.

I moved my hips toward him. Just my hips. And I felt my nakedness connect with his denim sheathed body and there was that power again. 'No.'

He pinned me harder, pushing my upper body so I couldn't move. The other hand trailed down from breastbone to belly button. The small muscles there leapt and danced for him until he smoothed them with his callused palm.

All of my world had zeroed down to this. The radio was a fuzzy back noise, the wind outside just a whisper, even the light was dimmed by my one track mind. His hands on me.

'This just proves that whatever you think I want, you'll do the opposite.' He swept his fingers – fingers that had just been caressing wood and ripe tomatoes – across my hip bones and the tug in my cunt became unbearable. So swollen, so ripe, so ready – so fucking needy. I was ready to beg him. I was actually on the verge of weeping. And it scared me.

This was no blueberry bush farmer field fucking. This was no 69 for stress release. This was visceral. Primal.

Honest.

My entire body started to tremble as his hand slid just an inch lower.

'Say it.' He leaned in so close I could see the very places where the whiskers peeked through his tan skin to form a beard.

I shook my head, reared forward and kissed him, biting his lips so hard I felt him go tense.

His hand dove lower then, sliding down my close-clipped mound, finding my wet centre. He plunged a finger deep into my sex and flexed that finger so my body bowed. Like he had a secret map to all the buried treasured places inside of me.

He pulled his finger free and stroked my clit so that my arms ached with my efforts to restrain myself. 'I don't like how crazy you make me feel,' he said, his voice low and dangerous

'So this is about you, is it?' I smiled but the smile fled when he expertly pinched my engorged clit between his fingertips. 'Shit,' I sighed.

'It's about me. And you. And this us thing, the weirdness.' Fingers returned to my pussy, pushing deep inside of me. Not one this time. A fat bundle of three and it made me groan. 'Sorry.' He didn't sound sorry at all. 'You were so damn wet I figured you could take three.'

I didn't respond, just chewed my lower lip and prayed for him to finish me off. Instead he pulled out of me again – drawing a sob out of me with his fingers – and played the wet tip of one over my clitoris.

'Shepherd,' I sighed. It was the closest thing to a plea I was willing to give him.

'Christ,' he said and drove his fingers back in. Deeper this time. His touch zeroed straight in on the tender bundle of nerves that begged to be played. My knees sagged and my breath froze in my lungs. I chewed the inside of my cheek gently to try and keep quiet. My eyes were shut.

'Open your eyes. Look at me when you give me what I want.' I opened my eyes to see him dip his head and my brain tried to count how many colours I saw in his slightly wavy hair. The lamplight bounced off of brown and a reddish colour, a slight hint of blond from the summer sun and sterling silver. But then he bit my nipple and I did make a sound.

Shepherd checked to make sure I had my eyes open and then he was grinding the edge of his thumb to my clit, fucking me with his strong fingers, watching my face like a predator.

Hungry for my submission.

My knees sagged a bit more and I worried wildly that I'd rip the whole damn shelf down on top of us. He stuck a big thigh between my legs to steady me as he cupped my sex with his hand and held me.

'You can still say it,' he reminded me. 'I'm just a distraction.'

He was wrong. So wrong, but that all fled from my mind when his mouth covered mine and he thrust up hard with his hand. Driving into me so my toes were the only thing touching the ground for a moment. Pushing into me hard so that I was completely filled by his fingers, so that I cried out hard into his mouth when I came. My pussy clasping his probing hand. My body shaking like I was dying. For a moment I feared I was, my vision going spotty around the edges when I opened my eyes.

I stared into those big, brown, serious eyes that were studying me so intently and said, 'Kitchen.'

There was a flicker. A fleeting vision of his disappointment and yes, maybe hurt, and then he gave me a business-like nod and reached up to free me from the bungees. His jaw was tight, eyes hooded, stance stiff. He was not going to show me even a chink in his armour.

'I still owe you that sweater,' he growled.

'And bra,' I said, snagging his big hand. I put it over my breast so he could feel my heart, its rhythm still wild and ragged.

He flinched like I had burned him and when his fingers started to curl against my skin I saw him force himself to stop.

'Kiss me,' I said.

He stared me down but made no move.

'Please, Shepherd, kiss me.'

'Is this a goodbye kiss?' he asked. But his hand had clasped the back of my head, huge and strong and calming. He drew me in and tried to joke – but it came out brittle – 'Is this the great kiss off?'

'Kiss me,' I breathed and parted my lips for him. I inhaled

132

his anger as he poured it into the kiss, clutching me a bit too tight, kissing me a bit too hard, barely containing his turmoil.

I wrapped my arms around him and pushed my naked body to his clothed one. 'I said kitchen,' I said.

'I know, I heard you,' he almost barked.

'It was the only way,' I said, ignoring his anger. Rubbing myself to him. I felt his cock hard and imposing pressed to the wet split of my pussy. I pushed myself to him and felt an unuttered groan rumble in his chest.

'I don't get it,' he said. Now one hand clamped the small of my back so I was crushed to him. He clutched the sweater to the small of my back even as my exposed nipples rubbed his pullover. I could smell the small bit of worn leather at the collar.

'It was the only way you'd undo me. Let down your guard.' I kicked off my boots, shook free of my jeans. Then raised my leg to wrap it around his waist. Opening myself, the heat of me surely seeping through the denim that covered him. I could smell my lust in the small cool space and by the look on his face ... so could Shepherd.

'I never let down my guard.' That hand in my hair tugged just enough for a frisson of pain to sparkle along my scalp.

'I know. But now you have and I need you.'

He froze.

'I need you,' I repeated. 'I don't know if I can promise you anything right now. Not now. I'm too ... fucked up. But right at this moment, I need you, Shepherd Moore. And I want you. I want you to take me. However you want. Right here. While you smell like sawdust and anger and tomatoes.'

I pushed all the words over my lips quickly. Saying them as soon as they rushed into my head so that I couldn't censor myself or fuck it up. I wanted to be honest with Shepherd – about more than how I wouldn't commit to anyone. I wanted to be honest with him about how I felt. Period. And if I let myself think about it, I'd tame my emotions and edit my words and that wasn't what I wanted.

I wanted to say it all. I could worry about the rest later.

He shook his head like he was about to say no and my heart

dropped. Then his arms banded round me and he plucked me up and started moving. Fast.

Chapter Twenty-one

HE SLAMMED ME TO the hardwood counter on the wall. Bolts
and pencils and pieces of sandpaper rained down on the floor. I
was thankful for his neatness as I didn't get a nail in the ass.

'Put your feet up,' he growled.

I put my feet up, allowing him to pluck my socks from my
feet. He tossed them aside and positioned himself between my
legs. I wrapped my thighs around his waist and took his kiss –
starved, gritty and more than a little bit raw.

'Shepherd,' I started and he shook his head.

'Don't talk.'

Sinking my fingers into his beard I scraped my fingernails
along the fragile skin beneath. So that he moaned and yanked
me hard against him. 'Shep–'

'Hush.'

'Shepherd, please take those fucking jeans off,' I said in a
rush so he couldn't cut me off.

'Getting there.' Yanking my hair in two big clumps, just
enough to make my spine tingle with pleasure and pain, he
tilted my head back and scraped his teeth along the length of
my neck. The bite he had administered throbbed in sympathy.
My cunt picked up the beat and kept time.

I had never felt so very frantic for a man. Never had the
urge to beg been so overwhelming. I grabbed his cock through
his jeans and squeezed. I wasn't gentle, he was so damn hard,
that would make my point. That would make him hurry.

'Fuck.' He pulled his hands out of my hair and worked his
buttons.

'Exactly,' I said and felt a blush heat my chest and my
cheeks. I slid a finger below his waistband and touched his skin

softly. Like a breath instead of a stroke.

He growled at me.

When aroused or tormented or angry he very much reminded me of a huge bear. Which turned me on enormously, more than I ever thought it would. 'Spread,' he said, cock free, jeans pushed down.

We both thought of it at the same time. Both of us stalling out.

'Condom?' I asked.

He shook his head. 'You surprised me.'

I shook mine. 'I slunk over.'

He started to pull up his jeans muttering, 'House,' but I stilled him with my toe.

'Do you want to know how much I trust you?'

His expression became unreadable and I couldn't quite get a deep breath. Someone had stolen all the oxygen from his tiny underground lair.

'Tuesday, you don't–'

I toed his cock and his eyes flickered like they would slam shut. Moisture slid from me onto his wooden counter. Hopefully he wouldn't mind.

'I trust you. Are you clean?'

He nodded, mouth a tight seam, eyes burning with intensity.

'I am clean as a whistle. Got my pedigree in January at my yearly Gyn appointment.'

'But–'

I didn't know if the but was about me or him but I cut him off this time. 'And I haven't been with anyone without protection for a very long time.'

He made a sound that was half excitement, half frustration.

'And a very long time means years,' I said softly.

When had it gone from chilly to hot in here?

'Tuesday.' He took my foot in his hand, the span of his grip suddenly encircling my ankle like a manacle. It was the most erotic thing I'd ever felt. His bigness encircling my smallness. His grip caging my bones.

'I'd like you … like that,' I said, my voice a ghost of its normal self. 'Bare.'

136

He grunted and stepped in still holding my ankle. 'You don't need to prove–'

'Shut up, Shepherd.' He was close enough now that I could reach down and take him in hand. All of him – the long, hard, exquisitely silken bulk of him.

He cupped my head with his free hand and kissed me again. Muttering things that weren't quite words. Using my ankle as a guide he pushed my leg high so my heel rested on the edge of the counter. I moved my other leg to match so that my heels pressed the lip of the wood and my whole body was open to him.

And then he stepped back to look at me – swollen, wet, ready and red. He shook his head, pleasured sounds rumbling out of him and said, 'You are fucking stunning. Do you know that?'

'Don't.' It made me feel shy the way he ate me with his eyes. I was so wet I could feel it and it made me wetter to realise he could see every single bit of glistening arousal. Every slippery bit of proof that showed my need for him.

'Shh.' He reached for me but did not touch and my entire pussy tingled. Like he was touching me without touching me. Like he was magic.

'Jesus, God, Shepherd,' I said, my voice breaking with emotion. 'Please. Please don't torture me any more.'

He broke. Moving between my legs, watching his own movements as he worked my slick split with the tip of his bare cock. And then we both exhaled at once as he nestled the helmeted tip of his erection just inside my body and then slid home.

It had been a long time – a very long time. To feel a man slide into you bare, flesh to flesh, heat to heat was an intense feeling. One I had not felt since before Phil. The realisation that he and I had never even done this and I had considered us a couple slammed me and I shook it off. Focusing solely on the feel of Shepherd's body crushing against mine, pushing into mine. Parting me and filling me and riding me so that my body already had begun a sweet lazy trip toward release.

'You're so goddamned tight,' he said against my ear. 'You

are so amazingly hot. Sweet. Sweet tight little pussy. Sweet mind fucking Tuesday,' he murmured.

I came with his words – sticky, sweet, messy glorious – me and his words.

'Yes,' I said. I didn't know to what but I meant it.

'You're in my head you know?' His fingers bit into my ass as he held me. My feet still planted to the wood, I braced for his thrusts. But he had other plans and now he gathered my legs to circle his waist. He pushed his hands under my ass to anchor me and tilt me as he drove into me harder.

My head hit the wall, hair brushing my shoulder and making me shiver. He was in my head too.

'In my head and my gut. And in my chest. When I think about you something in there squeezes. And when I saw you with that … man …' He broke off. I squeezed my pussy up tight and he sighed, moving a bit gentler but with more intention. 'Something in me raged.'

That scared me but I didn't speak. Trailing fingers over his sweater, I touched the very top of his leg and then pushed my hands up under the pullover to feel the heated, lightly furred expanse of his stomach and chest. I could ride out the fear for another staggering orgasm was sneaking toward me. The first tentative spasms had sounded and it was all downhill from there.

'But I'm not demanding anything from you, Tuesday,' he said.

Good. I don't know if I can give it.

'But I am warning you. That's all. You make me …'

I was coming. It had slammed me that hard and that fast that it surprised me to the point of silence. Shepherd felt it and his body stilled, hard and hulking and then he sighed out something that sounded, in tone, like a prayer and thrust once more before emptying into me. Shaking against me. Feeling for that one blissful moment in time fragile in my arms.

'You make me crazy,' he said softly. 'But I'm not putting any chains on you, Tuesday.'

He pulled back to look at me. 'Except maybe the ones you ask for,' he amended.

'Deal.'

I'd agreed to dinner. Out of town. No chance of running into Reed or Adrian or anyone who hadn't seen me and wanted to chat.

We headed out of town on the lake road and I watched out of town cars fly by, one after another.

'What the hell?' I whispered. I'd pulled on a slate grey sweater coat and a long sleeved red blouse. My jeans were tucked into my nicest and most beloved leather boots and I'd worn my hair up in a crazy twist with chopsticks.

Then I beat Shepherd off with a stick when he tried to take me in the great room of my house. I'd resorted to demanding food and no other sustenance.

He chuckled, patting my leg. 'What? No one told you?'

'Told me what?'

'The apple festival?'

'What festival? What apples? There are no apples.'

'Tuesday, not every single thing is right there on the lake front. There are apple orchards. And we draw quite a crowd every year to partake in the death of summer and the harvest of apples.'

'Hunh,' I said, pressing my forehead to the cool glass. 'Go figure. I guess I never came in the fall. Or I came after the festival.'

'That's when I travel every year. To get the fuck out of Dodge.'

What? Travel?

I blinked but he couldn't see me as he guided the truck into a right turn onto a much better paved road. 'You're travelling?' I asked, tempering my voice.

'Yeah. I was gonna tell you at dinner. I go every year when they do this shindig. I travel, sign autographs, hook up for a bunch of promo stuff.'

I thought hard and turned to him. 'Cage Fighters for Cancer!' I yelled.

He snorted and shook his head. 'I'll be damned. I was hoping you'd never–'

'I think it's great,' I said. 'You use your former ass kicking for good. How many kids, young men especially, look up to you guys? It's good that they see you using your personalities and names for good.'

He nodded, face unreadable. 'Thanks.'

'See, you're famous too! Not just Reed. So you should cut him some slack.'

He made a noise like an angry lion and I remembered that this man, who had just exposed a raw nerve of having feelings for me, had seen Reed and I doing the nasty on the kitchen floor.

Bad idea talking him up.

'Sorry. The point is you have a following too.'

'It's extra money that helps me keep my house and the charity stuff is for a good cause. I lost a sister to cancer,' he said quickly and then, 'Hungry?'

'Sorry,' I said softly. 'I mean, expert segue but I am sorry.'

He looked away and then laughed at himself which lifted my heart just a bit. 'Yeah, that was pretty fucking bad. But are you? Hungry?'

'I'm starved.'

He turned onto yet another small dark road and I saw a restaurant coming up on our left. Brilliantly lit like a golden mirage in the country darkness it looked welcoming. 'Good, they have the best cream of crab soup here. And Porterhouse. Oh, and Chicken stuffed with ... never mind. Order anything. It'll be good.'

Chapter Twenty-two

WHAT WAS NOT GOOD was our waitress, Lucy. One look at her and how she was looking at Shepherd and I knew he'd fucked her. And that, for whatever reason, set my teeth on edge.

I was sure a hypocrite, wasn't I. Couldn't admit my feelings, refused to give him a shred of emotion, refused to promise anything and yet here I sat annoyed and jealous over a perfectly nice girl who was being perfectly kind to me.

Bitch.

We ordered after our drinks arrived. Shepherd, a Porterhouse, steak fries and fresh green beans with new potatoes. Me a crab cake, Yukon gold fries and a huge garden salad with Allister Lake's signature Ranch dressing.

'So tell me about little Miss Lucy,' I said.

He cocked an eyebrow at me and I had a mental flash of me pinned to his workbench, heels riding the edge of the counter, Shepherd watching himself slide into my body. All of me erupted with goosebumps and then warmed to a volcanic heat in a heartbeat. The man did weird things to me.

'We dated. She's from out of town so that made it better.'

I tore off a piece of roll before popping it in my mouth. When it hit my tongue I paused to give an almost orgasmic moan.

He brushed my bangs free of my eyes and laughed. 'Oh yeah, they bake 'em fresh.'

'Dear Lord,' I said, and took another bite. 'Heaven.'

Shepherd took a swig of his beer and outside lightning split the sky. The needle fine spear of energy was visible as a blue-white flash through the restaurants slanted skylights. 'Weird weather,' he grumbled.

'Nice try. Now tell me about Lucy.'

Shrugging, he grabbed his own roll. 'Allister Lake is so damn small it helps to date out of the gene pool so to speak.'

'Because of the ...' I wiggled my fingers in the air, not wanting to say it aloud in such a quiet environment.

He grinned with only one side of his mouth. It turned me inside out when he did that. Shepherd leaned in. 'Whips, chains, hot candle wax on the–'

'Games,' I interrupted.

'If that's what you want to call them. Yes. But a) game indicates it's a regular thing and b) that it's light-hearted. It's not either usually. It's the right girl at the right time with the right desire.'

I blushed. 'So you and she ...'

I really didn't want to know so I really didn't know why I was picking it like a raw scab.

Shepherd blew out a sigh and thrust his fingertip under my palm and turned my hand so he could squeeze it. 'We went out a few times, fu–had sex twice and only one was like that.'

I nodded. 'Why did you–' I shook my head. 'Never mind.'

This was not the time or place.

'Why did I tie you up? The other time you asked me to take you to that place you needed to go. Why did I do it today?'

He had leaned in so far I could smell his soap. We sat bent over the table like we were sharing secrets. Because we were.

'Yes.'

'You needed it. You could have been free at any time. I wanted you to realise that you were stronger than you thought. But that I was ... safe, too.' He shrugged again. 'Tuesday, it's very hard to put it all in words. The things that happen at times like that. I think that's why people do it. It's not a words thing, it's an action thing. And it can be good or it can be bad. It all depends on–'

'Whose hands you're in,' I said. I squeezed his hand and sat back when Lucy came with my salad.

'Enough of that,' I said, drizzling my salad with dressing. My first bite drew another orgasmic moan from me.

'And that's why it's signature Ranch,' he chuckled.

'How often do you come here?' I asked.

'Once or twice a month.'

'I'm surprised you don't just camp out on the lawn.'

'In the winter when I get really hungry and work a lot outside, trust me, I've considered it.'

'So your sister,' I said.

'Pancreatic cancer.'

'Wow.'

'Yes, and very young. So the yearly trip to stockpile a bit of money to keep being the town handyman and not starve is important. But the cancer work is why I really go.'

'Good for you.' My throat felt suddenly tight. It was one thing to feel all kinds of weird and strange and somewhat unwelcome sensations and needs in my body for Shepherd. But when my heart flexed that way, when my belly warmed with something akin to but more than affection – it terrified me.

He swigged his beer again and I could tell it hurt him to talk about her. 'Any other family?'

'My mom's in Florida. Went to live with my uncle. I only see her once or twice a year but I tend to call her once a week or so.'

'Your dad?' I ate another piece of bread and let it warm my tongue before chewing.

'Ran out when I was three. You?'

Wow. The bread turned to sawdust in my mouth. 'I'm sorry.'

'Stop saying that. I'm not some pity party you know.' There was a flash of real anger in his dark eyes and I was momentarily stunned. Didn't know what to say. Rare for me, I usually had something pithy to say to everything.

'I know. I'm just … sorry is all. I don't mean to–'

'Sorry. Right. Now you. Parents?'

'Dead.'

'Both?' I could tell he'd almost said he was sorry but I let the opportunity to rib him about it glide right by.

'Yep. My senior year in high school. Car accident. Wrecked me – no pun intended,' I blurted, blushing. How stupid was I? 'Until I was about 20 I lived on my own because I was legal when it happened. I guess to a degree, I became the child of my parents' neighbours, friends and acquaintances. Eventually, I thought I fell in love, I moved in with a dork, beat him with a bat at a later date, yada yada yada. Then I ended up here.'

'Why didn't you just come here when it happened?'

'Good question,' I said, levelling a finger at him. 'I wanted to finish school in my school for one. In my mind it leant normalcy to it all. And I was … too stubborn?

I sat back because here came the food and what pretty food it was.

'So, I was right,' he said, tucking into his steak.

'What?'

'You are a warrior.'

It didn't escape me that warrior had been one of my words for him.

Lucy had been nice but not hovery. How she managed that after being with a guy like Shepherd was beyond me. But I ended up liking her, despite my best efforts.

'I have to get used to these country roads,' I said. It was pitch black out but for squiggles of rain on the windshield and flashes of that lightning in the sky.

'What's to get used to?'

I watched his face in the darkness, speckled only by some light from headlights. It was unreadable but entirely handsome. My body got to craving by just looking at him and I considered putting my hand in his lap. I also considered the consequences of making him crash his truck.

'It's so dark and deserted and–'

A crack of lighting, very close, cut me off and I yelped.

Shepherd laughed. 'I see what you mean. You're very much a city girl, aren't you?'

I snorted. 'I mean, come on. Where're the billboards? Where's the neon? Where're the spotlights?'

'Back in the city,' Shepherd said. 'I don't like it, though.'

'What?' More lightning and I realised I was gripping the door grip hard. What was wrong with me? I'd never reacted to weather. But the potting shed light and the unidentified noise

144

and the newness of blackness and quiet at night all added up to make me a tiny bit uneasy.

The deluge started and Shepherd slowed the truck. 'What are you doing?' I gasped.

He pulled onto the shoulder in a thicket of bushes so we were boxed in on all three sides but for the driver's door.

'This section of road tends to get iffy during sudden storms that dump a large volume of water.'

'Iffy?' I breathed. I was barely audible above the sudden thunder and rage of the weather. And then, yes ... hail.

'Washes out, trees fall, best to sit here for a few moments while it passes. They never last long. Especially this time of year.'

He cut the engine and immediately our breath began to fog the windows. I shivered and waited for the dying summer's last hurrah to fade.

'I'm sorry I pried,' I said.

He turned a bit in his seat. 'That was prying?' he asked. 'Then you're a keeper.'

His words slammed me and I went completely silent. So did he.

Rain slashed the windows from all directions and wind wracked the truck, buffeting it so it shimmied like a small boat in a rough sea.

'I meant–'

'It's fine. We both need to stop clamming up every time someone says something that could indicate ... feelings,' I finished weakly.

'I have to leave in the morning,' he said, taking my hand.

'I know. Have fun!' The last sounded so very stupid and kiss-off-ish even to me.

He tugged me so that I had no choice but to face him some. 'For the first time that I can remember I wish I didn't have to go,' he said.

'To your events?' I asked.

'No. Away from someone.'

That scared me too, but fear was food to me. Had been for many years. I groaned and turned my body more to him.

Getting up on my knees I threaded my finger into his beard and kissed him.

'I am terrifying myself to say that I wish you weren't going,' I whispered.

Shepherd grabbed my leg and swung it over his lap. I straddled him, my butt brushing the hard steering wheel.

'But I'm not asking anything of you. I don't know if I could even. I think I'm fucked up and you're–'

'Twisted?' I rocked in his lap until I felt the hard hump of his cock press to the lips of my sex.

'Slightly less fucked up.'

'Do me,' I said against his earlobe. 'Save me from the scary lightning and lake monsters.'

Under it all, I thought Shepherd wanted to save someone. Maybe because he hadn't been able to save his sister. And me … I wanted to be saved. I went after abusive men with my Louisville Slugger but I wanted to trust someone enough to save me.

Neither of us was quite there yet, but we could pretend. For this storm. For this moment in time.

'I don't have … I wasn't thinking …' Each breath came out in a puff of air. I rocked and rocked and he made a sound like a man breaking.

'It's OK,' I said. 'In for a penny, in for a pound.'

'I'm flattered that you think it's a pound–' He started to joke. I kissed him quiet by sliding my tongue past his lips and over his tongue.

'Tuesday,' he finished.

'Do me, big boy,' I laughed and the lightning flashed and I squealed and then we wrestled with our clothes and the truck and the closest quarters in which I'd ever fucked someone senseless.

Chapter Twenty-three

THERE IS SOMETHING TO be said for doing it face to face in the cab of a truck while Mother Nature has a temper tantrum. I relished the feel of his hands on my hips – eager, strong, possessive. The strobe lightning lit his face and then threw it back into darkness – the whole effect was of being off balance. Of being held and controlled but free falling.

Shepherd drove up under me, filling me with his length and biting along my shoulder so I shivered and rippled in his arms. The steering wheel kept me from wandering and when I moved my hips from side to side and squeezed my internal muscles to milk him he groaned.

'You trying to push me over the edge?'

'Maybe,' I said. I was so fucking close to coming. The wind and the rain and the storm only heightening the dream quality of it all. 'Maybe I want you to tip with me, Shepherd.'

He bit my nipple through my blouse and then shoved the whole thing up to take me more gently between his lips. My pussy clenched, my stomach tingled.

'I loved it when you said my name,' he said, licking from one breast to the other so the heated trail cooled as he went. 'And I hate my name.'

'I love your name,' I said rocking harder, grinding my clit to his pelvic bone as his hands cupped my ass.

'Fuck me, Shepherd. Do me, Shepherd. Make me come, Shepherd,' I said, being clever.

But he chose that moment to slide a long thick finger into my ass and press. The sensation snaked through my lower half and filled my pelvis as easily as smoke.

I came, rocking harder and simply saying, 'Jesus,

Shepherd.'

He yanked me down as he thrust up harder, one more deep go at me, and then he tipped. All he said was 'Tuesday. Tuesday, Tuesday, Tuesday …'

And my heart seized up in my chest.

The lighting calmed and the storm blew out. Shepherd got out, big and bad in jeans and boots and yes, go figure, a nice shirt. He was back within moments as I got my clothes situated and buckled in.

'Road's fine. Few limbs. I tossed them aside. Now we can get home without ending up in the creek.'

He said creek the way Nan had which was crick. It made me smile. And yes, miss her yet again. It surprised me when he leaned over and kissed my temple gently before cranking the engine.

We watched the lighting strobe far off over another part of town. I felt it again, that lightning strike between us. That was what it reminded me of and the storm only solidified it. 'Pretty,' I said.

'Gorgeous. I love weather,' he said. 'I'm happier in the crazy weird weather than sunshine. I guess I'm not a sunshine guy.'

I almost laughed but stifled it. 'Me neither.'

'Then I guess I don't have to worry about you in your new house in this crazy shit. I was a little.' He looked away like he was embarrassed for his concern.

'Nah, I'm fine. I will admit, I got a bit spooked last night.'

He grunted and I couldn't tell exactly what that meant.

'Adrian's still in the barn, too. So if there was a true problem–'

'You could protect him,' Shepherd said.

It caught me so off guard I started giggling. 'That's mean,' I snorted.

'Come on, you and your bat skills and life experience far outweigh that boy. You could probably kick his ass with one of your feet tied behind your back.'

'Now there's a mental image.'

'About as realistic as the mental image of Adrian protecting you.'

'Well lucky you, I don't need protecting.' It felt like a lie when I said it. Or maybe it was just that I liked that he had the urge to protect me.

He grunted again.

'Would you like a rock to go with your caveman grunt?

'No, but I'd like to toss you in that field right there and fuck you again,' he said.

Desire flared all over me and I had to concentrate on not shifting in my seat. The pressure on my pussy would only make the need worse. It was my turn to make an odd noise.

I caught him grinning. Brat.

I'll even cop to feeling a tad let down, even sad, when he pulled up to my house. 'I know you're not ready for a bunch of … stuff,' he said, shaking his head. 'And I know I'm not. I know we're both still dented goods. So, I'll just …' He didn't finish. Simply leaned in and kissed me, holding my shoulders hard. Real or imagined, every place his teeth had touched me throbbed when he gripped me.

'Wow.' I sat back, my lips tingling. 'Thanks for dinner and … the bondage, I guess.'

We both burst out laughing and I felt a weight lift from my chest. We were good. We were both really fucked up people and we had no real ties but we were good. There was a chemistry and an energy and at least, an understanding.

It was a start.

I leaned in, kissed him once more, feeling like a teenager again. Because I wanted to. Feel that jolt and feel that youth and the sharp burst of joy in my chest.

'Thanks,' I said again.

'I'll be gone three days. Be safe.'

I gave him a mock salute. 'Yes, Sir!'

He grabbed me by the front of my shirt, twisted it, hauled me in and kissed me. 'Better believe it. And you do realise how very nice I'm being by letting you loose tonight, right? I am not a man to show my cards easily. I showed you most of my hand tonight.'

I nodded. Unsure of what to say. 'I'm ... progressing,' I whispered.

'Me, too,' he said. 'Because apparently, you fuck with my head. Big time.'

I scattered before I could change my mind. When the truck pulled off, tossing white streaks along my windows, I shut the front door. I peered through the window to see if the barn looked like anyone was moving. I saw nothing. I thought I saw the potting shed door move and possibly a light, but when I looked again, nothing.

Nerves.

I had to shake off the night, because I was feeling something ridiculously close to ... happiness? Satisfaction? I didn't know but I couldn't afford to get close yet. I wasn't even that far from what had happened with Phil.

Dropping my clothes in a pile on the way, I slipped into the bathroom, turned on the shower and lowered the window blind. As an afterthought I locked the door and climbed into the shower. Fifteen minutes later I was in batik leggings, a tank top and yes, no shit, Shepherd's hoodie.

The house temperature had dropped even more. I considered a fire or turning on the heat but going the lazy route, I simply pulled on some thick wool socks.

I tugged the hoodie ties and whispered, 'We have to stop meeting this way, Mr Hoodie.'

I curled onto the sofa and put the TV on some cooking show. Dialling Annie, I had a moment of homesickness and then she answered yelling, 'Goddamn it, Bud, it's a rat. Just kill the thing! Hello?'

'Wow, I was feeling homesick and now ... not so much.'

'Kid! How are things?'

'Good.' I gave her a brief rundown of my night and then asked about her kids and her boyfriend, Toby.

'That no good son of a gun. He's a pain in my ass but he's good.'

Bright white-blue light backlit my windows and I sighed. 'I'm going to have to go in a moment. We're having another lightning storm here.'

'Really? We haven't seen rain or anything since before you left,' Annie said.

'Maybe it follows me,' I laughed. But maybe it did. One of my patented waves of gloominess rolled over me and I rode it out. 'Just kidding. Anyway, I just wanted to say hi. Everyone behaving?'

'Well, haven't seen Stan since you left. No word on Phil. Someone said he left town. Don't know if it's true or not.' She sounded unsure of telling me but truth be told, I didn't care a lick about Phil or him leaving town.

The storm got louder and I said, 'Real fast, did Rachel have the baby?' Rachel was a single mom-to-be who called the boarding house home. We'd thrown her a baby shower before I left for the lake.

'Not yet, but soon. She is ready to pop, that's for sure.' There was a pause. 'Damn it all. We have a rat in the house, hon and I–'

'I know, I can hear. You take care, Annie. Call soon.'

'Love,' she said.

'Love,' I replied.

Something slammed on the side of the house and I hurried to the window. All I saw was dark and rain speckles and more flares of light.

'You had to be all brave. You had to be all lone wolf type person,' I growled to myself.

Nan's "bar" held a whole slew of bottles. I chose some rum and a high ball glass. 'Drink anyone?' I asked.

'Why yes,' I answered. 'Hope there's lime.' I paused. 'Damn, Nan, is there lime?'

I truly needed to get an animal to share my house. I'd look less crazy.

Another bang and the lights flickered. Rain hit the side of the house sounding like a million ping pong balls. I opened the fridge thinking *do not panic* but feeling a bit frantic anyway. I'd never been afraid in storms before but that was in much smaller houses usually with other people in them.

I'd never truly been alone. But for now.

There was lime juice in the door. 'Yes,' I said. 'Thank you

bar gods.'

I assembled a nice rum and cola and found some cheese crackers in the pantry. Getting myself situated on the sofa involved shoving my feet between the frame and the cushion, sipping my drink and nibbling crackers.

The scent of Shepherd wafted off his jacket and I caught myself inhaling deeply to capture as much as I could.

There was another loud bang and then a shuffle by the front door. Fear streaked through my gut and up into my chest. Then I got pissed.

'Right!' I yelled in case the boogie man outside heard me. I stalked to a stack of my moving stuff, yet to be unpacked from the trip. The pile leaned precariously against the wall below the loft steps. I rummaged until I found it and then took a practice swing.

'Hello, Louis. How have you been?' I took another swing with the Louisville Slugger and tried to decide. Front or back.

Another rustling at the front door decided it for me and I didn't let myself think. Thinking would mean fear and second guessing myself. I took four running steps, unlocked the door and threw it open. Brandishing the baseball bat I yelled, 'What the fuck!'

Adrian took three big steps back and damn near fell down the porch steps. 'Jesus fucking Christ, Tuesday. What is wrong with you?'

He was soaked through, looking like a drowned rat. Anger burned hot in my face and my stomach. My fingers twitched on the wooden handle.

'Look, I know we fucked. I know maybe I gave you the wrong idea. But—'

'I thought I saw something,' he cut me off.

'What?'

But being rude and on edge, I stepped out into the rain instead of letting him in.

'I wasn't sure because … ya know …' He threw his hands up, rain flattening his hair. 'The Apocalypse is here!'

'Where was it?'

'Around the side and around the back. But I just circled the whole house, and FYI a big branch hit the side of the house … and me.'

'Sorry,' I muttered. That must have been what I heard.

'But nothing,' Adrian finished. 'So, before you beat me with a hunk of wood, I'm going to go put on some warm clothes and look at internet porn.'

Anger made his eyes narrow and his lips thin. He nodded with tight politeness and stomped away.

'Thanks,' I said, barely audible above the rain.

Back inside, I shook myself off, and considered changing. Truth be told, the rain and damp had brought the smell out of the hoodie even more. I'd dry …

I watched through the window as Adrian went into the barn and slid the big door shut. The potting shed, from this angle, appeared closed and locked and innocent.

So what the hell was going on?

I made it an hour – an hour later into the night – an hour later into boring TV. And another furtive sound slithered through my big home and I snapped. I turned everything off and pulled on some boots. I couldn't find my damn umbrella so I used a garbage bag from Nan's pantry. I locked the house, put the key in my pocket and took off running.

There was a final huge flash of lightning and when I turned I swore I saw a man shape standing in the darkness.

Nerves? Maybe.

Adrian? Hopefully. At least that would make sense.

Chapter Twenty-four

HE WAS ON ALERT when he ripped his front door open. I could see the stance and the look on his face and the breadth of his chest as he stood to full height, prepared to fight. I almost laughed.

'Tuesday,' he said.

'Sorry,' I whispered.

'I can't hear you,' he rasped and yanked me inside. 'Are you hurt? Are you OK?'

'I am … a pussy,' I said. It was only then that I realised I had the bat with me.

Shepherd took it from me gently and put it by the front door which he locked and bolted. 'I doubt that. But are you OK?'

'I changed my mind,' I said.

'Did you?' He cocked an eyebrow and almost smiled at me.

'I did. Can I stay here? I'm spooked. I admit it! I'm spooked and there was lightning and noises and then Adrian and–'

'Adrian what?'

I explained. 'I think it's harmless. I believe him. He probably saw what … a bear?'

'Doubtful. But in this light it could have been anything. Or nothing. Or he just wanted an excuse to talk to you.'

Shepherd pulled me in with one big arm and I felt the press of his biceps to my cheek. He kissed the top of my head. 'Want a drink?'

'No.'

'Want dry clothes?'

'No.'

I was shivering but his arms around me made me feel much more stable. And now that I was here, I knew what I wanted.

'I was off to bed. Early morning drive to the airport tomorrow. You want the spare room or to be in my bed?'

Lust marched up my spine when he uttered "in my bed". I nodded. 'With you,' I said. Wanting him so much more than I already had today. And tonight. And since the moment I laid eyes on him.

He led me upstairs. A nightlight was plugged in low on the wall right above the baseboard in the hallway. Shepherd took me to the main room and I saw he had a balcony off his room, too. The view would be the great room down below. But for now the room was dark barring camera light flashes of lightning through the skylight.

'Come on. Get warm.'

Off came the leggings and the hoodie and the tank. I stood before him naked and he pressed a kiss to my belly. 'Now I'm warm.' I slid my fingers into his thick hair and rubbed the pads of my fingertips along his scalp.

Shepherd looked up at me, kissed my bare stomach once more and slid my arm back in his hoodie. Then the other. When he zipped it up I was a bizarre mixture of confused, hurt and offended.

'But–' I shook my head, catching myself. I would not beg him to have sex with me. That was ridiculous. I could get Reed or Adrian or … wow. How quickly I reassured myself with conquests.

'Come on. Get in here and get warm. And calm. Don't be mad.' He pushed his bulk back into the huge bed – it had to be a King size and patted the bare spot.

I crawled in next to him. Letting him cover me. Letting him drop a huge arm across me and spoon up behind me.

'Don't be offended, Tuesday,' he whispered into my ear and chuckled softly.

It had been a confusing night.

'I'm not,' I said. Both of us knew I was lying.

'Sometimes the sexiest foreplay is to do nothing. Let me just hold you. But I promise.' He nipped the back of my neck and my pussy flared with heat and moisture. That fast. That easy. His hard cock pressed to my bottom and I wondered why it was again that we weren't fucking right now.

'I promise you I'll have you again before I go,' Shepherd finished. 'Now get some sleep.'

'Yeah. That'll happen,' I sighed.

I was slightly surprised to feel myself drifting when I did. Even more surprised to feel the bump and crush of a body a few hours later.

Acid green numbers showed me the time: 2.03 and I blinked. Shepherd was splayed against me, his breathing deep and even. I was sure he was asleep until his lips touched the back of my neck, spiking my nipples, stealing my breath.

Teeth scraped where lips had been and he pulled me into him, covering me a bit more with his body. Heat baked into me even as a trembling shiver racked me. I exhaled loudly and then sucked in a breath when his hands cupped my breasts through the sweatshirt material. He pinched my hard nipples and worked his lips lower under my hair, along my shoulder.

'Are you awake?' I asked dumbly. Then I grinned at myself in his dark room. The storm had passed.

'Nope. These are sleep advances.'

'Me too,' I said, gasping. There was a rush of cool air as he kicked off the covers and shoved up his hoodie. He kissed the line of my spine, fingers smoothing along my ass as I pressed my face into his bed. It smelled like him, everywhere – I sucked in as much air as I could. 'I am totally asleep.'

His mouth touched my right ass cheek and I moaned. His tongue was a hot streak on warm flesh. He held my upper thighs flush as he tongued secret patterns over the skin of my bottom.

'Spread your legs a little,' he said but he didn't give me the chance. His big hand separated my legs with ease.

His face pressed to the place in between and I felt his tongue on my back hole. I tensed for a moment but he slid a finger into me and flexed it while working that tongue again. 'Relax. I'm not going to do that.'

I relaxed.

'Not tonight,' he said and a fear shiver shook me. But it was a good feeling. That forbidden dirty wish that I knew I'd let him make come true if it came to that in the future. He was the first man I'd even consider letting go there.

The thought fled my mind when his tongue continued to circle my hole, breaking only to bite the plump flesh of my ass. A second finger joined the first inside my cunt, flexing and thrusting and working me to a frenzy. Getting me going to the point that I could barely stay still. Constantly trying to shift and move under him despite his strong hold on the backs of my thighs pinning me down.

When I thought I'd start babbling he pulled me up on my hands and knees, posing me like his own personal doll. Which only served to make me wetter and want him worse. I was powerless in his grip, bent to his will, doing his bidding – and it was good. I did not need a baseball bat here. I just needed to surrender.

I heard him searching in the dark and I whispered. 'Twice might as well be three times.' Meaning without a condom. There was some secret thrill in letting him take me bare. Letting him shove into me with nothing between us but breath and need.

He groaned and I barely heard him even in the deafening silence of the country when he said, 'Just saying that to me makes me almost lose it.'

I pushed my ass back toward him, opening my body, inviting him in. Another groan and then the marble-smooth, hot tip of his cock as he ran it along my juiced opening.

'Hurry,' I said, surprising myself.

'Shh,' he answered, going slower. Playing me. Priming me.

'Shepherd,' I sighed.

He drove into me swiftly. I didn't see it coming. One moment he was lulling me and the next he was taking him. Hard.

I dropped my head to the mattress, steeling myself with my forearms as he gripped my hips hard and fucked me. Then he froze and I made a desperate surprised sound. Shepherd arched over me, reaching under me to find and pinch my nipple. It was a rough, but perfectly executed, pinch that made my cunt ripple around him.

He groaned and I sighed and then he was inching back into me, lubricated by my ridiculous arousal. I couldn't recall ever being so turned on – ever being so pliable. Moving back, I took him as much as I could, as much as he'd allow. He still had a death grip on the flare of my hips.

Shepherd laughed softly and then his movements were inching me across the bed. My head banged the wall a bit and he rasped 'Touch yourself, Tuesday. Rub one off for Shepherd.'

Christ. So dirty. So bad. So crude. So fucking perfect.

I did it. I found my body slippery and wet already from our coupling and my clit was a hard little knot under my fingertips. I pressed it once and pleasure unwound in my cunt like a long warm ribbon.

'Oh,' I said.

'Yes, oh,' he echoed, his voice barely controlled. 'Do it!'

His fingers tightened, his voice grew deeper. Again he found one hard nipple with his fingers and he pinched it into a painful point of flesh. The perfect amount of discomfort bled into the firm circles I ground out on my clit and I was crying. Tears streaking my face as I came – harder than I could recall. Even with him.

My visions sparkled with phantom light and he said, 'Tuesday. Baby. Fuck.' And that was that. He held me tight, not letting me move as he made one final thrust and spilled.

Then I was sobbing for real. Not crying from my orgasm or the shock of it. This was coming from a much deeper release.

'Do you need me to stay?' he asked in the dark, pulling me to him.

I thought of his work and his income and his mission. I thought of my embarrassment and how I felt laid bare and exposed and silly. I thought of working the diner during the cluster fuck that seemed to come with the Apple Festival and how I'd be busy. I thought of how it wasn't safe to want or need something like security from someone. How the last time I'd done it, I'd had to resort to a baseball bat and fleeing the home.

'No, I'm fine. I don't know what's wrong with me,' I said.

He smoothed my hair and kissed my head and wrapped around me. I wasn't too eager for morning to come. I wasn't too eager to be independent in the morning light.

Chapter Twenty-five

I WOKE HIM BY straddling him. Taking back my power in my own mind. I made him hard with my mouth while he slept and when he cracked his eyes open he smiled at me. He got the power thing, I think. His hands came up to thread with mine when I straddled him. I pressed down as he pressed up and I bucked my hips eager to get us both off. To remake our final fuck memory before his trip into something fun. Not me bursting into tears like a lunatic.

'God, you are fucking beautiful.' He enunciated each word with a powerful up thrust of his hips.

I studied the lines of his muscles and the light hair on his chest. The cut of his jaw and the warmth of his eyes. And that goddamn crooked grin that put me on the edge of orgasm when fully clothed and in a room full of people. 'You're pretty darn beautiful yourself.'

'Please,' he chuckled, rolling his eyes. 'Men are not beautiful.'

I thought of Reed and pushed the image away.

'Handsome.' I rocked from side to side, driving his cock into all the tender places I needed it most. I watched him bite his lip – he didn't seem to know he was doing it – it was the sexiest fucking thing I'd ever seen.

'Boring word.' It came out on a puff of air.

'Hot?'

I let go of his hands and draped my body over his, pressing my breasts to his warm chest. I kissed him on one eyelid and then the other.

'Strong, powerful, sexy, scary, dominant,' I whispered. I licked his earlobe and his arms banded around me, pinning me to him.

Now he was fucking me, only I was on top. We both knew it. He drove up hard and filled me and said, 'Broken.'

I came kissing his hair, shaking in his arms as he came too. 'Me too,' I said.

'And that's OK, Tuesday,' he said and kissed my neck.

It was strange to watch him pull away two hours later and feel that ache and twinge in my chest. To feel my heart sink and my gut turn with missing him. He wasn't even out of sight yet.

'No fucking for a few days,' I said to myself. 'Figure yourself out, woman. Because you are twisted up as hell.'

'Jesus. Happy Apple fucking Festival,' someone said against my hair and I jumped, spilling a soda on my apron.

I let out a whoop that even had Irv turning to see what I'd done. 'Sorry! 'I yelled and he smiled at me, giving me an, it's-all-right wave. Thank God Irv was nice because the diner was mobbed thanks to the apple people. At least that's how I'd come to think of them.

I'd barely had time to moon over Shepherd or try and figure out what I wanted or felt or any of that emotion crap.

It was Reed. Looking handsome and friendly and kissable. He was much safer, it occurred to me. Like some pretty bauble I could touch and play with and simply put on a shelf when I was done.

He made me feel, sure of myself – sexy, wanted, funny, flirty. But not sobbing, crumbling real stuff that made me want to confess my past or my dreams or any of that.

'Hi,' I said. 'Sorry, so-so busy.'

'Can I buy you a late dinner?' he asked. 'When you get out of this zoo?'

'I … don't think so,' I said. 'I have some stuff to do. I'm sorry. Did you want a table?' I rushed on, hoping he'd just let it go.

'Yeah. If I can get one.' He touched my hair just for an instant. 'You have stuff? Like baking? I could come help you bake.'

I laughed, remembering us fucking on my floor. Remembering that Shepherd saw and feeling that weird mix of shame and satisfaction. He'd seen – seen me with another man. One he didn't like, at that. And he still wanted me. He'd still offered to ... stay.

'No.' I smiled. 'No baking. Writing I think. I was supposed to do that you know. So I'm taking a few days ...' *Until Shepherd is back or I know what the fuck is going on in my head.* '... To write,' I finished weakly. 'Sorry,' I said, nodding to the man whose soda I still held. He was raising a hand to get my attention.

'You sure?'

'I'm sure. I'm just very ... overwhelmed,' I said. 'I'll be back to get your table.'

When I pushed past him, his fingers slid along my waist. The touch was warming and unassuming and I remembered how good we were out in that field. How easy it was with him. There were no complications. Just orgasms.

'Right back,' I whispered and hurried to the table.

It was just long enough to catch my breath so when I went back I was more composed. 'Hope you don't mind being stuck back here in this little nook,' I said.

The very back booth under the windows was on the small side. Irv had told me to only seat two people there, never four, or they'd be like sardines in a can.

'I like it. It's cosy,' he said, taking the back seat so he could still watch the action in the dining room. 'You OK?

'Flustered,' I laughed, nodding to the crowd. I bent to wipe his table real fast and he caught me by my shirt and kissed me. It was firm but gentle and his tongue touched my lips before slipping past just enough to connect with my mine. A jolt of electric want filled me and I sighed.

This was too hard. It was all too hard. On a cellular level I wanted this man. But the woman who'd burst into tears a moment after climax in the wee hours of morning was confused.

If I had any brains at all, I'd step back and just figure my shit out.

'Your order?' I whispered, pulling back. Fixing my hair, begging him with my eyes not to get me in trouble.

Reed nodded and grinned his TV star grin. 'Chicken pot pie, side salad, blue cheese dressing, sweet tea, and a piece of lemon meringue pie for dessert.'

'Thank you,' I said, touching his hand. And I hurried back to place his order.

Thankfully, any further conversation was lost in a flurry of apple people. Irv cut me loose at ten thirty after I wiped down all the tables.

'Good job, kiddo. Virginia would have been proud. Go home. Rest. Tomorrow won't be any better.'

Great.

The Grenada poked two little white holes of light in the lakeshore night. Jesus but I had to get used to the darkness of the country.

Outside Nan's house I put my car in gear and sat there. No rain or storm or flashes of electricity tonight but still … creepy. The potting shed was dark and sealed, the barn too. My porch light burned, a welcoming beacon for me.

'Stop being a wuss, Tuesday,' I sighed. I grabbed the door handle and my food that Irv had insisted I take. Dinner on the restaurant, he'd declared. Came with the job. If I could get my scared ass inside I could eat some slippery pot pie, salad and apple pie.

If.

I flopped my head back against the headrest. 'No one is waiting for you.'

What if it's Phil?

'It's not Phil. Don't be a baby. Just because your big scary handsome fuck-buddy is gone doesn't mean you need to turn all woozy,' I told myself.

I popped the handle and let out some weird banshee yell before walking – not running –very fast to my front door and unlocking it quickly. Inside, I slammed and locked the door and took a shuddering breath. My face was hot and flushed with anxiety but my hands were freezing cold.

'What the fuck? You're spooking yourself.'

Someone knocked on the door and I yelled, dropping my dinner on the floor. Thank God it was in a bag.

I peeked – Adrian. Blowing out a sigh, I straightened up and cracked the door.

'You OK?'

'I am.'

'You were yelling.'

'I know. I … thought I saw a snake.'

'In the dark.'

'Yep.'

He frowned. 'You sure you're OK?'

I sighed outright this time. 'I'm fine. Just tired and ready to eat and go to bed.'

His eyes tracked me from head to toe and I added, 'Alone.'

Adrian held his hands up and I had a twinge of guilt. 'Hey, you don't have to tell me twice. Clearly I've been dismissed. I'm no foo–'

'I'm sorry, Ade,' I said. 'I'm just …' I pressed my head to the door jamb. 'My life is a wreck right now. Out of a relationship, losing Nan, moving. All that shit. It's not you …'

He started laughing and shook his head. 'Please do not say, "it's not you, it's me".'

I smiled.

'Hey, I was just trying to be a good guy. I wanted to make sure you were OK. Now I'm going to veg out. If you change your mind, Tuesday and want some company, dirty or otherwise, you know where to find me.'

I nodded. 'Will do.'

And that's how I ended up on the sofa with a cable knit throw over me, tepid slippery pot pie on the coffee table, an alien abduction show on the tube, writing a short story long hand.

Go figure it was full of angst and fear and sex and bravery. But it wasn't the time to analyse it. It was just the time to get it out. Disgusting as it may sound, writing – to me, at least – was often the emotional equivalent of lancing a boil. Nasty, horrible, relieving and necessary.

Somewhere around the middle of the night the alien

abduction show turned to a ghost hunting saga. I watched briefly, with burning eyes and a throbbing hand from a night of writing out a story long hand.

When the sky started to turn periwinkle my eyelids gave up. I fell asleep. Wondering if ghosts and aliens felt loss, guilt, pain and love – the stuff that made us human.

Chapter Twenty-six

SOMEONE WAS STORMING THE castle. It's what Annie always called it when someone knocked way too hard and way too loud, way too early. I fell off the sofa, landing on my notebook. I had a numb arm and lucky for me and my vulnerable eyeballs, I avoided falling on my pen.

'Fuck.'

I got up on hands and knees and caught my bearings. I must have passed out on the sofa. I crawled a few feet before realising it might be a good idea to stand.

More knocking.

'Jesus. I am coming!'

I threw open the door without thinking and blinked at the light in my face.

'Um … hi?'

'Hi.'

'Reed? What time is it?'

He checked his fancy watch that probably cost more than my car. 'Eleven.'

Shit, I had only about five hours before another shift at the restaurant. Another evening of Apple Festival hell.

'Come on in,' I said, stepping back. 'I fell asleep …' I waved my hand wildly at the sofa. Remembering the last time he showed up so early I blushed. 'I'll be back.'

I ran to the bathroom and peed, brushed my teeth. After a glance in the mirror, I gave up. There was no fixing this bed head meets wildly stunned look I had.

He was in the kitchen making me coffee. 'I came to see what happened.'

'What do you mean what happened?'

'I thought we were having fun, you and I.' He snapped the lid down on the coffeemaker and pressed the button to turn it on.

'We were, I mean … we did.' I opened the fridge for food and found very little.

'Damn,' I said. 'Never did go to the grocery store.'

'We have fake creamer and sugar. What more does a person need?' He flashed his shiny smile at me and tucked a lock of his hair behind his ear. It fell in mild waves today, probably due to all the rain.

I had the urge to touch it.

But I'm not asking anything of you. I don't know if I could even. I think I'm fucked up and you're–

'Twisted,' I whispered to myself remembering my conversation with Shepherd.

'Pardon?'

'Nothing. Sounds good, the coffee, I mean,' I said.

'We'll have this coffee and …' Reed opened my pantry like he owned the joint. A feeling he was probably used to. 'Um …' He reappeared holding a box of grocery store Danishes, individually wrapped. 'These!'

'Ech,' I said, but reached for it anyway. 'Gimme. I'm starving,' I giggled.

'And after we fortify ourselves with sugar, fat and salt, I'll show you the grocery store.'

'Yes, thank God.'

It was innocent. A trip to the grocery store. Plenty of time to think and not fuck. Right?

Right.

We picked at our Danishes and drank the good coffee and he told me about the Apple Festivals beginnings. This was the tenth year and every year it got more insane.

'Guess we should get to the store, then. In case it's super mobbed.'

Reed nodded and took my empty mug. 'Go get dressed, I'll clean up.'

'Oooh, the perfect man,' I said without thinking.

He caught me around the waist and pulled me in. His

fingers slipped below the hem of the hoodie I still wore and then hooked in the waistband of my leggings. 'I am the perfect man.' His mouth came down soft and humid on the slope of my throat. My nipples pebbled and my stomach tingled. God, his mouth on me made me forget the thinking I was supposed to be doing.

And I wasn't stupid. I was afraid of a lot of what I was feeling for Shepherd. This was the perfect distraction. Feelings? What feelings? Why have feelings when you can just fuck.

Reed pushed his hands up higher, spreading his fingers wide over my ribcage so I shivered. It tickled just enough to make me jump in his grip.

He almost touched my breasts. I almost felt the heat of his touch on me and probably the pinch of his fingers on that tender pink flesh. But I backed up fast and said breathlessly, 'I'll get dressed now. You don't want me to starve, do you?'

'No, ma'am.' He grinned.

He almost let me get away but snagged my hood and pulled me back. One hard kiss and he let me go with a, 'I'm not done with you yet, Tuesday.'

'Good lord,' I muttered, scurrying up the steps. What a fine mess I'd gotten myself into.

'This is a grocery store?'

About 20 minutes from my house sat an enormous green barn. One whole section was a huge opened spot with tables and chairs where folks sat drinking coffee or eating sandwiches. You could see the huge sliding barn door off the right. When it was open there was a semi-outdoor patio for patrons.

'Yep. This is Cooper's. Was once the main farming land for the whole lake. Now it's the grocery store, café and over there is a carwash.'

'Wow,' I said. 'I'm … impressed. It's so quaint.'

'Wait till you see the prices,' he said winking. 'I think you'll change your mind.'

'Uh oh,' I snorted.

Before I could get out, Reed caught my hand in his. He dropped a proper, but somehow smoking hot, kiss on my lips and I parted them to accommodate. His tongue tasted like cinnamon and I let him kiss me deeper. He slid a hand inside my blue sweater and held me, his thumb sliding along my cotton tee and teasing my nipple erect almost instantly.

I shifted a little. My panties were wet, and I was willing to wager that Reed Green not only knew that … he'd counted on it.

'Have I done anything?'

'No. I'm just overwhelmed. Can we shop? Because if you kiss me like that again,' I said. 'I might have no control and that would upset me.'

'Careful. Don't show your hand.'

I nodded and popped the car door latch so I could escape.

Showing my hand was bad. Acknowledging, accepting and embracing that he was a pretty distraction was probably also bad. Remembering how good he was at fucking –definitely bad. I hurried over the gravel parking lot with Reed on my heels.

He came up on me and I felt his energy. It made me prickle and pick up speed. He laughed softly, staying right on my heels.

'You running from me, Tuesday?'

'No.'

'Liar,' he said and followed me inside.

We bagged lemons and limes and some late season cherries. Reed held up cucumbers and tomatoes and some lettuce that was the colour of healthy green grass. When half the cart was full of produce we hit the nuts and dried fruit section.

'You gonna be like your grandmother? Always prepared? Always fully stocked?' He sipped a sample of something pink.

I shrugged. 'I doubt it. Nan was always … on guard. Ready. I tend to fly more by the seat of my pants.'

We were back behind a display and his hand splayed my ass, worming into my back pocket and squeezing. 'These pants?' he said in my ear. He was pressed right up behind me, his breath hot on my neck.

My mouth went dry. 'Yes.'

'These pants I want to peel off you?'

'Um ...'

'These pants I want to use to fucking tie you up so I can have my way with you?'

I tried to think. I tried to focus and process and stay calm but I felt to be shimmering with attraction and lust.

'Um ...'

'Hurry up and shop, Tuesday. We have some business to take care of.'

Shepherd had said he didn't expect anything of me. But I expected something of me – and I needed a clear head to do it.

I turned fast, pressed to him, our lips almost touching but not quite. 'I can't sleep with you, Reed. Not today. Not till I'm straight in the head.'

He grabbed the back of my head and yanked me in hard enough to steal my breath. 'That's fine. We can do stuff besides fuck, Tuesday. I'm very inventive.'

He pushed the cart past me and I watched him continue to shop. I wanted to be blasé about what he'd said. Instead I felt a war of guilt and excitement in the pit of my stomach.

I followed him down the aisle and tried to keep my attention on the business at hand.

Shopping.

Chapter Twenty-seven

TWO HUNDRED DOLLARS LATER, we were headed home.

'This food better last me about a year,' I said. 'I think that was all the money on my bank card.'

A look of concern flashed over his face and I laughed. 'I'm kidding. Plus, Reed, there's a settlement from Nan's will. And oh, hey, let's not forget my pay check from Irv.'

The concern was replaced with relief and I patted his leg. 'But thanks for worrying.'

'You know if you ever need money. If there's ever an issue you can come to me,' he said.

'Sure. You're my friend,' I said. Not telling him that I'd rather eat the gravel we were driving on than ask most folks for help.

Reed's lips compressed to a thin line and he said, 'Yeah, we're friends.'

Then I realised what I had said. That I had somehow offended. He pulled into my drive and I glanced at the barn which looked deserted – Adrian's small blue pickup was nowhere to be seen – and then the potting shed which looked completely harmless. What was I so worried about. How had I become so spooked?

We carried the bags to the house in twos and threes. I'd insisted on buying some of Cooper's reusable burlap bags. So much more fun than the plastic ones made in the city. Each was stamped in a different coloured ink to resemble a bulk package of coffee or rice or beans.

The final trip and I dropped my bag. Reed put the final grocery sack down and began to crawl around to retrieve my crap.

'Great,' I growled.

'No big deal.' Reed shoved a make-up case toward me and then a pad with a pen. Lipsticks, hair clips, a bandana, tampons, earrings and then he was clutching a small clear pouch.

'Um–'

'I recognise all the other female debris but what is …' His face broke out into a wildly thrilled grin when he accidentally hit the button and the pocket vibe jumped to life. 'Nice.'

'Give me that,' I growled and made a grab for it.

Reed was too fast, he pulled his hand back and up and the small toy continued to buzz merrily while I blushed like a fool. I sat back, legs folded under me, and sighed.

'So this is for sexual emergencies?' he asked. Thankfully he'd dropped his voice and leaned in instead of shouting. Not that anyone was around to hear right now. But still.

'Reed …'

He was fast. He pressed the toy, still in its case, to my thigh and I felt the buzz sound through me, thrilling me. 'Do you like this little toy?'

'Yes,' I said, trying to remain calm and straight faced. I got to my feet and I brushed my jeans off. 'I am a grown woman who likes sex and has a vibrator in her purse. I am also a grown woman who is going to go put her groceries away before her meat spoils and her ice cream melts.'

Then I turned and stalked to the house leaving him where he sat.

'Fine!' he called good naturedly. 'But you are no fun, Tuesday Cane!' And then he followed me into my house.

Everything was put away when I heard the thing jump to life. I was hanging my jacket on a hook in the cubby off the great room that Nan had used as an office.

'Give that back,' I said, half heartedly.

'This?' And then he pressed the button. On-off-on-off. So the small thing went buzz–buzz … buzz–buzz like a bumble bee with ADD.

'Yes, that,' I snorted. Reaching for him. My hand sank into his yellow and grey chequered shirt and I tugged. We were playing. No big deal.

Reed surged forward. I hadn't expected him to do that. I'd expected some good natured tugging and pulling and whatnot.

Instead he had me pinned to the office wall with his free hand and the rest of his lean self. 'I told you, I can't–'

'Fuck me,' he said. His words were blunt but his gaze was complicated. 'Who said anything about fucking?'

Buzz–buzz ... buzz–buzz ...

'Reed, I–'

His dark brown eyes were hooded with a hunger when he pulled back to look at me. Clean shaven and smooth under my fingertips his skin was hot. I meant to keep him from kissing me. But his mouth was a pale pink pout and his eyes were so warm and he said 'You're the first woman in a long time to really make me ... miss her when she's not around.'

Oh God. He missed me, too? The fear I felt at all my twisted emotions for Shepherd reared up and bit me. I needed to come down, detangle, disengage.

I kissed him. I kissed him and he found his opening, pressing solid against me, stalling my breath and forcing the hard crest of his cock to my pussy through our clothes. It was breathtaking, the feel of him. The thrill of breaking my own personal rule.

'No fucking,' I said, my voice little puffs of air.

'Fine, fine.' He pulled my top up exposing my pale pink bra and ripped the cup down so he could get at my nipple. Teeth clamped down on that tender pale flesh and I hissed, my fingers curling into his silken brown hair.

I wanted to say a million things right then but said none of them. The pleasure ate up every clever thing I had to say and I simply moulded myself into his embrace, pressing my breast to his seeking mouth.

'It's that fucking cage fighter, isn't it?' he said almost to himself.

He'd dropped to his knees, exposing a wide band of bare skin above my waistband that he proceeded to nuzzle and bite and lick. My pussy flexed wetly, my skin erupting in goose flesh. A fine tremor worked through my body and I felt the fine

173

hairs along my scalp sway.

'Don't talk … about … just don't. Please,' I said. If he started talking Shepherd, I was done for.

He nodded, somehow understanding that and popped the button on my jeans. Shoving the denim down, he scraped one hipbone and then the other with his teeth so that my body went on high alert, my nipples painfully hard, my breath thin and panting.

He got my jeans off after I kicked off my clogs and put his mouth to my mound. 'Open your legs.'

I did. Taking one step out to the side so my body opened for him. Reed pressed the whole of his mouth to my pussy and licked.

I grabbed his shoulders for support and let him lick me with a force that pressed me back to the wall. He held my hips steady and drove his tongue into my cunt so my knees threatened to buckle and dump me on my ass.

'Reed, I–'

'Be quiet, Tuesday.'

He was working his belt and his jeans, pulling them down around his hips and I had a flash of fear that he'd try to fuck me. And then a flash of fear that I'd let him. Because part of me was sure I would.

His hand slid along the curve of his erection and I realised he was going to jack off while he ate me. A very naughty thrill galloped through my stomach and I gasped.

Reed nibbled my clit while pressing his forearm to my belly to hold me still. Then he pulled back forcefully, cock still in hand to grab something from his jeans.

The toy.

It was out of the plastic case and buzzing before I could question him. He dipped it between my legs to get it wet and then touched it to my clit.

I had no words. I just said, 'Oh.'

Reed's fingers were cool and long as he slid two into my cunt, pressing the dancing toy to my clitoris as he thrust. I tried to grab the panelled wall but my fingers skittered and skimmed the smooth surface finding no purchase.

'I'm going to come,' I confessed. Realising that I had sworn off fucking but he'd found this dirty alternative anyway. It fuelled my orgasm. I was hopeless – shameless and wicked and cruel.

Shepherd's face flashed in my mind. Him pinning me to his work bench, my feet resting on the edge, my cunt open for his examination. His eyes eating me before he fucked me.

I came. Reed's fingers nudging my G-spot with expert ease, the toy buzzing a line of heated bliss through my pussy. I thought he was done. He wasn't.

Reed turned the toy off, set his mouth back to me and began licking up the wet evidence of my orgasm. He shoved a hand between my legs, rubbing me, getting his fingers wetter. Then he started to masturbate again, his now slick hand making sinister sexual noises against his cock.

I made a small sound when he sucked my clit hard and then thrust his tongue into my juicy pussy. 'Come with me. Come for me again,' he demanded.

I watched him handle his cock, his fingers pulling and twisting and moving much harder than I ever would have had I been the one jerking him off. He tugged to the right it seemed but just the sound and the sight of him tugging at all had me sinking down the wall in the grips of the first tentative flickers of orgasm.

'Jesus, Reed ...'

'Yes, ma'am?' he teased. But then he groaned, the rumble vibrating his teeth against my mound and the sensation of his noise filled my pelvis.

'I'm coming,' I said softly and grabbed twin hunks of his hair and pulled.

That did it. He gave a final jerk with his well manicured hand and a spray of semen flew across my lower legs. He moved just a bit, still keeping his mouth on me, and the final jet went a bit higher.

His come was as warm and wet on my skin as his mouth. The final spasm twisted in me and the heat in my womb started to subside. I tugged that luxurious hair again and said. 'You are so fucking confusing.'

Reed looked up and grinned, his mouth smeared with my wetness, cock still in hand. 'Ditto, kid.'

Chapter Twenty-eight

'SORRY, IRV.' I HUSTLED in and literally tossed my bag into the office onto a chair.

'Sorry for what?' He handed me my apron.

'I'm late.'

He looked up at the clock showing a slice of pie. 'By what? A minute?'

I grinned. 'Yeah.'

He rolled his eyes. 'Jeesh. If only they were all as conscientious as you.'

'I'm a keeper,' I teased. Outside the doors, people from out of town were already lining up to eat. I wiped down a few tables.

'You doing OK with the insanity of apple time?' He was doing his best to buff the countertop spotless.

'I think it's good for me to be busy right now,' I said.

In the kitchen the cook was singing to the radio. La Bamba had never sounded so fun. I laughed. Irv rolled his eyes again. 'He's a great cook. Can't carry a tune in a bucket, though.'

I moved on to the next table and watched more folks join the throng waiting outside. 'Do you put drugs in the food, Irv?' I asked. I smiled at him.

'What?' he yelped.

I nodded to the crowd. 'Look at that.'

'Oh.' He chuckled. 'We serve the only decent burger and fries for miles, is all. So you need to be busy?'

He flipped the conversation back to me and it flustered me a bit. 'Yeah.'

'Missing Virginia are you?'

My throat tightened up and I tried to shake off the blanket

of emotion that settled over me. 'Yeah, some. OK, a lot.'

I moved on to the final table and he came up behind me to pat my shoulder. 'We all do, kiddo. It's normal for you to miss her a lot. So don't feel bad about feeling bad. A new life takes time to break in. Just like shoes.'

I stared into his friendly face and wondered about him and Nan again. For some reason the thought of him wooing her made me very happy. 'Like shoes,' I echoed.

Irv went to unlock the door and in the jostling cluster of people I thought I saw a flash of a familiar face. But as fast as it appeared, it was gone.

The fine hairs on my nape stood at attention and my stomach bottomed out some.

I was back to freaking myself out it seemed.

Ten o'clock had never looked so good. Despite searching the apparently starving crowd repeatedly I saw no one I knew. No dark figure lurking around the corner to come and get me. No boogie man, no ex, no stalker.

The Grenada chewed up bits of the lakeshore road, spitting gravel here and there as I went. The barn and the potting shed still appeared abandoned. My story was calling – shockingly I was eager to get back to it. Even though it felt sort of full of angst to me, all the bullshit writers write about when they're trying to process their fear and pain.

'I also have some pot roast, new potatoes, soft carrots and vanilla pudding waiting for me,' I whispered patting my dinner packed by Irv himself.

I made myself walk normally from car to door. Made myself unlock the door and slip inside as if nothing in the world were bothering me and none of my bells and whistles of anxiety were going off.

'It's living in a big house alone and missing you, Nan,' I said aloud, locking the door. 'And desperately needing a dog. Maybe a big one. A pit bull, or better yet a German Shepherd.'

Shepherd.

'I could name him Tiny,' I snickered.

In the kitchen, I unpacked my meal, put on a pot of water to boil for tea and poured some wine. I'd eat, shower and then pass the time the way many, many writers – wannabe and otherwise – before me had passed an evening. Slugging down drinks and writing pretty words.

I wrote GO TO SHELTER on the small dry erase magnet board on Nan's fridge. At the top she had written my phone number at the boarding house. It appeared to be the last thing she wrote on the board before she died.

I dialled Annie while the water boiled. The phone rang and rang and rang but no one answered. She was probably out drinking beer at Jimmy C's and playing Keno with her man. The machine greeted me and I simply said, 'It's me. Checking in on y'all. Love.'

Then I hung up. There was a face at the window and I screamed, dropping my wine. Now would be a really, really good time for that dog named Tiny. I kept waiting for the figure, distorted by the pebbled privacy glass, to wave or laugh or yell out a greeting. Instead it stayed still and did nothing. Finally, it turned away.

Man. That had been all I could tell of the figure.

I grabbed the ever present bat – propped in the corner of the kitchen where I'd stored it –and took off out the back door. Part of me had tempered my knee jerk nature and let him have a head start. On the side of the house I heard a noise and I rounded the corner, bat brandished. Adrian was facing me with a Maglite in one hand and a chunk of wood in the other.

'What the fuck!' I screamed at him, losing my cool. 'Are you trying to scare the shit out of me?''

He stalked toward me, his face angry in the weird streaks of pure white light from his flashlight. 'What are you talking about? I saw someone around here and came to help you for fuck's sake, Tuesday. I am the caretaker. Until you fire me. I'm taking some goddamn care.'

My rant stalled out and I stood there, anger wavering. Was he telling the truth? Had he seen someone or had he been the person at my door? I simply didn't know. I remembered why Adrian and I hadn't worked out to begin with. He'd been a bit too needy in the knight in shining armour department. He had required constant reassurance of any affectionate feelings for him, his prowess in bed and his appearance. It had been too much high maintenance stroking for me.

'I'm going in.'

'Wait, Tuesday, are you OK?'

'I'm pissed. I'm hungry. I'm cold and I'm tired. But yes. I'm fine.'

I started to walk away and he grabbed my arm. 'Do you need me to stay inside?'

I grinned. Was that what this had been about? Had he baited me so I would want him in the house?

'No,' I said. 'Thanks. I don't need you.'

Even in the dark I could see the war of hurt and anger and petulance cross his face. 'I just bet you don't need anyone, now do you, Tuesday?'

'No,' I said. 'I don't.'

I slipped back inside and pulled the kitchen door shut behind me. I locked it, kicking aside a bunch of leaves that blew inside. 'Good way to stay safe, Tuesday,' I said. 'Leave your damn door wide open.'

I poured my tea, picked at my food and finally stored most of it, giving into the temptation to just eat the pudding.

Four new pages into my story, which was becoming way longer than just a story, and the phone rang. The house phone.

I grabbed it assuming it was Annie calling me back. 'Hey there. I hope you're behaving because I sure am not,' I laughed.

'Good to know,' the voice rumbled.

Shepherd.

'Oh, hi,' I said.

'So, tell me. What exactly are you up to?'

I threw myself back on the sofa, put my feet on the back of the cushions and started to tell him. All about the apple people, the busy diner, the man and the window. About finding Adrian outside and the bat and my anger. And the pages. He was the only one I told about the pages.

'Do you need me to come home?' he asked. He'd gotten very quiet when I told him about the man and running out and lugging a baseball bat around in the dark.

I paused, almost saying yes. Yes … it was on the tip of my tongue. And when I realised it, I was so terrified by the urge that seeing the figure at my back door seemed like nothing more upsetting than a spilled drink or an unexpected sneeze. True need scared me more than strangers, I now realised.

I wanted him to come home. I wanted him to be here so I'd feel safe. I wanted him to come and take care of me – and I hated myself for it. I hurriedly said, 'No, no, no – you do your thing. Charity is more important than some stupid stalking caretaker.'

'Are you sure it was him?' he asked, his voice low – he was trying very hard to control it, I could tell. And he didn't sound convinced.

'Completely,' I said. 'And don't worry. I can handle Adrian. I did it last time, I can do it again.'

When I hung up it hit me. I knew that I'd just lied to Shepherd. That was a no brainer. What I hadn't realised until his voice was gone was that I felt guilt over it. I didn't like lying to Shepherd and I really did want him to come home – now – and the thought of him home made me feel safe in my skin.

I poured myself more wine. 'You know what that means,' I said to the TV that was showing a sitcom starring Betty White.

'You. Are. Fucked.'

Chapter Twenty-nine

I SLEPT ON THE sofa again. It was becoming a habit. Maybe because I was alone in a fairly large space for the first time in my life. I felt more contained and therefore secure in the main room facing the TV and hiding snuggled down in the high backed sofa.

The sun was bright and it lit the inside of my eyelids so the world was red. Sun or not, I heard the wind before I even opened my eyes.

I needed coffee and I needed it fast. My neck was sore, my feet cold and I had to figure out the heat.

I'd have to ask Adrian.

'Adrian,' I sighed, measuring out the dark rich coffee carefully into the basket.

Thanks to Reed, there was food in my fridge and I made myself a slice of toast with some of Cooper's signature peach preserves. I probably should have eaten more but I didn't have much of an appetite. My urge to ask Shepherd to come home still haunted me.

It was only early October but the wind blew and I felt some phantom curls of cold air on my arms. The A-frame was old enough to be draughty and if I didn't want to freeze my ass off tonight, I'd have to figure out the goddamn heat. I had tried simply turning the thermostat on but nothing cut in and no heat came out of the vents.

'Fucking heat. I guess that's what a caretaker's for,' I growled and went upstairs to get dressed.

I rehearsed what I'd say in my head as I made my way over to the barn. I'd simply say I was startled and I was sorry for yelling and accusing and could he come and teach me how to do whatever I needed to do with the heat so I didn't asphyxiate myself and die a beautiful corpse. That made me snort and then the wind blew hard and I hustled my ass across the yard.

Pulling open the barn door I poked my head into the dusty, draughty expanse of emptiness. 'Hello?' I whispered.

Flashing back to my whispering to Shepherd in his secret underground workshop and how that had turned out, I called out a bit louder. That would not be happening with Adrian, that was for sure.

We'd had our fun when I first showed up, but carrying on with a man like Adrian any more would have been unfair. He'd start expecting something ... more. And that was something I didn't have to give him. *More.*

'Hellooooo?' I semi-yelled. 'Adrian?'

I made my way past the empty stalls. Past Shepherd's snow plough. I repressed the need to go push my hand against the cold metal simply because it was his. Simply because I thought it might somehow be imprinted with his energy.

'Boy, I'm not 14 or anything, am I?' I rolled my eyes at my own damn self. 'Jesus.'

I heard them when I got a bit closer. And I knew I should stop right there and then. Do an about face and leave and come back later in the day. But I didn't. I pushed my feet forward because I was nosy and brazen and a bit crazy, I think.

His door was cracked. I mean, who was here to see him, anyway? I'd made it clear he should take a hike and my grandmother was gone. Adrian was spread eagle on his double bed while some girl with a shock of honey blonde hair sucked his cock. One arm was tied to a metal ring set in the wall – originally intended for horses not a caretaker.

'You like that, baby? Do you?'

I wanted to laugh at how ridiculous the whole thing was, but it wasn't. Not so much. They were raw and energetic and they thought they were hidden.

He muttered something to her, putting his free hand in her hair and guiding her to take him deeper. I couldn't hear what Adrian was saying but I could hear the tone and it was one of appreciation.

He tugged a hunk of hair and she gasped but followed his lead as he tugged and tugged until she moved. She sidled up to him on her knees, her back still to me, nothing but a pair of almost sheer mesh panties on despite the barn's chill.

Something told me Adrian and his guest weren't chilly.

She straddled him, going higher and higher and higher until thanks to his murmured words, she straddled his shoulders and he set his mouth to the front of her panties. His lips latching to the fabric before I lost my view of Adrian's face and she blotted him out. Her hips undulated and she met his mouth with eager thrusts of her hips. When Adrian tangled the fingers of his free hand into her panties and tried to tug, she laughed, hair tossed back.

It was her profile that gave her away as Tammie at the bank. Irv had sent me over for change the other day and we'd met. Her breasts were small but jutted up with perfect pink tips that stood out in erect arousal. Her stomach was flat and a single beauty mark rode above her hip bone. Tammie ditched the panties and returned to him so he could hold her close with that one bold, strong hand and eat her.

Adrian was good at eating pussy. I remembered as my own sex gave up a rush of juices at seeing them together this way. Better than porn and with the sneaky factor to amp it up, I watched. Knowing I should go, but not quite able to make myself do it.

She came with a long lusty cry, letting her head fall back and making her honeyed hair ripple with the pleasure that slid through her body.

Tammie yanked his open jeans lower on his hips and at his bidding, grabbed a condom from the dresser. She rolled it on and then climbed aboard, taking his free hand and pinning it to the bed frame so he couldn't touch her.

She rolled her hips and laughed and then leaned in to kiss him and I watched Adrian's toes curl. I must have kicked the door to his room because they both froze and I stepped back into shadows. She turned her head a bit and called, 'Hello?'

I hurried out of the barn, laughing at myself. Eager to find my little bullet that Reed had abandoned somewhere in the great room. And maybe take a shower to relive the voyeurism I'd just enjoyed.

'Pervert,' I hurried through the wind back to my home. I'd leave him a note later about the heat. Or make more noise the next time I went to ask.

The door was ajar and I froze. Had I done that? Had I neglected to pull it closed? That had to be what had happened.

I poked my head in and looked around. Everything in its place – which meant strewn about the great room. I had to be careful or the main room was going to start resembling a dorm room.

'It's my house,' I said to myself just to hear a voice.

I grabbed the bat from where it rested by the TV, I'd kept it close the night before after my back door visitor. Doing a quick tour of the house, I saw that everything appeared OK. The laundry pile in front of Nan's storage room looked a bit off, but it was a pile of dirty laundry. How was it supposed to look?

I popped my head in the room and glanced around. Nada.

There was no attic and the basement door was locked from the outside when I checked it. Which meant that only a supernatural visitor could go into a basement and then lock the door behind them.

'Right. Stop it, you lunatic,' I muttered.

But I really did need to go to the shelter. I thought I might feel much better with some furry, mega-toothed, protective company.

I had time before my shift at the diner. I decided to take a run and then call Annie. I wanted to check in on the closest person I had to family. I prided myself on not having roots, but feeling uprooted was an entirely different sensation.

Standing in my big, empty and cold house with Shepherd gone, Reed at arm's length and sweet sexy Adrian out there in the barn fucking a bank teller – I was feeling uprooted.

Maybe I wasn't as independent as I thought.

'There she is!' Irv shouted as I rushed in. The crowd was already starting to gather. Either I'd imagined it or I'd felt a hand sneak up my spine as I made my way through the crowd to the diner door.

'Here I am,' I said, pushing the worry away.

There was quite a cluster of out-of-towners out there waiting to be fed. The hand on me had probably been an accident. Or an over-eager husband trying to get a handful of stranger.

Odder things had happened to me.

'When is this apple festival over?' I laughed tying on my apron.

'Two more days. But don't rush it. We make good money while they're here. And that means a nice Christmas bonus for you.' He winked.

'Christmas bonus?' I snorted. Was he serious?'

'Yes, ma'am. My servers are family. The apple festival dictates how generous Santa Irv can be.'

I blew him a kiss. 'I'm starting to see what my grandmother saw in you, Big Irv,' I said.

He actually blushed.

'Who says that Virginia and I–'

'Save it, Irv,' I said. I gave him a grin and retrieved my spray bottle and rag to wipe down the tables. 'You can't fool me.'

He blushed again and turned away. 'Let's hustle this along, Tuesday. We have hungry people to feed.'

Again, I thought I saw it. I was really freaking myself out, it seemed. I was seeing fleeting glimpses of lovers past everywhere. Or at least boogety boos. Whatever I was seeing, I was tired of seeing it.

It was Friday and I had Saturday off, Irv had said. I'd get snookered tonight and then hit the apple festival tomorrow.

Irv opened the door and all my plotting flew out the window. I was too busy filling orders and bussing tables and laughing at strange men's jokes and admiring strange women's recently purchased from the festival wool sweaters.

When we locked up I realised that Reed had not come in, nor Adrian and that I was relieved about it.

Which made me feel a bit too wound up to sleep.

Chapter Thirty

THE PHONE WAS RINGING.

'Hello?' I dropped my purse and my dinner bag at my feet. Tonight Irv had insisted on packing me meatballs, brown gravy, rice, veggies and a piece of apple cake. Made in honour of the festival, dontcha know.

'Kid!'

'Annie.' I grinned. 'How's tricks? Any more rats in the house?'

'No ma'am. But soon there'll be a baby!'

'Oh, Rachel had him? Her? It?' I snorted. 'Well, not it.'

'Him. Jacob Samuel Saunders. Quite a mouthful for a little bundle of screams and poops.'

I laughed, shook my head. Annie had two grown children so she knew what she was talking about. I couldn't help but find amusement in her summary of procreation.

'When will they be home?'

'Day after tomorrow. It was hard on Rach so they're keeping her a little.'

'I want to send a gift. What does she need?'

'Everything,' Annie said. I heard her light a cigarette and she read my mind. 'Don't worry. It's just one. I'm down to two a day, kid. Per our agreement.'

I'd been begging her to quit for quite a while.

'Good. Now when you say everything …'

'Diapers, food, diapers, clothes, diapers …'

'I take it babies need a lot of diapers,' I teased.

'Are you kidding? That's all they do for the first three months – cry, pee and poop.'

'And yet I can tell by your voice you're dying for that kid to

187

be in the house and in your clutches.'

She chuckled. 'Shut up, smarty pants.'

'Better than being a dumb ass,' I countered.

'Very true.'

'Now, what else is new?'

Annie sighed. 'Not a damn thing. Fall is here sometimes, the next moment it's summer again. We're fluctuating between low 60s and high 90s and it's driving me ape shit. And before you ask–'

I shut my mouth because I had been about to interrupt.

'I haven't seen either of your men.'

'They're not my men,' I corrected.

'Your former men.'

'Well, that's good news,' I said.

But did that mean the flash of familiar I'd been seeing was a glimpse of a man I'd recently assaulted with a bat? And how good was that for me?

Someone knocked at the door and I jumped. 'I have to go, Annie. Someone's knocking.'

'You being safe out there in the boondocks?'

'I am. I am. But I am thinking about a dog. I am talking to myself a lot.'

'Just as long as you don't answer yourself, kid,' she said. 'Love.'

'Love,' I answered and hung up.

Adrian stood on the other side of the door. His face unreadable. His hands shoved in his pockets.

I opened the door. 'Hey, there. I wanted to ask you about the hea–'

'You dropped something,' he said, pushing an earring toward me.

I stepped back and he stepped in. Wind rushed in around him and some mail scattered off the side table. 'Come in,' I said and shut the door behind him.

'Did you enjoy the show?' he asked.

I felt myself blush but there was no denying it. The matching earring was in my ear. I fingered it and cleared my throat. 'Yeah, about that. Sorry. I came to ask for help for the heat and you were … busy.'

I laughed and I was surprised when he joined me. 'Did you enjoy the show, Tues?' he asked again.

Adrian moved fast. He plucked my hardened nipple through my tee and when I made a startled sound he slid the other between my legs. Knifing his hand and putting pressure on my clit through my jeans.

'Adrian,' I said.

'I know. I know. I'm off the menu now but it doesn't keep me from wanting to touch you. How about a goodbye kiss.'

I rolled my eyes but let him kiss me. His mouth covered mine and the edge of his hand sawed in and out between my legs – almost but not quite getting me off.

'Now what was it I can help you with?' he asked, suddenly backing up. He put his hands in the air like he was under arrest and though he had a hard-on that was evident; he made no move toward me again.

'Very evil, Adrian,' I said. I shook my head and sighed mightily. 'The heat won't cut on. I tried but it just clicks at me.'

'I have the main switch set to away. I meant to switch that when you came home. I'll go fix it.'

My body beat with one big pulse from his kiss, his pinch, his touch. My panties were too tight, my pulse too fast and I wondered what the hell I was gaining by denying myself him. But I knew I would continue to do it.

Within moments he was back. 'Yep. It was off. I changed the setting when Virginia passed and the house was empty,' he said, shutting the basement door and latching it.

'To keep the boogie man out?' I asked.

'Critters. It looks like something got in down there. I'll check tomorrow and see if a trap needs to be put down.'

'Critters? Traps?' A mild but very real panic flared in my gut.

Adrian grinned and tried to cover it with his hand. 'Relax, Tuesday. This isn't the big city. It's getting cold and animals aren't stupid. They like warmth and comfort too. But it's no big deal – you might even say it's normal around here.' He winked at me, simultaneously making me feel better and about five years old. 'I'll come back and double check tomorrow. But for now, I'll get out of your hair.'

The heat kicked on and I jumped a bit. The smell of baking dust began to fill the A-frame.

'Unless, you'd like me to stay …' he sing-songed, but it was a teasing, friendly tone.

'Good night, Adrian,' I said.

He shrugged and kissed me on the cheek. 'Can't blame a guy for trying. Oh and …' He tugged my hair just rough enough to flare my arousal again. 'Just a reminder – I'm around for you should you change your mind. You know, in the orgasm department.'

'Thanks, Adrian. I know you'd sacrifice just for me.'

'You know it,' he said and stepped out into the wind. 'Just keep that door locked even if there is a critter down there, you'll be fine. They don't have thumbs and all that.'

I locked the door behind him and when the phone rang, I jumped again.

'This is getting ridiculous.' I grabbed the phone and feeling stupidly silly I said, 'Tuesday's house of horrors.'

'Do tell,' Shepherd rumbled and that small spark of arousal in my gut flared into a full blown fire.

'Hi,' I said.

'Hi back. So, Tuesday …What are you wearing?'

'Hold on.' I set the phone down, tossed my food in the fridge, shucked my tee and my jeans and walked to the sofa in my striped knee highs, black panties and nude bra. 'Not much,' I said honestly.

'What's not much?'

I told him and he rumbled appreciatively.

'And what are you wearing?' I teased.

'I am wearing a towel. We just finished a cancer spot for TV, set to run during the holidays and then I hit the gym in the hotel and took a run and then a swim and then a hot shower.'

I imagined him sweaty and then soapy. I imagined his big body with nothing but a small white hotel towel slung around his hips. I imagined water in his hair and in his beard and in the divot of his navel.

'Stroke your cock,' I blurted.

'Ah and here I thought I was calling you to be dirty. And you beat me to the punch.'

'Do it,' I said and slid a hand down into my panties. I hadn't lowered the blinds but felt pretty sure that from where I was lying, sunken into Nan's comfy flowered sofa, no one – not even Adrian – could see me.

I tweaked my clit with my fingertips and a shuddering sigh escaped me. The thought of him handling his cock brought me down to a whisper when I said 'Are you? Are you doing it, Shepherd?'

'Jesus, woman,' he whispered. I thought I heard the faint whisper of flesh on flesh as he jacked his cock for me. 'Even long distance you fuck with my head, do you know that?'

'Are you hard?' I asked, slipping a finger deep in my cunt. Pushing it hard against the suede marble patch of my G-spot. My clit ground against my palm and a lethargic kind of pleasure seeped into my limbs.

'I could pound nails with this thing,' he said.

'I wish you were pounding me,' I said.

He groaned again and this time I was sure I heard it. His hand working his erection. In my mind he was there, bare but for some flecks of water. The light bouncing off all the colours in his hair. The silver strands and flecks being the sexiest.

'Tuesday,' he laughed. 'I'm going to pound you until you can't walk straight when I get back.'

'Promises, promises,' Pulling my fingers free, I rubbed the slippery juices on my clit. I was so aroused, so sensitive, so ready to get off, I thought I'd pass out.

'I do promise.'

'I wish I was sucking your cock,' I confessed.

'Now you're just fighting dirty,' he said. The sounds I heard were more hurried, more erratic. More frenzied.

'No, I mean it.' My voice was barely there and this time I plunged two fingers into my slick cunt and flexed them right where I needed it most. My clit throbbed with the approaching orgasm. 'I wish I were sucking your cock. That first slide of a

191

smooth cock, hard and ready against my lower lip always nearly pushes me over. I almost get off just from the feel. And you, Shepherd, have a perfect cock. Big and long and very, very talented.' I laughed softly.

'I'm going to come. I am. I swear to fuck. And all I can think about is coming on those black panties you're wearing and then streaking those last few threads of it through your pretty blonde hair.'

'I like it in my hair,' I confessed. 'I walk around and squeeze it to feel the crunchy texture. If you come in my hair, Shepherd, I'm going to want to walk around with that secret invisible evidence in my hair all day.'

'Fuck,' he growled.

'I'm coming.' I said it when I heard the vulnerability in his voice. The most perfect sound to me – a man coming undone. A man losing his tiny thread of self control. A man who was now groaning loud, coming with me. Because he'd lost his hold on himself.

Because of me.

Chapter Thirty-one

BEFORE WE HUNG UP he said, 'I'll be home tomorrow. I'm taking the early flight.'

'Good,' I said.

I realised I'd be happy to have him home. Back on the grounds where I could get to him should I want to.

'I missed you, Tuesday.'

A heavy nervousness settled over me and I could tell he felt some anxiety over it too.

'Me, too,' I said.

'Does that bother you?' I could hear him smiling.

'Would you be mad if I said yes?' I chuckled.

'Yes.'

I went dead silent, all the words drying up on my tongue.

Then he laughed and said 'Of course not. That was a joke. I wouldn't be mad at you for feeling anything you feel. But I hope when it comes to me, it's mostly good.'

'It is mostly good,' I said. 'But in a very unnerving way.'

'Well, I did my good deed for the year. Earned my nest egg for the next twelve months too. And when I get home, I plan to fuck you entirely and also good enough to last a year.'

'It won't, though, right? I mean that won't be the last time you fuck me for the year?'

'Not on your life,' he said.

We hung up and something scratched in the basement. I remembered what Adrian said. Keep the door locked and leave the critter be.

I cracked my notebook and started writing. I liked the slow but intense pace of my emerging – I liked that I felt cleaner after I wrote. I liked that I was already thinking of how to put aside enough money for a laptop or even giving into the urge sooner rather than later and signing on to Nan's computer.

But for now I was content to write it out long hand. Capturing the words and emotions as they bubbled up to the surface. Focusing on that instead of missing Shepherd or acknowledging that I was looking forward to seeing him again. Naked. Between my thighs.

Something made a sound in the basement. But I wasn't afraid of raccoons or possums or even skunks. The only real thing I feared was Phil and that was because Phil had hit a point where he felt he had nothing to lose. A man who had nothing to lose was a dangerous man. I glanced at the basement door and the small skeleton key hole. Nan had the key somewhere in the kitchen but on this side of the door was a bar lock because she hated to fiddle with the old fashioned key. She said it was easier to go modern. A simple lock worked just as well.

'You just stay on your side, Mr Raccoon,' I muttered. At one I put on an 80s movie and rubbed my tired eyes. I fell asleep watching John Candy flip a huge pancake with a snow shovel.

The next day, I was in the shower when I felt it. That unmistakable wave of invisible energy invading your own. The same as being in a silent room and feeling that someone has walked in.

I poked my head out and looked around, brushing shampoo bubbles off my face as I looked.

'Hello?'

I wanted my voice to be big and booming. I wanted to hear myself be aggressive and sure. Instead my call came out breathy and messy and kind of scared.

'Adrian?' I asked. Yes, feeling hopeful if you must know.

Nothing.

Shepherd was a plane ride away in New York. He said he was leaving early but that included a layover.

Down in the great room the phone started to ring. It dawned on me that the phone was down there, the extension in Nan's room, my cell was somewhere at the bottom of my purse.

My eyes skittered wildly around the room for a weapon. The hiss of the shower filled my head and I took a deep shuddering breath. I had simply felt something. There was no evidence that there was anything at all to worry about.

But for my gut feeling, that is. And my gut rarely failed me.

My gaze found the medicine cabinet. An old fashioned barn cabinet salvaged and redone in a distressed white. Nan had been a very, very talented crafter and had made many old things new again. Inside her new-distressed looking medicine cabinet rested a large, sharp pair of hairstyling scissors. I know because I'd moved them the night before while rifling for a bottle of pain reliever.

'Scissors,' I said to myself.

'Nan?' I called. I'd take a ghost over a human intruder.

Maybe it was the raccoon or whatever critter Adrian suspected.

I rinsed my hair and my body, shutting off the water to hear better. All I heard was the high whine of tinnitus in my ears from the dump of adrenaline in my system.

I tied my robe and found those scissors and pocketed them. Slipping from the bathroom as quietly as possible, I walked softly through the bedroom. Nothing. I found the cordless phone from Nan's nightstand and stuck that in my other pocket. Then I poked my head into the storage room. With the stacks of stuff, the armoire full of clothes and the slanted walls that were the earmark of A-frame walls, it was hard to tell if anything was out of order. The house had no attic proper and I wondered if one of Adrian's critters had found its way into what was basically the storage area of the home.

I stood there silently for a moment and not a single thing moved. Nothing appeared disturbed.

From the lake shore I heard a radio playing. Some classic rock song about making love. I heard what sounded like a weed whacker and I wondered if Adrian was out there fixing and testing equipment.

Another furtive sound but thanks to my distraction, I could not tell its origin. There was no way to tell if it was inside or outside or as simple as an innocent nosy squirrel scooting across the roof.

Great – paranoia, fun for all ages …

I pulled on motorcycle boots, well-loved faded jeans, a linen swing top and a crocheted vest. I had the day to putter and fuss around the house. The main room needed to be tidied and probably vacuumed. I remembered to return the scissors to the medicine cabinet so I didn't impale myself the next time I wore my robe.

Maybe I could go through the storage room for more vintage clothing finds, that might distract me. But the idea of poking around in that abandoned room made me prickle with nerves.

Maybe not.

Downstairs I looked out the front door to see Adrian coming across the driveway and I threw the door open. 'What is that?'

'That is a raccoon cage. And this is a can of tuna,' he said, climbing the steps. He looked handsome and doable in his jeans, work boots and flannel. A feed cap covered his brownish red hair and when he smiled at me I wondered why I had given up all the fucking.

Oh yeah. To figure out my own damn self.

'Come on in. Can I get you coffee?'

'Yeah, sure. I like it sweet like my women.' I didn't see it coming. The slap landed on my ass with a hefty crack and I yelped. 'Sorry, sorry. I know I'm not supposed to touch,' Adrian sighed but then he grinned.

I shook my head and went to get our coffee. He really was a hottie. I hoped that Tammie appreciated it. She seemed a bit ditzy but very nice. Probably the perfect girl for the likes of Adrian. He'd constantly be told what a big, strong, strapping man he was. What a fierce player he was in the sack. What a good man he was.

And he was.

We had our coffee and he peeked out my back window at the lake. 'Who the hell is sitting out there with a radio in this? I mean it's sunny, but Jesus. It's windy as hell and only about 50-something degrees. Not really sunning weather.'

I shrugged. 'I've been told that the Apple Festival brings all kinds.'

He laughed, rubbed his eyes and yawned. 'Yeah. That's true. We had a woman who came as a vendor one year who was selling sweaters made from Alpaca hair.'

'That's not so weird,' I said.

'She brought the Alpacas and promised to spin the fabric on site.'

'Oh.'

'Yeah, oh. The sheriff's department had a field day with that.'

'I bet.'

'I have a date with a critter and then a real one for lunch later. Best get moving. You sure you're OK, Tuesday? You sleeping well? You look a bit tired.'

'Gee, thanks. How flattering.'

Adrian shrugged. 'Sweetheart, you are always hot. That's a no-brainer. I just want to know if you're OK.'

'I'm fine,' I said, deciding not to tell him about my weird feelings. It was just the new life I had to settle into. It had me all off balance. I had seen zero evidence that anything besides my overactive imagination was going on.

'Good. Now I'm going to go put some stinky tuna fish in your basement – 'kay?'

I snorted. 'You are a prince.'

I saw him off and when the phone rang I dove for it. Something about the long day stretching out ahead of me had me on edge.

'Hello?'

'It's me.'

I knew that me. Shepherd. 'Hey, you. I thought you were in the air.'

'Delay. Some technical difficulties.'

'Boy that's reassuring,' I said.

'Tell me about it,' he growled. 'For some reason I wanted to let you know. It seemed important.'

'Because I'm that awesome?' I teased.

'Yes,' he said. His tone dead serious.

Flustered, I twisted my hair around my finger and sighed. 'You are awesome too.'

'I want to be home,' he said.

'To commence with the fucking?'

'Yes, but also because … I'm just being the pain in the ass overprotective person that I am. But just pay attention,' he said.

'To what?'

'Your surroundings. I have this bad feeling. Last time I got it, I told my mom and she laughed at me. She got mugged the following day.'

'Jeesh,' I said. A wave of unease threatened to drag me under. 'Thanks for that.'

'I know. I'm Mary fucking Sunshine. But can you just humour me?'

I wasn't about to tell him I had a similar feeling. 'Sure. No problem. When is your flight?'

'If they can pull their heads out of their asses and pull some spare parts out of their attics, maybe around lunch time. Which will put me home after my stopover around dinner or so.'

'OK,' I said.

He told me he missed me. I told him I missed him too. I almost told him to hurry but I didn't want to be a big dramatic girl about it. Instead I whispered, 'Be safe.'

'You too,' he commanded.

I hung up.

'I'll try.'

Chapter Thirty-two

MORE TIME TO BURN, so not what I needed. I changed into running clothes and laced up my shoes. I'd take a run, get rid of some of my tension and settle something in my mind.

I ran down the lake shore road. Thankful for no tourist traffic. The stretch along Main Street had been mobbed since the apple festival began, but I didn't see much change along the lake road.

Noises, possible vermin in my house, strange men at my window. There were three men in my life currently. One who was away. Two still in town. There were two others I'd left behind and one of those two I feared. I wasn't quite convinced this was just me freaking myself out.

My feet crunched and popped gravel and crushed shells as I ran to the picking fields and yelled 'Hey!' to the figure in the middle.

Reed looked up, his hair blowing around his face when the wind kicked up. He raised a gloved hand and dropped a handful of berries into a basket.

'Working your own farm?'

'I am. Just the end of the season stuff. Marilee out at the general store makes preserves with it. She sells them around the holidays and I get a 50 per cent split of the money. If I take it.'

'But you don't?'

'Hell, no. That pays her Christmas bills for her kids,' he said.

Good man.

I nodded and put my hand on my hips, bending at the waist, trying to catch my breath.

'How about some tea? Water?'

'I'll take the water,' I gasped.

I followed him in and waited while he washed his hands, then I took the offered glass. When it dribbled down my chin Reed chuckled and took his finger to sop it up. Then his finger, warm and clean and smelling of soap pressed my bottom lip and desire arched through me.

I had not promised Shepherd anything. And he hadn't asked. For all I knew he was out there in New York fucking every girl to bat her lashes at him.

'You have that look,' he said with a grin.

'What look is that?'

'The fuck me look.'

Heat rushed to my cheeks and I looked away from him. I wanted to be fucked. I just didn't know by who. Or was it whom? As if that mattered right now.

'Oh,' I said. Then I cleared my throat and barrelled on. 'You haven't been um … lurking around my house, have you?'

'Lurking?' His ocean coloured eyes sparkled with amusement and when he licked his lips that desire flared in me again. He had fabulous lips. Hot and sweet and plump. Good kisser, Mr Reed Green was.

'Maybe not lurking. You haven't been … screwing with me? Trying to scare me? You know, messing with me, Reed!' I laughed, suddenly feeling very, very stupid.

'Nope. The only time I screwed with you, babe, you were completely aware of it,' he said. He stepped into me, pressing his full lean length against me. When my heart sped up this time, it had nothing to do with the run.

His cock was hard.

My breath fled my body in a shuddering sigh and I said, 'OK, just checking. Thanks.'

'You still on the no fucking policy?'

His fingers walked over the front seam of my running pants and my clit thumped to life.

'Trying,' I breathed.

'So if I did this, you'd be averse to it?'

He kissed me, his tongue warm and gentle. His hand sliding

below the elastic waistband of my pants. I was already warm from the run, but his touch made me warmer. I felt my body respond almost violently, growing plump and swollen and wet for his fingers.

And then there they were. His fingers. Sliding down lower and entering me, inching in slowly to draw back out and press my own wetness to the nub of my clit. I gasped into his mouth and Reed took the opportunity to kiss me deeper.

He slid his fingers back into my cunt, flexing then hard and then driving them deep. The kiss grew more aggressive and he pressed his cock to my leg. I felt him fumble for his button and his zipper and then the whispery sound of his fist around his erection.

'I won't try to fuck you.' He murmured it against my throat, licking the cooling sweat off my pulse point. The pressure of his tongue – just on my skin – made me moan.

'No. No fucking,' I said, not even sure myself at this point.

I did not want to be exclusive. The thought scared the shit out of me. Me and exclusivity –commitment – did not mix. Our history was bad. And yet my heart seemed to have another opinion because even though I arched my body to meet his probing fingers, I didn't cave.

He rubbed his cock a bit harder and I reached out to get him in hand. I stroked him, feeling the silken steel length of his hard-on. 'Oh, she's touching me this time.'

'Shut up, Reed,' I said.

He chuckled, biting my shoulder gently through my sweatshirt. 'Beggars can't be choosers, babe.'

I grinned and kissed him, turning fast to pin him to the counter this time. My hand sliding up and down to work him, pausing only to run my thumb over the weeping tip of his cock.

'You have a little precome there, man,' I said, laughing.

He stuck his tongue deep in my mouth, sweeping it over mine and nipping the very tip of my tongue so I jumped. He brushed a tender bundle of nerves deep in my pussy just then and the first blissful flex-shiver of my orgasm flooded my pelvis .

'I don't know why. It's not like you turn me on or

anything,' he growled. Reed wrapped his free hand in my hair and I pictured Shepherd using my braids to guide me as I sucked his cock.

Reed tugged a bit tighter as my cunt flexed around his fingers and I started the long slow unravel of a climax. 'Oh,' I said as he tugged again.

But it was more due to me imagining Shepherd fucking me from behind. Pulling my hair. Whispering dirty, dirty words to me as he did me hard.

I came with a rush and a sigh and as my pussy worked around his fingers he gave an almost tortured groan and came with me. His come jetting out over the top of my fist, across my sweatshirt. The salt water smell of it heavy in my nose.

We paused, eye to eye and he grinned at me. 'You make me feel like a teenager. As just evidenced.'

'I know the feeling,' I said. He pulled his hand free of me and then of my pants and Reed said, 'You sure I can't make you that tea?'

I shook my head no. 'You sure you're not messing with me just to be funny or anything?'

He nodded, blue eyes suddenly honest and sombre. 'I'd never do that, Tuesday. Especially if I knew it spooked you. I'd cop to that for sure to put your mind at ease. Do you need me to come stay there until your ...' He cleared his throat, frowning. 'Neighbour comes back.'

I barked out a laugh and kissed his nose. 'No. I'm fine. I don't need a babysitter. I just wanted to double check with you.'

Before things could get any more sticky between us – so to speak – I gave him a wave and ran out the door.

I took off at a good clip for home. The apple festival was calling me. I'd go and walk around and eat and see what there was to see. It would distract me and let me soak up my new home's environment. And it would give me time to think.

Something I felt I desperately needed.

Not a lot of people look like me in Allister Lake. Most of the women wear jeans and riding boots. Big wool sweaters that have been made by other local women. They have long corn silk coloured hair or hair the colour of warm rich cocoa. They wear just enough make-up to accent but not enough for you to be able to tell for certain they're wearing it.

Basically, I stick out.

But no one said a word and a good number of the locals I recognised nodded or raised a hand in greeting.

'Ah, so you came out to see what there is to see.'

I turned to find Irv in a fishing cap and a chequered barn coat. The wind was biting today, the air chilled. It wasn't cold-cold yet, but it was definitely fall and the nip in the air was the perfect atmosphere for the gathering.

'I did. I'm almost out of good home baked treats in my freezer,' I said. We stepped out of the path of the main traffic and under an apple tree heavy with fruit and buzzing softly – if you listened – with lazy bees.

'You bake?'

'I fake,' I laughed.

'Written that great American novel yet?'

I rolled my eyes. 'Hardly.'

'You know, Virginia always told me that your biggest obstacle is yourself?'

'Me?' I was shocked. Had my grandmother really thought that of me?

'Yes, you. She said your fear that you couldn't was the only thing stopping you.'

He raised an old-man bushy eyebrow at me. 'Wow.' I'd had no idea she felt that way.

'Yes, wow. So enjoy our festival and your two days off. I plan to work you like a dog when you get back. You're turning out to be a fine addition to Irv's.'

'Thanks, Irv,' I said and impulsively kissed his cheek. Whether it was for the compliment or the unknown information about Nan, I didn't know.

'Now I have to go buy six pies for the dinner rush. Maryellen Erickson makes the best and only does it once a year for the festival. Beyond that you have to be in her good graces and get one as a holiday gift. If you're lucky ... for your birthday.'

'I'll keep that in mind,' I said. 'Might need to buy a few myself and tuck them in Nan's magical freezer.'

'Your magical freezer,' he said. 'You need to think of that house as yours now. It's how Virginia would have wanted it.' As I turned to wander off he said, 'Oh and Tuesday?'

I paused and turned back to him. My stomach growled at the smell of fried dough and some sort of spice in the air. 'Yeah?'

'When the estate is settled you won't have to fret so much. I think if you keep working with me to keep active you'll be A-OK to take life a bit slow and write that novel. Your grandmother said it was in you and if there's one thing I learned in all my years of knowing Virginia, it was to trust her instincts. She could pick a winner from a mile away. And she thought the world of you.'

I smiled at him and turned away before he could see me cry.

I bought three pies, a sweater, a handmade leather bookmark and some second hand books. Storing my loot in the Grenada seemed like a plan. I shoved it all in the trunk and decided I also needed some apple preserves and maybe some of the wool socks I'd passed about six times. I had a hard-on for wool socks. Socks were my Achilles heel so to speak.

When I re-entered the throng of festival goers, someone knocked into me. Hard. Difficult to imagine someone hitting you that hard by accident.

In the clamour of voices I was fairly certain I heard a guttural "slut" and it put my hackles up.

Spinning in a circle but trying to avoid innocents, I saw nothing. A broad back retreating could have been familiar, but I'd been in town long enough that I recognised people now. Was it familiar from the past or the present?

My body speckled with goosebumps that had zero to do with the chill wind.

'You OK?' a woman asked me. I knew her face from the diner. 'Diana,' she said, patting my arm. 'Diana Palmer. You've waited on us at Irv's.'

I smiled. I nodded. And yet I remained mute.

'I could see you trying to place me. Are you OK? You look a little … freaked.'

'I am freaked.' I laughed wildly and felt stupid for it. My nerves were jangling. 'I'm sorry. Someone just really banged into me and I guess it rattled me, is all.'

'Oh no. You have your wallet right? Because my dad was a police officer and he said that the first thing a pick pocket does is bang into you …'

I patted my purse, popped it open. My wallet was there and when I cracked it open so was my money. 'It's fine,' I said. 'I guess it was just a mistake. I'm probably just on edge.'

'Anything I can do, honey?'

I shook my head. 'No thanks Diana. Thank you, but I'm probably just overreacting.'

'A busy time with your grandmother passing and all. Hard stuff.'

I nodded. 'Yes. Hard stuff. Thank you.'

I was officially done with the apple festival. The voice and the tone and the hard hit made me ache for home. I'd go home, eat some pie and wait for Shepherd there.

Chapter Thirty-three

MY DOOR WAS OPEN. What the fuck?

Another storm was kicking up. The air had the same electric quality as it had the night before Shepherd left. The hairs along my scalp – the tiny fine ones that were invisible unless you felt them as opposed to saw them – were all at attention.

I glanced to the barn and dug for my always-missing cell phone in my bag.

DID YOU LEAVE MY DOOR OPEN?

I texted Adrian and waited, stomping my feet on the front steps, for him to answer. It didn't take him long, the phone jingled in my hand and I read: NOPE. WHY?

'It must have been me. It must have been.'

I stood inside the front door for a moment and waited. Nothing. Plus, didn't it stand to reason that if someone at the festival had malicious intent toward me, they couldn't be here too. Right?

'Hello?' I called out. I tried to keep my voice bold and loud. But it wasn't lost on me that I was doing the typical horror movie heroine dealio where I called out to the villain as if he'd pop up and say, "Oh, hi there"!

Holding my breath, I listened for any noise in the basement. Any indication that someone was down there, or even a critter as Adrian suspected.

Not a sound. Well, nothing but the thundering pound of my own pulse in my ears. I rushed forward, nearly diving across the floor. The bat was stashed under the sofa. I don't know why I put it there, but I had. My hand found the smooth wood that had been my protector more than once and I tugged it free.

Still nothing. No noises.

It seemed a good idea to spin in a slow circle. I'd become convinced that someone had entered behind me and was waiting to grab me up, but no one was there.

'Of course,' I hissed.

Right about now I could have gone for a gun. Or a harpoon. Or a rocket launder. I rushed through the great room, checking any nooks and crannies – which were few and far between. The small, cosy kitchen was bare. Even the pantry was empty of bad guys when I tossed the door back ready to attack. A box of tea bags slid off the shelf, spraying small white packets all along the floor at my feet. That was the most excitement the kitchen offered. I hurried on, leaving the mess for later.

The office space was bare as Nan had left it. One chair, one standing lamp, one roll-top desk with a computer on it. A closet with an accordion door that stood open baring its bookshelves full of books and papers and bins that Nan had neatly arranged.

The woman had owned two basketfuls of clothes she wore. They were all up in her room. This had been her "paperwork hub" as she'd put it and she'd cleverly used this closet as a filing cabinet of sorts. To the right were fat colourful bundles of holiday wrapping paper. The shelf overhead stored gift bags, old books, and various other day-to-day stuff in big round wicker baskets.

No intruder.

I took the steps two at a time, my boots frantic on the steps. Upstairs, my bed was a rumpled mess. The closet door was open. One of my duffles tossed on the closet floor among Nan's neatly arranged shoes. Her clothes still hung from the rod and her neat purses and tote bags still marched across the top shelf overhead. Her big leather bag, her red leather satchel, her straw beach bag, her "market" purse made of canvas that had seen better days. A gardening bonnet, a funeral hat, a cowboy hat that had been my grandfather's.

No one hiding in my room.

Bathroom empty.

Storage room a wreck but as I poked around with the tip of the Louisville Slugger, nada. No one. There was a trunk and stuff that appeared to be mail-order items she planned to give for Christmas. I found a black sweater that was peppered with teeny tiny skulls that appeared on first glance to be polka dots.

'Gee,' I paused. 'I wonder who this was for, Nan?'

The sound of my own voice spooked me. All that remained to be checked was the basement.

I went back down the steps on tiptoe. I didn't want to announce my failure and my return. When I rounded the corner, my eyes registered a broad back, wide shoulders, a bent head. In the kitchen.

Fed up, adrenaline flooded and ready to kill someone, I gave a big yell and rushed the guy. Who the fuck was he to be in my new house? Who the fuck was he to scare me when I was just getting used to my new life?

He turned fast but it felt like slow motion. The profile came into view as the big body stood and he turned. Even as my brain screamed *ShepherdShepherdShepherd!* my body refused to slow down.

I jabbed him near the solar plexus with the business end of the bat and when he flinched and reached for it – even as my mind was screaming for me to stop – I cocked the bat to hit him properly. The blow was glancing – too slow and low – and part of that deceleration, thankfully, was the start of my mind overriding my body.

When I made another sweep, wondering in some surreal way why I was still moving –Shepherd reached for and caught the bat. He grunted, flinched when I fought him and then my ears picked up his words.

'Tuesday, Tuesday … it's OK, Tuesday. It's me. It's OK, kiddo. Hey …' A running monologue of calming words.

'Oh, fuck!' I hiccupped. The fear had bubbled over into stunned shock and I dropped the bat. Only he was holding the broad end so it didn't hit the floor. Shepherd laid it gently on the counter and caught my upper arms in his big hands.

'Oh, shit,' I sighed and I started to shake.

'Are you OK?' He bent his knees just enough for us to be eye to eye.

'Are you OK?' I yelled and then laughed like a hyena due to

my shredded nerves. Sexy.

'I'm fine. I just want to know what's got you so worked up you're coming at people with that bat of yours.'

That bat of yours … I snickered. My history and reputation with the bat was really starting to stick, wasn't it? But … good. Better to be known as an ass kicker than a cry baby.

'Someone …' I shook my head.

'Someone what? Broke in?' I felt his body tense so close to mine and I shook my head again.

'No, no. Someone's been around here. I think. I feel. I mean I saw someone one time but I don't know who it was. It could have been anyone, someone lost, a kid. I thought it might be Reed or Adrian. I thought … I don't know.'

I shook my head repeatedly and wondered if I'd shake my damn brains up too much.

His lips were tight and he kicked the tea bags out of his way. 'Come on. Come home with me and then I'll come check around here proper.'

'And there could be a raccoon,' I added mildly. 'And my car is full of apple crap.'

He stared at me. 'Apple crap?' He was trying not to smile.

'Pies, preserves, sweaters, a bookmark. And someone at the apple festival called me a slut and almost knocked me down and …' I blew out a mighty sigh and ran a hand through my hair before realising I'd braided it and had to untangle my fingers and rings.

'Come on. Come home, have a glass of wine and slow down so we can figure this out.'

I nodded. 'Fine. But I want my pies.'

'Sweetheart,' he said, wrapping his arm around my neck, tugging me in and kissing the top of my head. 'I want your pies.'

I turned to leave. I wanted out of the house for the moment. Shepherd called me. 'Tues?'

'Yeah?' I looked over my shoulder to see him offering me the bat. 'Don't forget Old Faithful.'

I rolled my eyes and snorted at him but put my hand out and took the bat. 'Shows how much you know. His name is Louis.'

Shepherd followed me out and we solved the apple crap issue by driving the Grenada the few hundred feet to his house.

We spread the apple fair loot out in the kitchen and Shepherd found a bottle of wine and glasses. 'Now tell me what the hell is going on.'

I took the wine, sipped it. 'After,' I said.

'After what?'

I put the glass down and walked into him. Fast and hard, we collided and my fingers wound into his beard, my body pressing to his so I could feel his heat.

'After you fuck me,' I said, between kisses.

'I'm worried—'

'I'm worried you're going to argue.' Pushing my pelvis to his, I felt the heated line of his erection. His belly pressed my belly, his heart beating so fast its cadence tapped against my breast.

He pulled back, holding my face in his hands. His dark-dark eyes studied mine and finally he growled, tossed me over his shoulder and turned.

'Are the doors locked?' I gasped as he took the steps two at a time.

'See, you are worried.'

'Only mildly worried,' I corrected.

'They're locked. Don't worry. And if anyone comes within a foot of you they'll have to go through me.'

He dropped me on the bed and slid to his knees. Pulling, twisting, yanking at my jeans until he had them down around my knees. He pressed his face between my legs, nudging me with his tongue, his beard an added sensation against my skin.

'I had dreams about eating your pussy while I was gone.' His words were muffled by my inner thigh, but then his tongue found my slick hole and he thrust it inside of me. And then his words didn't matter a lick.

I laughed, though. I thought he was kidding.

'I'm dead serious,' he said and when he sucked my clit and then soothed the swollen bit of flesh with his flattened tongue I came. So full of adrenaline and having missed him and all that stuff. I came and he muttered, 'Good,' and flipped me on my belly.

Chapter Thirty-four

'YES, GOOD,' I SAID. 'Good, good.'

He paused. I knew what for. 'Go,' I said. 'Do it. We're good.' Then I chuckled at our copious amount of goods.

Shepherd ran his stiff cock along the length of my wet opening. I kept moving back to meet him, wanting him so bad to enter me but he didn't. He was teasing me. Slipping the smooth hot head of his cock into me and then moving back to simply tease the edges of my cunt with my own moisture.

'Jesus, God, please,' I said and moved back a hair to force his hand.

I should have known better. The feel of him disappeared entirely until he was brushing the arch of each bottom cheek with my own wetness. Painting me with the head of his erection and laughing softly.

'How much adrenaline would you say is in you now?' he asked conversationally.

'A gallon.'

'I agree.' A blow landed and I hissed but the bubbling melting pleasure that spread along my skin and spasmed through my sex was pure bliss.

'I am turning inside out,' I admitted, shamelessly pressing up to where his hand hovered without touching me.

'Don't do that.' Another blow. Hard and fast and perfectly placed so I was ready to come just from the burst of pleasure-pain.

'I know. I know. Please, Shepherd.' I was begging and that was OK with me at the moment. I'd say anything if he'd just fuck me. And keep hurting me just enough.

'You hit me with a bat,' he said and three blows rained

down.

I hung my head, moaned low. 'I know.'

'Even after you saw my face.' Three more blows.

A tear slipped free of me but my cunt was so swollen, so ready, my entire body throbbed with my heartbeat.

'I was too … amped up.'

One … two … three. He shoved his thumb in my ass and then the head of his cock was pressing, pressing, pressing into me so fast. I was so wet. So, so fucking wet.

We both made a sound like people being saved and then Shepherd gripped me up tight in his free hand and fucked me long and easy until I started to come.

I moved back to meet him, toes curling, fingers gripping the bedding so tight my knuckles turned white. 'I'm going to come. I am. I'm going to–'

I came and Shepherd waited for that final spasm before pulling free. His thumb was still in my back hole and I knew what he was doing.

'Tell me not to.'

I couldn't. The feel of him there was staggering and a bit scary and I wanted more of it. I said nothing.

He slipped a finger and then another into my still tender cunt and flexed those fingers, tickling another small spasm out of me. Then he slid those fingers into my ass, using my own slick juices as lubricant.

'Tell me not to, Tuesday,' he said again and positioned the head of his cock to my asshole.

I held my breath, my heart pounding in my ears, my body wanting this so bad I didn't have a rational thought left in my head. I said nothing.

And then he was inching into me. Slowly. Three thick fingers pushing into my pussy even as his cock slid lazily into my ass.

I could feel his fingers sliding against his cock with just my pink flesh between pussy and ass as the barrier. The thought alone stole my breath. I was full of him. Entirely full of Shepherd Moore and it was perfect.

'Have you ever done this before, Tuesday?' he asked me

softly, rocking into me with an almost indifferent rhythm. But I could tell by his breathing, by the thickness of his voice that he was far from indifferent. He was on the edge.

'No,' I whispered. I pushed my forehead to his bedding. It smelled like him. The thick scent of leather and cold air and man.

'I'm your first?'

'Yes,' I said. My voice had drawn down to nothing but a barely there breathy exhalation.

'Do you like me in your ass?'

'Yes.'

'Say it.'

His big hands slid over the arc of my ass cheeks. He palmed them softly and the skin he had just spanked responded with a tingling pleasure to his now soothing touch.

'I like you in my ass.'

'Do you want me to come?'

His fingers shoved back into my cunt – deeper this time – and he teased my G-spot while thrusting deep into my ass. 'Yes,' I sobbed. My whole body was only aware of one thing. His presence inside of me.

'Are you going to come?'

'Maybe.' I moved back to take him and this time he made the deep desperate noise in his chest.

'If I let you touch yourself will you come?'

I could hear the tension in his tone. He was trying so damn hard to sound in control and I almost smiled. But then he drove into me forcefully and stole that chuckle right out of my chest.

'Yes. I think.'

'Then do it,' he said and began to move smoothly in and out of me. His fingers mimicking his cock.

When I added my own trembling fingers on my clit to the fray I came with a low moan and Shepherd drove into me once, twice, thrice and came. My pulse flickered under my skin like silverfish in shallow water – fast and skittish but sure.

We stayed that way for a moment when he stopped emptying into me. Me bent in submission before him. His hands now splayed along my lower back. My face pressed to the mattress.

I realised I wanted to say something to him. I wanted to tell him I loved him. The urge was just as strong in me as the urge to fuck him had been.

Instead I said, 'Let me up.'

He let me up but hooked an arm around me as I turned from him. He pulled me back and kissed me, simply saying, 'Don't run from me.'

I eyed him. Wanting to do just that. But when I took a breath to still my fear I said, 'I won't.'

We ate one of the pies standing at his kitchen island. Wine with homemade country apple pie heavy on the cinnamon. Yum. My hair was still damp from the quick shower we'd taken but I'd braided it loosely to keep it at bay.

'So this person at the fair?' Shepherd prompted.

'Slammed into me. Hard. I mean, almost knocked me off my feet kind of hard. And called me a slut. Which doesn't really bother me. Sticks and stones and all that shit. But the hit was so unexpected and that …' I shrugged.

'Rattled you.'

'Exactly.'

'Then what did you do?'

'I came home.'

'Hunh,' he said.

'Hunh? What does hunh mean?'

'I'm just wondering if perhaps the person who bumped you and all that was herding you out of the fair.'

'What does that mean?'

'That they wanted you to run home.'

'If they called me a slut because they've been watching me since I got here and–' I broke off, not wanting to get into the whole Shepherd-Reed-Adrian triangle.

He held up a hand. 'I know I didn't ask anything of you, so I don't want to know. But just for the record …' He popped the last bite of the pie in his mouth and I shrieked with faux rage.

But then I swallowed hard. 'What?'

'I'm getting there. Getting close to asking something of

you. So you keep that in mind, OK?'

'OK,' I said.

Then he leaned against me, kissed me and said 'I'm going to go check your house out.'

'I'm coming with you.'

He eyed me, trying really hard not to smile. 'Why didn't you let one of your other knights in shining armour help you while I was gone?'

'They asked,' I said, rubbing my neck hard to loosen some tension. 'But I told them I didn't need them.'

'You let me help you,' he reminded me.

'I ...' Tilting my head back I blew a big breath out toward the ceiling. 'I guess I need you.'

Shepherd grinned – it was a very victorious grin – and then he patted my ass. 'Sweetheart, watching you with that bat, you don't need anyone. Not physically. But I'm glad your heart is starting to think it might need me. Maybe, possibly ...' he teased, jostling against me with more playfulness than I'd ever seen from him.

He seemed downright happy.

Which made me happy. And terrified.

'Maybe,' I said, sticking my tongue out at him.

'Careful. When you put it out like that, I want to put it to good use.'

'Possibly later,' I said and grabbed the Louisville Slugger from his hand.

Chapter Thirty-five

'SEE, HE SHOULD HAVE known it wasn't a raccoon. They don't jimmy basement windows.' Shepherd pointed to the old painted window frame that had been messed with. Even the ancient, faded white paint was splintered in places. 'Good thing you kept your top basement door locked. Whoever was down here could have waltzed right up there otherwise. As it stands, he used this to get out when he wanted to.' Shepherd kicked a stack of old but sturdy orange crates.

I wanted to shiver but repressed it. Freaking out wasn't going to do a damn thing. And I'd already assaulted an innocent man once.

'You don't think it's Adrian do you?' I asked quietly.

'I doubt it. He's a douche bag but not dangerous. He's just ...' Shepherd shrugged. 'Clingy? I mean, from what I've seen. He's a guy who needs–'

'Stroking,' I said.

Shepherd chuckled. 'Exactly.'

'I don't see former TV star Reed hanging out in the basement.'

'Not when he can woo you with money and wine and fine fast cars and all the berries you can pick.' His mouth was tight again. Every time he talked of Reed. But I reminded myself I'd promised him nothing and had done nothing wrong. It was the going forward that counted.

'So that leaves?'

'A local whacko? Someone from your past?'

Now I did shiver. 'Maybe an ex someone who's met my bat?'

'Maybe. Any idea where that charmer is?'

'Annie – the woman who owns the boarding house I lived at – she said she has no idea where Phil or Stan are.'

'Phil or Stan?'

'Phil's the ex and Stan's the guy I dated right before I moved.' I shrugged. 'The …' I trailed off.

'The rebound guy?'

'Yeah, for lack of a better word.'

We walked around the basement. It was pretty bare and pretty dusty and damp along the foundation in some spots. 'The beauty of lakefront property,' Shepherd sighed, toeing the stains. 'Seepage.'

'I can live with it. Looks like not much goes on down here but storage and intruders,' I snorted.

He pulled me close so fast I let out a yelp. His arms were big and warm and strong and I let myself feel soothed for a moment. 'Don't make fun. It makes my blood boil to even think about someone being in this damn basement when I was gone.'

He steered me toward the steps and I followed his lead.

'Is Nan's potting shed haunted?' I asked as we headed up the steps. They were horror movie steps. The kind that had treads but were open at the back. Perfect for a malicious hand to reach through and grab your ankle. Perfect to fall to the bottom, break your neck and die.

So I'd spooked myself. I sped up enough to almost run right into Shepherd's back.

'You OK?'

'Fine. Fine. I'm just a little freaked out.'

'No shit. You're staying with me until we have this worked out.'

We went to the front door and Shepherd pulled it open and looked at the potting shed. 'That potting shed?'

'It's the only one.'

He grinned. He barrelled down my front steps and grabbed the potting shed door handle. It was locked. Just like last time.

'May I?' Shepherd indicated the meagre hasp and lock and I shrugged.

I gave him the bat and he whacked the coupling. It fell away taking the padlock with it. All of Nan's fancy stuff – her painted pots, some bags of soil, old yellow gardening clogs. Her gorgeous gardening tools she kept spotless for her spring plantings lined the shelf and the counter space. They always looked like they should be decorating a brightly painted wall instead of working in a garden. She painted all the handles bright colours and often would sit and paint flowers or butterflies on them too.

'She liked prettiness for its own sake, Virginia did,' Shepherd laughed, picking up a small spade dotted with what looked like Black Eyed Susans.

'True story.' I couldn't look at any of it too long. It made me want to cry.

We turned and looked out the high windows above the door. Through smudged glass an upper window was visible. 'What's that?'

'My room,' I said, my mouth going dry.

'You walk around up there with the lights on?' He stepped back some to examine the view.

'Well, I do prefer walking around with lights on as opposed to stumbling around in the dark.'

'Smart ass,' he said and patted me on mine.

'Better than being a dumb–'

'Ass. Yeah, yeah. Let's see.'

The potting shed wasn't huge but it was big enough. Shepherd took three more big steps back until his back hit the potting shed's long wooden counter. 'Yep, perfect view of you, my love.'

My body rippled at the words, "my love".

'So how did he get in a locked potting shed? These windows are sealed on.'

Shepherd squatted tapped a few of the windows. 'These are fragile and the panes are stacked one atop the other. If one of them broke a bunch would and ...' He bent over and then squatted down. His knees popped like shotguns. I wanted to ask if that was from being an ultimate fighter.

'Ah, here we go.'

'Here we go what?'

'There's a section back here that was patched. Probably someone hit the wood with a tiller or lawnmower or something. Or even a car. Possibly wildlife chewed their way in for bird seed or something. Anyway, it's big enough that perhaps a person even my size could wriggle through there if he was desperate.'

'Can't be Adrian. He could just unlock the fucking thing.'

I turned in a slow circle. Dusk was starting to fall and now I felt exposed. Someone had been watching. Sneaking about at the lake – following me if the slut remark was to be believed. Either a local creep who I didn't know, or my worst nightmare – a creep I did. Phil.

'It's not Adrian, and that's why you're going to go pack a bag. You need a fucking dog,' he grunted as we left.

I had to laugh.

'What's so funny?'

'I was thinking about that when you were gone. A shepherd.'

'Nice,' he said and put his arm around me. The barn was dark. Adrian's car gone.

'Named Tiny,' I snorted and then started to giggle. The giggling was good. A pressure release for my pent up anxiety and the worry that now the psycho from my past was back.

Phil had been a good man until life had beaten him down and he'd sought comfort in the arms of alcohol instead of mine. Then it had been a nightmare. He was an all or nothing man. Good when sober. The devil when drunk. After he lost his job, he preferred the devil.

'That is completely unfunny,' Shepherd said, but I felt his big body vibrate just a bit as he suppressed a laugh. 'Tiny ...' He shook his head.

'Come on. I chose a shepherd just for you.'

He stopped on the doorstep of my house. 'Would you choose me just for me?'

I swallowed hard. 'I think if I were at a place where I could feel that way, I would. Life didn't just beat me down, Shepherd. It beat me down, rolled me up in a rug, ran me over and dropped me in a river.'

'Because of one man who didn't know how to keep his hands to himself?'

'Nah. Parents … dead. Man … turns bad. Nan, light of my life … dead. It's just been building.'

'Well, you know I learned something a long time ago.'

'What's that?'

'Never give up. Even if both your eyes are full of blood and you're pretty sure you lost a tooth.' He tapped his canine and said 'Cap.'

'And what else?' I asked, smiling at him. I touched his face, grateful he was here.

'And when you see something you want grab it. Don't wait.'

He hugged me to him fiercely. I allowed myself to press my body to his. The heat of him was blissful. The memory of him entering me the way he had, in a place no one else had been, made my whole body flash hot.

'So, I'm grabbing you, Tuesday Cane. All you have to do is grab me back.'

Chapter Thirty-six

'OH, PACK THESE FOR sure,' he said, dangling a pair of neon green and black striped over-the-knee socks at me.

'You like those, do you?'

'You in these and nothing else? Hell, yeah.' He leered at me and waggled his eyebrows.

'Perv.'

'You know it.'

I tossed them in my duffle. I carefully folded and tossed his hoodie in, too. 'You know you're not getting it back, right?'

'How about the smell. Won't it fade?' He winked at me.

'OK, you can have it back once a week to wear and smellify and then it's mine again.'

'Smellify?'

'Made a word up for ya, there.'

He palmed the back of my head and guided me in gently. His mouth was soft at first but then intense. His tongue stroked over mine. How about you in that jacket and those socks, just for me? Bent over, opened for me. Taking my cock hard and deep and–'

I pushed a finger to his lips. 'Stop or we're doing it right here. And I want out of here until this whole silent stalker Nancy Drew mystery is solved.'

'Hurry up and pack then,' he growled.

'Help me.'

When he turned from me and I caught his profile, I felt a rush of affection and lust and something more. Something I pushed back and away and out of me.

Not ready. Not ready …

I put a toiletry bag in my duffle even though I knew I'd be

stealing his stuff so I could capture his scent.

When I grabbed my things and followed him downstairs I called, 'See, I ask you to pack and you go and run awa–'

My words broke off because he was sitting on the sofa, the sofa where I'd been sleeping (nesting like a raccoon, really), with all my writing stuff stacked in his lap. Shepherd's eyes skimmed the pages of the notebook where I had been working long hand on my short story.

'I see why she bragged about you,' he said to me without looking up.

I cleared my throat, at some point a huge gob of something had become wedged in it. Emotions, I think. 'Yeah, well, she was a bragger no matter what. Deserved or not.'

I came down the final few steps and suppressed the urge to race over and snatch the book from him. It was embarrassing, someone reading your words when you didn't expect it. The emotional equivalent of showing up at a swanky dinner party in your underpants.

'The praise is deserved,' he said and turned a page.

'Hey!' I said a bit too brightly. 'It's bad luck to read a writer's work before it's done.'

Total lie.

'How about you wait until I finish?' I said and held my hand out to him. Praying he wouldn't balk. Praying he would humour me.

He smiled and shut the book. Placing it in my hand, Shepherd stood and gathered all the other writing debris he could find. 'When you asked me to help you pack, I figured I'd know how important this stuff was even if you didn't.'

We heard a noise and both of us froze. It was dark now and the noise had come from the kitchen door. Where I'd seen my phantom shadow man peering in the mottled glass.

My neck spiked with goosebumps and Shepherd turned very slowly toward the sound. Then he took off at a run still clutching my notebooks.

Damn!

'Motherfucker,' he hissed when I almost slammed into his broad back. Out on my deck, he stood watching the thick trees that bordered the lake. 'Someone was here but he took off before I could catch up. I heard him go down the steps. Fell in that bush over there,' Shepherd pointed. 'I guess he didn't see it. But he was fast enough to get away. And I'm stupid but not fatally stupid. I'm not ploughing through those trees in the dark.'

'For all you know he has a gun,' I said, grateful that Shepherd was a manly man but a smart man. Now I wouldn't have to chase him through the woods worried he'd get hurt.

'Right. Let's get your shit and go.'

He locked my back door and chained it. After a spot check of all the other windows and the door that led to the basement, we left by the front door, locking it behind us. Carrying my bags, we trudged across the expanse of open space to his house.

'Gotta say, I feel super exposed,' I said softly. My voice was barely audible above the crack and pop of our boots on the gravel.

'I agree. But I don't think he has a gun. I think he has a thing for you. And for right now the spying is working for him. Now that I'm back and I'm relocating you ... well, now I'm not so sure.'

'You think it'll make him violent?'

Shepherd shrugged, my duffle rising and falling with the motion of his wide shoulders. 'Don't know. But I want you with me if there's any chance of that.'

I tapped my bat on the ground as we walked. He laughed softly. 'What?' I asked as we neared his house. A house had never looked more welcoming to me.

'Remind me not to piss you off,' he said nodding toward my weapon of choice. Then he put his arm around me.

'Who do you think it is?' My voice was way too meek for my liking. I poured us each a glass of a red from a local winery and took a shaky sip.

'No idea. Whoever he is, I'm gonna beat his ass if I catch him.'

'Not if I catch him first.'

Shepherd swigged down half of his wine and said, 'No doubt.' He set his glass down and took mine.

I let him wrap me in his arms. I let him tuck my head to his chest so I could feel his heart. I didn't like to feel need for someone besides maybe Nan but here I caught a fast and flickery dance of that need inside my belly. It wasn't a need for sex. It was a need for a specific person.

And it scared the shit out of me.

'So one girl who fell out of love with you can't be why you were all monk-like when I showed up. But for the fucking.'

He chuckled.

'You don't seem the sort to let just one instance get you down. Not for good.'

He let out a long, slow breath and I held mine – waiting.

'I was in love once upon a time – before her. Before that girl, before the UFC stuff. I think that's why I went into it. I was big, I had rage and it was a legal way to let it out. Even earn some money from my anger.'

My hair brushed his pale blue tee as I nodded against his chest. But I didn't speak. I thought it might break the spell of him confessing this bit of himself to me.

'And I went to pick a ring for that long ago girl. There are not a lot of places around here as you can imagine. I travelled to neighbouring towns and I finally found the perfect antique gold settling. She loved old things.'

I held my breath. I listened to the thump of his heart. I smelled the cotton-salt-leather smell of him and my own heart thumped in sympathy.

'Anyway, I bought it. I asked her. We were going to be in love and married and have babies and all that bullshit.

Silence.

I didn't think it was all bullshit, but I sure knew it could feel that way should your heart get mangled badly enough. Should you get stomped on and hurt.

'And she said no. She had actually picked the same night to tell me that she'd fallen in love with an older guy. Forty to my twenty-four. She walked away from me. But what can I say … she'd warned me.'

I looked up at him then, realising my eyes were stinging with unshed tears. So two women had walked away from his love when he offered it. Part of me realised he probably had love to offer me. That was mostly what he'd been saying to me without actually saying it. But I was sending signals that I couldn't deal with it. That I would push him away.

Jesus. What a train wreck we were.

'Warned you about what?' I prompted.

'That she loved old things.'

I stared at him then started to laugh. 'Oh, punch line. At least you can work that into your story to lighten the mood, am I right?'

He grinned down at me, his finger sliding below the waistband of my jeans. Making me gasp a little and wriggle to get my skin closer to his skin.

'Hey, you have to find laughter where you can.'

'True.'

'And you never pass up an opportunity to touch a beautiful woman,' he said. His hand worked lower and he turned it so his fingers pressed right above where my clit throbbed merrily waiting for him to stroke it.

'Also true,' I breathed.

'I think we need to do something, you and I.'

'What's that?' I found him hard under my hand when I touched his jeans. I thought of how he'd taken me just hours before. I thought of giving myself to him in a way I'd never given myself to any other man.

How much trust had that required?

A ton.

And I had given him that part of myself without questioning it once.

It took some effort but I slid my hand down into the front of his jeans to find him hot and stiff and soft as sin in my hand. I slid my fingertip along the slit of skin on the head of his cock and felt the dot of precome spread over him.

'We need to recreate a kitchen scene. I need to claim that back in my mental terrain. When I think of kitchens, I want to think of me and you. Not you and Reed.'

My heart fluttered. It sounds stupid, but it did just that. It jumped like some tiny animal in my chest and my pussy grew slick and warm. I pressed my knees together but it only made the urgency in my cunt worse.

'Oh,' I said. Because I didn't know what else to say.

He gripped my shoulders tight and kissed me. When his hands moved to hold my head so he could deepen the kiss and thrust his tongue against mine, the breath fled my lungs. I moved against him, trapped in some sinuous dance that only came from one source. Arousal.

God, how badly I wanted him. Again. It never seemed to end – my lust for this man. It was maddening and insane and entirely comforting.

He dropped to his knees, stealing the warmth of his body from under my hand. I made a low desperate sound and watched him peel back my jeans with big blunt fingers. His mouth crushed down – lips only, so surreally soft – on the sensitive skin just above my mound. My pussy took up the steady beat of my heart and a small rush of fluid escaped me. By the time he got my jeans and panties down over my hips, I could feel the wetness at the very tops of my thighs.

My breath rushed out of me and he kissed my mound firmly so I felt his energy all along my skin. The fine hairs on my body prickled with it. My pulse slammed with it. My cunt flexed with it.

'Please,' I said. Feeling foolish but totally OK with it. 'I might actually die if you don't–'

But I didn't get to finish the sentiment because he seared me with his open mouth. His tongue and teeth and lips pressing over my clit – surrounding it with his heat. And when he sucked the swollen bit of flesh into his mouth, my knees did dip a bit but he steadied me with strong hands cupping my ass cheeks.

'Stay still,' he murmured and suckled at my clitoris again. He drew it in hard and then soothed it with his tongue. The rigid tip of that talented tongue teased me until more of my juices sluiced from my eager cunt. I gripped his shoulders, holding on like I was drowning, holding on like I would fall.

But utterly willing to fall if need be. Because I was falling for him.

I let the thought go when he nibbled each of my outer lips – plump and swollen – and then drove his tongue back into my folds to find the little hard organ. He bit me there gently, just hard enough for the sharpness to register and then burrowing two thick fingers into my cunt, he got me off.

And off I went like a shot. My knees sagging and Shepherd holding me up with only his free hand.

'I … you need …' I was tongue tied. A minor miracle for the likes of me.

He shook his head and shushed me and pulled me down to my knees. His mouth had the rich humid musk of my sex and he pushed his tongue to my lower lip and swept it back and forth so my own scent filled my head.

'Take your pants off,' he rasped.

I tried to get them free of my body with hands that were shaking terribly. Finally, I dropped to my ass and he helped me by yanking then off by the leg cuffs. With one big hand splayed between my breasts, he pushed me back so I was supine, my braids tickling the edge of my jaw.

I unzipped my sweater and he filleted it open to reveal my bra and my breasts and my quivering stomach.

'Leave it on. It's cold in here,' he said, suckling my nipples through the sheer mesh of my bra. Each halo of pink flesh stood at attention as if seeking his mouth, his tongue, his teeth.

He tugged one rosy disc and then the other, his fingers painting invisible patterns on my stomach. I shook with the sensation and when he pressed a thumb to the very centre of me, I drew in a shuddering breath.

'Fuck me,' I said.

'I will.'

'Take me,' I said, my voice a ghost of its normal boldness.

'I plan on it.'

'Use me.' I was almost crying and I didn't know why and I wasn't going to question it. For once, since the whole disaster of my life had unfolded, I was going to just go with the visceral feelings that pounded through my veins. Thick and syrupy, sweet and terrifying, gorgeous and transformative. I would just shut up my own chatter and give in.

He grunted, pushing my thighs apart so that I was spread wide for his examination.

'In the best possible way,' he said as an answer. 'I'll use you.'

His cock was flushed and thick, and in his hand almost resembled a weapon. We had passed the point of niceties and the clever condom dance. I was safe. He was safe. And I trusted him to be in my body unsheathed. That alone spoke volumes and we both damn well knew it.

Shepherd slid the head of his erection up and down the length of my slippery split. He nudged me but did not enter me. Parting me with his tip just enough to make me move up to meet him and then he withdrew.

He was watching me. My body, my movements, my face. He covered me with his body and kissed me and then backed off again. I wanted him in me, filling me, moving in me, but he seemed to be waiting.

Chapter Thirty-seven

MY FINGERS FLEXED FOR him, my body rising up to try and touch him. He continued to watch, his face stoic, his mouth set, but his eyes soft. His eyes, those big brown eyes – fuck, they were so ... full.

'Shepherd,' I said, laying a hand flat on his hard abdomen. Feeling those muscles ripple and buck beneath my touch. Tracing a finger down that trail of hair from navel to pubis, I remembered how I'd wanted him home.

How I'd missed him.

How he was the only one I'd let help me.

I bit my lip to keep it at bay as he ran that silken helmet of flesh along my cunt opening again. I gasped, moving toward him in a tiny thrust but failing to engage. 'Shepherd,' I said again, echoing myself. And finally I crushed down my own barrier and simply said, 'Love me.'

And that was that. He thrust in deep. He filled me up. Crushed his warm firm chest to my breasts and kissed me like I might disappear. I didn't know if those were the words he wanted or just some variation. It didn't matter. I wrapped my legs around his thick waist and opened my body to him. Relishing the feel of his cock slamming the tiny bundles of lust-fattened nerve endings in my pussy. I was so plump, so ripe, so goddamn sensitive I seemed to sway under him. It felt like I was underwater caught in some invisible current.

The room moved, the earth moved, the air moved ... with us.

His shoulders were hot under my hands as I gripped him tight – probably painfully tight, but he didn't complain. With his teeth, he explored the slope of my neck, the jut of my jaw, my earlobe and my bottom lip. Small sharp bursts of pain that quickly morphed to bliss exploded along my skin. His head lowered and his teeth found my nipples.

Bite … My cunt flexed.

Bite …A deeper flex, a moan from me. It swelled out of me before I knew it was coming.

Bite …A small flickering spasm and I was holding him, nearly pinching him.

He thrust hard and rocked his hips and bit the swell of soft flesh above my heart and I came with a cry that I had never heard from myself. I'd never made that sound before. How could someone not love this man? How could someone stop?

They were colder women than me, I guess.

As scary as it was to realise just how I felt, it was baffling to think of that changing. Which made me tremble with fear instead of pleasure.

Shepherd rolled off me and onto his side, gathering me in so we lay face to face. Strong as he was it was nothing to hold my right thigh up and steady himself. He moved so his cock was between my legs and looked me in the eye. 'Put me in you.'

I did. My hands still shaking, I reached down and guided the tip of him to my pussy. I rocked my hips to get him in and once he was in, he thrust deep, his fingers so tight on my ankle as he held me wide I feared I'd bruise – I hoped I'd bruise.

My urge at realising my true feelings was to run. To fuck him hard and then to run fast. I bit my lip to focus my mind and steel my heart.

I could not do that. I couldn't do it to him and I couldn't do it to me.

'You love me,' he said, snagging my wrists and trapping them above my head. He rolled half on me and let me wrap my legs around his waist. My wrists ground together and my body arched up on its own seeking the warmth of him.

I said nothing. It brought me down to a whimper – his words.

He held me tighter and rocked into me – a hard but soft rhythm that was both lulling and urgent.

'You love me,' he said again, his lips meeting mine, his

tongue seeking mine.

I did.

'You love me,' he gasped, fucking me harder, my hair rasping against his kitchen throw rug, my feet pinned to the back of his waist. I dug in with my heels, thrust up with my hips, opened to him to get him as deeply as I could.

'Say it,' he said.

'I …'

I blinked, shook my head, small traitorous tears leaking from my eyes and yet it was right there – on the tip of my tongue.

'Say it. It's true. You know it is.'

I swore I could hear him smiling but I kept my eyes shut tight.

'I …'

He growled in my ear, 'You can't be afraid forever, Tuesday.'

I swallowed, arched up and he drove deep and I came. I came so hard tiny white fairy lights danced in the darkness behind my lids and on the final exhalation prompted by pleasure I said, 'I love you, Shepherd.'

'Fuck,' he said.

'Not the response I was hoping f–'

But he was gripping me by the hips and driving his cock deep and kissing me like I was precious and when he grunted, giving one final thrust before emptying into me he whispered, 'And Christ how I love you, Tuesday. I think since the first time you smiled at me.'

Funny, I was full of so much then. Worry, joy, fear, love, lust, terror. I laughed. It was all I could do. I laughed and I laughed until I cried. And when that happened he held me. He wasn't offended. He was OK.

'I know, baby. It's the scariest thing I've felt in over a decade. But it's there. And I'm man enough to admit it.'

'Me, too,' I said. Then I snorted and he was laughing with me.

'Yes, you are man enough to admit it too.'

* * *

232

I stared at his kitchen ceiling.

He was lying next to me, tracing his finger from the space between my breasts down to my belly button to make my skin flicker and tremble. He smiled at me.

'What do we do now?' I asked.

I tried to ignore the anxiety balled in my chest like lead.

'We go day by day and we just … figure it out.'

'Do we burst into flames or anything?' I asked.

He chuckled. 'Nope.'

'Are you sure? The last time I let myself feel something – that trust me, was minor compared to this – it was a total disaster.'

'Me, too.'

'And I hit him with a bat.'

'And she left me and I fucked every woman that looked at me sideways.'

'And I had to run.'

'And I broke more hearts than any man should have in the name of protecting myself,' he countered.

'And–'

'And now we're here,' he said, and kissed my hair. 'And it will be OK.'

'I'll try,' I said.

Shepherd levelled me with his extremely unsettling gaze – it was so direct at times it was startling to the likes of me. 'Try what?' he asked.

'Not to fuck it up,' I said.

'Me too.'

I sat up and put my hands on his chest. Just feeling his heat and the soft thrum of his heartbeat. 'But what if we do?' I asked him.

My voice broke and I was so mortified, so terribly embarrassed, I waited to burst into flames. But if I couldn't be real with a man I was admitting to loving who the fuck could I be honest with?

'I won't let you and you won't let me. Now how about if you let me run you a bath. I have a nice deep claw foot tub your grandmother use to tease me about. And I'd love to see you in that thing – naked …' He slid his hand down over my hip and then my thigh. It felt so good when he touched me it was almost sinful. 'And wet.'

'What do you mean she teased you about it?' I leaned over to kiss him. I couldn't stop kissing him.

'She called it a panty dropper tub,' he said. 'Apparently, girls like tubs like that.'

'I bet she never expected it to be my panties.'

'I like to think she'd approve.' He brushed my too-long bangs out of my eyes. Touched my nose.

I warmed all over as girlish as it sounds. 'Plus, I've already dropped my panties for you. Lots of times.'

'If I have my way, you'll do it lots more, too. Maybe forever.'

More anxiety beating big black wings in my chest. But under it a warm comfort. A peace. My nan's unheard voice telling me to go ahead and take a goddamn chance. On him. On me.

I stared at it. 'It is a panty dropper,' I sighed.

It was the kind of tub my other grandmother back in the city had had. A big white porcelain claw foot tub with the lion's feet and everything. The skylight showed me a dark velvet swatch of night overhead and the room's soft lights made me think of amber or softly flickering fires.

'So drop the panties.'

'I'm not wearing panties,' I said and sat buck naked on his toilet lid.

Shepherd turned the water on and rummaged through a small cabinet by the bathroom door. 'I have bergamot, cinnamon, sandalwood. Sorry, I dated a woman who worked in one of those fancy-pants bath shops.'

'All manly scents,' I said, laughing.

'I guess. But which do you want?' He faced me and when I really looked at him, head to toe, from expression to stance – my heart seized up.

'What do you use?'

'None of them. I just can't see wasting them.'

234

'What's in your cologne?'

'I have no idea.' He was waiting and smiling and his cock was getting hard again. I watched it twitch a bit and fought the urge to crawl to him and take him in my mouth.

We'd get there. No rush.

'Which would you use?' I shifted a bit and caught his gaze lingering on my breasts and the small roundness at my belly. I spread my legs knowing my pussy would be flush and pouty again. Ready again.

'The sandalwood, I guess. That's the one that smells most natural and the least like perfume.'

I nodded. 'Good. Then I can get clean.'

'Then I can get you dirty again,' he said almost to himself. His voice a tumbling growl.

He squirted a healthy amount of the bath bubbles in and foam started to rise, filling the small but pristine room with sandalwood scent.

I said nothing, my throat a little tight, my heart a little fast. When Shepherd offered me his hand I took it in and climbed into the tub slowly. The heat made me hiss.

'Too hot?' He cocked an eyebrow.

'Yes. And just the way I like it. I love hot, hot water.'

'For real?' He didn't look convinced.

'Sir, when I get out of the shower, I am the colour of a cooked Maine lobster.' And it was true.

He leaned over me, his bulk eclipsing the pretty overhead antique light. 'I like that whole Sir thing. We'll get to all that soon enough.'

I eyed him, sank a bit lower in the molten water. 'Yeah?'

'Yeah. Any special requests?'

'Do you have a leather belt?'

His face was unreadable but the pulse at the base of his throat slammed for a second or two. 'Yes.'

'Good.'

'Done that before?' His fingers tangled in my bangs and then he kissed my eyelids one at a time. It made me feel dopey, the sensation of his lips on my skin.

'Nope.'

235

Shepherd sat back on the thin lip of the tub, balancing with one arm thrown across the width of the porcelain. 'And what makes you want to try that?'

'You.'

'My cock's hard,' he said and laughed.

'I should hope so.'

Out in the night a soft sound emanated. It was soft but not normal and when Shepherd said 'Be right back' and left to check it out, the way my gut bottomed out told me that what he'd find wouldn't be good.

Chapter Thirty-eight

'I'LL BE BACK.' HE was pulling jeans on and nearly tripping over himself. Then he set the Louisville Slugger inside the door and rushed forward to kiss me.

'Wait! What? What's happening, Shepherd?'

I was submerged in hot water damn near up to my neck and still I felt a cold shiver of fear work under my skin.

'There's a fire. By your house. I don't know if Adrian's there or even–' He grunted and shook his head.

'Well, just call 9-1-1 and–'

'I did. But it will take them too long to get there. I don't know who set it and I don't know if I can trust Adrian to tend to it and Tuesday, fuck, by the time they get here it'll have spread to the house.'

I watched him shove his feet in boots. 'Lock the door behind me and stay in the bathroom with the bat.'

'But–'

'Don't argue. I mean it. I don't want to leave you but if I don't go and turn the hose on those bushes and dried out weeds, it's going to really catch and then your house is in trouble.'

I opened my mouth to speak and he was gone. Pointing to the door and saying, 'Lock it.'

I heard his boots on the steps and the front door and just sat there like a goose in a pot of boiling water. 'What the fuck?'

I was stunned for a second but then angry. 'Fuck this shit,' I growled.

Shepherd would be much faster getting to the house and dealing with the beginnings of a fire. If Adrian were home, I knew he'd come to help even if he didn't like Shepherd.

237

Despite their dislike for each other, and despite what Shepherd thought of him, I knew Adrian was innocent. This was something else. Something worse than a jealous ex boyfriend I'd had casual sex with upon my return.

I shook off the sandalwood scented sheets of water and stepped warm, and soap covered from the tub. His towels were huge – to fit him I guess – and it wrapped around me twice. The ends of my braids dribbled warm water down my chest. They had soaked up water like twin sponges only accenting the unsettling feel of too cool air on my too warm skin.

I grabbed the bat and turned to lock the door and for a split second my brain didn't register. I heard the faint rustle of a person moving and my first thought was to assume it was Shepherd. But it wasn't Shepherd and when I did look up into the stern troubled face, I had a moment of recognition and normalcy.

Before it set in.

'Hi, Tues.'

'Hi, Stan.'

Not Phil. Phil was gone in the wind, it seemed. It was Stan.

Don't leave, Tuesday ... Or take me with you.

He wanted me to stay. He'd loved me and I'd very succinctly told him that we'd never been together. Never.

'I came for you.'

Funny, he didn't look crazy. And maybe he wasn't. Maybe just somewhere in his brain this would all work out – there'd be a happy ending. He was here to rescue me from a life I'd thought I'd wanted but I'd been wrong. In his mind, he was the knight in shining armour.

'I'm staying here, Stan,' I said, curling my fingers around the neck of the bat. The bat was becoming a fucking joke I was employing it so often.

'I don't think you should. There're critters in your basement.' He smiled at me.

Yep. Crazy.

'Just a big ole' Stan in my basement,' I said and tried to smile back. 'Nothing that would fit in a cage, right?'

'Right.'

'And my potting shed.'

'First place I could get into once I got here.'

'So, what? You were right on my tail all the way here?'

'Pretty much.' He took a step forward and the hair on the back of my neck stood up. I could see the manic flickering lights of the fire he'd set to distract Shepherd through the dark windows.

I had no cell phone. I had no gun. I had nothing. But my bat.

'Look, Stan, I don't want to hurt you.'

'You won't.'

Then he laughed at me. To him it was ridiculous. The thought of me hurting him. But I'd hurt men just as big and nearly as crazy.

'I don't love you.'

I took a step back.

'I told you, you're just a restless spirit is all.'

He took a step forward.

'Not any more,' I said. 'That's not what I am now. You set the fire?' I rushed on, just trying to distract him, eyeing up the small room for any way to help myself out of this situation.

'To distract your caveman.'

'Ah,' I said softly. 'And he went to save my house and ...'

'I slipped in the front door when he was gone. He really should have seen that coming.'

'Funny, I did,' Shepherd said from the doorway, his face a dark mask of rage.

I didn't ask any questions. I simply took the moment that was offered. When Stan turned, startled by Shepherd, I clocked him. I took a short but hard swing with the bat. I wanted to put him down and not kill him.

Stan made a sound that was half grunt, half cry and hit the ground on his knees. He slid in some water and I took the short end of the bat when he landed face down and jabbed him right between the shoulder blades. The air rushed out of him in a whoosh. That would help keep him down.

Shepherd rushed toward me and I dropped my ass onto the toilet seat again, the towel still damp but secure around me. My fingers started to shake first so I dropped the bat. Then my thighs started in, my stomach even trembled, my arms jittered and my teeth started to clack.

'What the hell?'

'Shock. Flood of adrenaline. All that good shit. Not abnormal for even a fighter. The more combative, the bigger the after effect.' As he spoke, he worked efficiently, wrapping a plaid robe he grabbed from a bathroom hook around me like a cape. I could barely hear him above my annoying clacking teeth. They sounded like the novelty teeth that walked on giant cartoon feet.

'I'm OK,' I said.

'Oh sure you are. Nobody fucks with you,' he said and wet a washcloth. Then he pressed it to the back of my neck.

Stan started to stir, pushing up on his hands and glaring at Shepherd.

'Stan,' I said to Shepherd and nodded.

It only took a second. I knew it would happen, but I let it. Sometimes you got what you deserved. Shepherd grabbed Stan by the back of his collar, reeled him back. 'I was hoping you'd wake up.'

Stan was up on his feet, wobbly but aggressive and I got to see my cage fighter in action. 'Wrong girl, wrong house, wrong lake front. Bad plan,' he growled and clocked Stan once. Just once. And Stan went limp.

'You didn't kill him did you?'

'Unfortunately, no,' Shepherd said.

'My house?' It was the closest I could get to asking if it was on fire.

'It's fine. Adrian came out to help and then the fire crew showed up so I rushed back. As soon as that door clicked behind me I felt bad – like something was off. I couldn't ignore it as worry any more, so I came back.'

'Should we call the police?'

'Already did.' He picked me up and I let him. He kissed my hair and I let him. I felt my need for him and I let myself. I let myself need him.

'Where are you taking me?'

'To get a shot of whiskey and away from this joker.'

I put my head against his shoulder and knew soon we'd be having an exhausting talk with cops. Cops who would fingerprint my basement and my potting shed and ask me questions and all that bullshit. I'd had to deal with that after I ended things with Phil. I hoped no one blamed me this time. I doubted with Shepherd in the vicinity that'd happen.

'Shepherd?'

'Yeah.'

Down the stairs we went and I allowed myself the pleasure of sinking against him. I'd wielded my bat and I'd taken down Stan but it was OK to feel this way I realised.

'Don't leave me alone with them. I need you.'

He stilled but then set me in a leather easy chair and poured me that shot. 'I'm not going anywhere, Tuesday.'

'Did you hear me?' I demanded almost angrily. 'I said I need you.'

He chuckled softly and handed me the shot. 'Drink it.'

My hands still trembled and I hated whiskey but I did it. I drank it and amber fire filled my throat, and then flooded my gut. I gave him the glass feeling damn near bratty.

Then he sank down next to me and pulled me onto his lap. 'I need you too, Tuesday. I'm not going anywhere.'

I let out the breath I didn't even know I'd been holding.

'I love you,' he said softly.

They were coming. The lights, the sirens, the invasion would be here any moment.

I turned in his lap and buried my fingers in his hair. He made a noise because I tugged that hair hard enough to hurt a bit. But I kissed him so hard and so long he made that noise that signalled fucking to come.

'You have to behave. They're coming,' I said.

'They won't be the only ones.'

'Careful, I have a bat and know how to use it. Don't be cheeky.'

'Know how to use it? We're getting that damn thing bronzed,' he said.

'Then it'll be even more dangerous.'

'True story.'

Then the doorbell rang. The police were here.

Epilogue

SNOW CAME TO ALLISTER Lake on December 14th. It just so happened that was my birthday too. It had snowed the day I was born so I had a natural love for it.

The apple festival had come and gone. Adrian had ended up with Tammie and had told me that he was going to propose by Christmas. He was still my caretaker, helping me get stuff situated around Nan's house but was moving on to another position soon. Stan had been arrested and was undergoing psychiatric counselling. Annie reported the boarding house baby as they called him was growing so fast and so big they thought they might have an NBA player on their hands. And Shepherd had asked me to move in.

'What about Nan's house?' I'd asked. Fear was in my gut. It would probably stick around for a while, but I knew when I'd been able to let Reed off the hook and assure him I had no further interest in him beyond friendship and his wonderful fresh berries, that I was done for. Monogamy so soon on the heels of swearing off serious relationships – go figure.

'Writing cottage. It's paid for, it's yours. You have plenty of time to figure out what you want to do with it.'

'Why here? Why not there?'

'We can go there if you like.'

That shut me up. A man who listened to me … respected me … considered me. I loved that he reminded me daily that I was a bad ass all on my own but he was always there to back me up.

'Well that took all the fun out of the bickering,' I snorted.

Shepherd pulled me in and said, 'I know how much she meant to you. If you want me to …'

'But your workshop. Your stuff. It's all here and I was just settling in. It's all Nan's stuff there and …'

'Scared?' He kissed me.

'Terrified.'

'I won't hurt you,' he said.

Tears stung the corners of my eyes and I nodded instead of speaking because my throat was so tight.

'Don't hurt me,' he said.

I clutched at him then and stood on tiptoe and kissed him. Hard. 'I won't.'

'Happy birthday,' he said.

'Yay! I'm older!'

'Better than the alternative.'

He backed me down the hall, kissing me all the way. My buttons gave up under his fingers. He pushed his hands in my jeans and then down in my panties as we staggered-stumbled-walked down the hall to a spare room.

'Ooh, new room. Kinky.'

'Your birthday gift's in there,' he said.

I never went in there. So it was the perfect place to store my present. I never went into his spare bedroom or anywhere else just yet. I was still worried I was overstepping my bounds. It was my hang up not his issue. And now he wanted me here. Every day. Every moment. Every room.

My ass hit the door and it popped open. 'I can't …'

I couldn't see or think because his finger was on my clit pressing me there with the perfect amount of pressure. It thumped through me like a drum beat – my need.

He yanked my jeans open and the button fly gave with a whispering sound. Then his arms were turning me and I was thinking kinky again and then I faced the room.

The room.

'Happy birthday.' He chuckled at my silence and pushed my jeans down along with my striped pink panties. I was bare there but for my long sleeved navy tee and black vest.

'Fuck,' I said.

'I plan to. Do you like it?' He bent me at the waist and my hands found the back of a heavily padded desk chair. I clutched it as he moved behind me. The leather of his belt hissed behind me and I shivered, my heart speeding up and my stomach dipping crazily.

'Is it mine?'

'Your office.'

'My office,' I said.

'I've been reading your work.'

'That's not fair. You're not supposed to do that,' I said as he slid the leather along the flare of my hip – the swell of my ass.

'Sorry. You can sue me if you like.'

The leather of his belt was a warm worn kiss against my skin. The small of my back pebbled with goosebumps and my nipples tented my soft cotton tee. He was going to whip me … he was going to whip me. I thought that conversation had been forgotten and here I was in my new office, my new office that was outfitted with …

'The bookshelf,' I said.

The bookshelf from the day he'd bound me in his underground work room and fed me tomato sandwich and fucked me and …

'It was for you. All along. It's for your books. Books you will surely have if you decide to write. Which you should … that's just my two cents.'

I hung my head as his fingers slid into my cunt and then withdrew to slide into my ass. I hummed low in my throat, curving myself up to meet his touch. Moving my body to accept his ministrations.

'Thank you for your two cents.'

'You have a real voice. A lot to say.'

I hung my head lower and my bangs draped my vision. Out the window the lake was shades of grey. Snow falling fast and furious. The house smelled like the cake he'd baked me and now the slight smell of varnish off the book case.

'I've been afraid to say it.'

'Don't be. Now … birthday girl … how many?'

I blinked, momentarily confused and then. 'I don't know. I've never … I don't–'

'It hurts,' he said. But somehow that only served to make

me want it more. To crave it more.

Then softly– 'But I'll make it worth the pain, sweetheart.'

'Four?'

'And one for luck,' he laughed. The tip of the belt licked my hip, my lower back, the top of the crack of my ass.

'And one for luck,' I agreed.

His bulk of his body withdrew from me and I felt the absence of it tingling along my skin. And then the belt tingled along my skin.

Each nerve ending went on red alert. A smarting, startling pain that stole my breath and then a brushfire rush of heat along my flesh.

'One,' he said and I sobbed.

'Keep going,' I said.

The second blow landed on the opposite side, a scalding stripe of pain. 'Two.'

My back bowed and sweat broke out on my upper lip. I felt the pulse and beat and swell of my cunt and the flicker deep inside of me that signified arousal. I gripped the back of the chair and let the tears roll down my face.

They weren't from the pain. They were from how much I trusted Shepherd to do this. The trust felt more intimate than the fucking.

He paused to slide a thick group of fingers into my pussy and when he flexed them I sobbed again, but for an entirely different reason.

The brutal kiss of the leather belt crossed the original welt and I yelped. His fingers returned, thrusting, driving, digging into the plump flesh of my pussy until I white-knuckled the leather chair and pushed back against his hand. The fourth blow crossed the second and in my mind I imagined demon-red Xs flared across my buttocks.

'And one for luck.' This blow landed horizontal.

He stepped out and to the side, emerging in my peripheral vision for a moment. Then flicked the belt so it crossed the top of both cheeks but below the small of my back. It hit the meaty part of my ass with a thwack and then the belt hit the ground and Shepherd stepped into me.

He pressed the hot head of his cock to my slit and slid into me, plunging so deep my feet – but for my toes – left the floor for a moment. He looped a big arm under my waist and held me as he fucked me. His words – a stream of heated chatter – slid into my head, filling my mind. But I couldn't make any one sentiment out, just the sound of lust and need and affection and love. He fucked me so that I begged him to go harder thought I doubted he could and all the while my heartbeat marched itself through all of me. Chest, throat, cunt and ass. I was my own pulse.

And he was part of it all.

His other hand came under me and flicked my clit. His thrusts had grown shorter and more intense. The base nature animal sensation of being humped during the throes of mindless passion is a wonderful thing. There is something so intensely dirty about it that it adds to the chemistry of arousal.

'Come for me.'

My bottom burned with fire that bled out to fill my womb and my pussy with a warm liquid heat. I was up, I was down, I was inside out – but above it all I was safe.

And without thinking, as I came, I said the catch word I used with the one person I considered family in my life. I came and I sighed and I cried out softly and simply said 'Love.'

And Shepherd echoed, 'Love,' as my eyes found the beautiful bookcase that this man, this amazing man, had been crafting for me before he even knew I could love him. Let alone that one day I would.

Also by Sommer Marsden

The Best of Sommer Marsden

From edgy and intense, to light and comedic, this collection of over twenty hand-picked dirty tales from Sommer Marsden runs the gamut of erotic fiction. Stories include a supernatural spurred ménage, a captivating Dom who takes control at a crowded house party, an irresistible alpha who makes recycling kind to the body and the planet. A husband encouraging his wife to take advantage of a girl crush and a woman who can't help but lose herself between two of her two best friends in a night of passion. A curvaceous woman gets stuck in her boot – that's right, just one – before an important interview with a handsome applicant and a public spanking makes a young woman reconsider the disposable nature of her rebound guy

ISBN 9781908086082   £7.99